BATTLE SCARS

LOVE IS MESSY DUET SERIES BOOK FOUR

EMILY GOODWIN

COPYRIGHT

Battle Scars: Book Two in the Love is Messy Duet
Copyright 2017
Emily Goodwin
Editing by Ellie from Love N Books
Editing by Lindsay from Contagious Edits
Cover Photography: Sara Eirew
Models: Amanda Renee and Brian Silvers

∼

To those who still believe in magic

BATTLE SCARS: BOOK FOUR
IN THE LOVE IS MESSY
SERIES

chapter
one

ANA

My eyes flutter open in the dark, and I sit up in bed, looking around the large master bedroom. Light from the city outside glows behind the honeycomb blinds, and I squint at the doorway, just knowing a dark figure will cross through the hall at any second.

My heart hammers in my chest, pumping adrenaline throughout my body. My fingers tingle and my hands shake. I thought I heard a thump. The distinct sound of someone pounding on glass. Like a window.

Calm the fuck down. No one is in the house besides me and Cole, who's fast asleep next to me. I saw him disarm the house when we got home after the release party. We stepped in and immediately turned the alarm system back on. It's not possible for someone to come in the house without us knowing.

Unless he's figured out how to disarm the alarm. Maybe one of his prison buddies told him how. Or he has some sort of device that temporarily blocks the signal and he forced a basement window open and has been waiting, watching for the right time to strike.

I bring my trembling hands up to my face and rub my eyes. My ex-boyfriend is not here. I had a nightmare, which makes sense since I thought I saw Steven just a few hours ago. I bend my knees up, letting out a slow breath. I need to calm down.

And be brave.

Swallowing my fear, I carefully peel the covers back and tiptoe out of bed. Nerves prickle along my spine and my feet don't want to move. If anyone saw me, they'd think I was walking into the belly of the beast, not creeping toward the bedroom door to look at what has to be an empty hall. There's no one there.

And yet my mind conjures up the image of a shadowy figure, standing right outside the door. He'll be cast in darkness, and I won't be able to make out his face.

But I'll know who he is.

"Ana?" Cole calls groggily from the bed. "What are you doing?"

"Uh," I start, trying to come up with a lie. But if Cole's been watching me, then he knows I'm slowly inching toward the bedroom door. In the opposite direction of the bathroom, too, so I can't use that as I lie. "I thought I heard something."

Cole sits up. "Heard something?"

"Yeah. Like a noise."

He rubs his face and gives me a half-smile. "Typically noises are heard."

I smile back and shake my head. "Right. It's nothing, I'm sure. I just wanted to go check."

He stretches his arms over his head and gets up. I fell asleep right after we made love and was only half aware of Cole carrying me upstairs and into bed. He was still dressed —well half dressed in his shirt and tie, I'd taken his pants off

4

— when we went upstairs. Now he's only wearing boxers, and I see a dark stain on the flesh of his shoulder.

"You got a tattoo?"

Cole grins and looks down at the ink. "Yeah. On Thursday."

I narrow my eyes, trying to make out the details in the dim light. "I like it."

"I'm glad you do." He comes over to me and takes my hands in his. "You're shaking."

"I'm cold." It's not a total lie. Outside of the blankets and away from Cole, the air is chilly.

He gives me a look that lets me know he doesn't believe me but doesn't push the issue. I'm so fucking glad. I hate feeling so afraid. I hate feeling weak. Feeling useless. Like I can't defend myself. Like all I can do when shit hits the fan is hide and hope someone else fights for me.

Steven worked hard to make me feel like that. He sunk his claws in and carefully peeled back layer after layer until there was nothing left but my tender beating heart. Then he tore that to shreds too.

"What did you think you heard?"

I shake my head. "Just a thumping, like someone was hitting a window. I'm a really light sleeper. Any tiny little noise wakes me up."

Cole's face tenses. "I'll check." He takes a step forward and I dash after him.

"I'm coming with."

We don't go far; Cole goes around to his dresser and pulls a tablet off a charger. He taps the black screen and a menu comes up. It's the home screen for his security system, and the thing is pretty damn impressive. There are cameras rolling live footage around the house, one in the foyer showing the front door, and another showing the back in the kitchen. The back stairs are in the bottom of the frame, and I distantly wonder if anyone from the alarm system company happened to check in every now and then. If they did, there's a good chance they saw Cole fucking me into oblivion on those stairs.

"Nothing got picked up," he mumbles. "But I'll go down and look."

"It's okay." I grab his arm. "Let's just go back to bed. I have very vivid dreams. A lot. Actually, I should have warned you of that before. Don't be surprised if I wake up thrashing. And sorry in advance if I smack you. It's not done on purpose, I promise."

Cole meets my eyes, holding my gaze for a second. He knows my ex has been reaching out to me, trying to get a rise and freak me the fuck out. Which he's doing, dammit. But does Cole think Steven is here too? He doesn't know the details, doesn't know the masterfully creeptastic extent Steven went to before in order to send me a message.

And I don't want him to know. There's no reason to bring that shit up right now. I'm trying to start new and move on. I won't go back unless I have to. And a nightmare is just that... a nightmare.

"All right." Cole takes my hand and leads me back into bed. We climb under the covers and he spoons his body around mine. I close my eyes, finding solace in the way his strong body feels against mine. He kisses the back of my neck. "Goodnight, Ana."

"Night, Cole."

~

I PULL OPEN the top drawer of my nightstand, brow furrowing. I push aside the various junk I keep in there. Where the hell are my keys? I'm careful where I put them since I've lost them so many times in the past and was late for work because of it.

I close the door and run my hand over my hair. I spent forty-five minutes trying to curl the thick strands. They're hanging in loose waves around my face now, which looks pretty even though it wasn't the look I was going for. I leave the bedroom and go to the front closet to look for the keys once more. I know I left them in my purse. I specifically remember seeing them when I pulled out my lip gloss last night.

"You won't find them in there." Steven's voice comes from behind me. I whirl around. He's smiling at me, gray-blue eyes glinting. *"Your keys, I mean. You're looking for them, right?"*

"Yeah," I start, annoyance building inside me. *"Have you seen them?"*

"I have. I took them."

My heart skips a beat but my mind checks out, refusing to process this. It's not the first time this has happened. It won't be the last time either. And yet every time, he says he's doing this for me. For us. And every time I believe him.

"Steven, I'm supposed to meet friends for dinner and I'm already running late."

His arms wrap around me. Tight. Tighter. Until it hurts. "But I want to have dinner with you."

"I'll be back in two hours. I haven't seen the girls in over a year. Katie came all the way from Bowling Green for tonight."

"So you'd rather spend the night with Katie, who hasn't bothered to see you in a fucking year, than me? I do everything for you. You are my life, Ana."

I shake my head. "I'm not choosing her over you. I'm not choosing anyone. I just want to have dinner with my friends."

"Are you going to order a drink?"

"I don't know. Maybe."

"People only go out and drink for one reason: to hook up."

I laugh. "I'm not hooking up with Katie, Jess, or Hannah. Trust me."

"It's not fucking funny, Ana! You know damn well what I

meant. And fine. *Fucking forget it. If you want to go out with your friends, then go.*"

"*If it's that big of a deal then—*"

"*A big deal? Of course it's a big fucking deal that you want to go out and get drunk without me. Besides, none of your friends will say it, but I will. Because I'm the only one who cares about you.*"

"*Say what?*"

"*That you really don't need the extra calories from a few drinks. I noticed how those jeans are getting snug on your ass.*"

I look down, subconsciously sucking in my gut. My jeans are tight. Way tighter than they were the last time I put them on. Yet I don't look any different. Maybe that happens when you slowly gain weight. You don't notice it.

"*I just...I...it's just...*"

"*See? You know you're fucking wrong. You'll never learn. Now, if you want to earn your keys back...*" *He raises his eyebrows and crosses his arms.* "*You know what to do.*"

Once again, I startle awake, breath catching in my chest. Why can't I have nightmares about spiders or the boogeyman like normal people? Why are my nightmares frame-by-frame replays of my life? And parts of my life I'm horrified and ashamed of at the same time at that.

Early morning light filters through the blinds, letting me know it's way too fucking early to be up on a Saturday. I stretch out and realize the spot next to me is empty. Heart still racing, I roll over and find a note on Cole's pillow.

Ana-
I went to get coffee and donuts. I'll be back soon :-)
-Cole

I SMILE, looking forward to donuts and coffee. And Cole. Definitely Cole. I fold the note and set it back down. His handwriting is small and neat, almost looking like a font. Way better than my chicken scratch. Which reminds me...I should start practicing writing my signature as Scarlett. Assuming people want me to sign books, that is.

Still tired, I get comfy and close my eyes. I should get up and shower or at the very least, take off yesterday's makeup and brush out my tangled curls. Well, what's left of the curls. Though if Cole and I are giving this a go, he can take me as I am, leftover makeup and all.

chapter
two

COLE

"*W*hat do you want, Steven?" My voice leaves my throat gruffly and I stare down the stranger on my front porch. I swear that man was sitting at the cafe just minutes ago. The feeling of being followed burns inside, filling me with unease and putting me on the defensive. My hands are full—the flowers and coffee are precariously balanced on top of the large box of donuts, but I'm not afraid to toss it all aside and beat the shit out of this creep if I have to.

Chill, I tell myself. I can't be certain this guy is up to no good. Not yet at least. He turns around, pushing sandy blonde hair out of his face. He eyes me up and down and a stupid grin plays on his face, one that's hard to read.

"You," he confesses and then laughs. "Sorry, I don't mean to be so forward. I didn't get the chance to introduce myself to you at the release party last night."

I take another step closer, coming up to my front door. Thank God I locked it. And turned on the alarm. Ana is asleep and vulnerable up there.

And naked.

Fuck, I want to go back to her. This guy is really irritating the shit out of me for showing up unannounced, especially if this has to do with work. It's the fucking weekend.

"The release party?" I echo.

"Yes, for Gregory Lawrence's book. I'm a friend of his, and he promised to introduce me to you but, well...you saw him last night."

I nod, mind going a million miles an hour over everything from last night. I was preoccupied with managing Gregory and his drunk ass. I know there was a lot I missed. And there's no way I can recall every fucking face from last night.

"Right. He was a bit distracted."

"That he was. He told me where to find you and said I should stop by. I'm a writer."

I sigh. Maybe this guy is harmless, but he's all the more fucking annoying now. It's not the first time an author has showed up uninvited either. Though compared to some of the stories I've heard from agents, this is nothing. Still...this is not what I want to be dealing with right now. Or ever. I'm not shy to give a constructive rejection, but when it's in person like this it's always awkward.

"I don't have a card on me, but if you have any questions about publishing, the Black Ink website should have all the information you need. And I don't accept unsolicited manuscripts."

The grin doesn't leave his face. There's not even a glimmer of disappointment. In fact, it's as if he *knew* this wasn't going to amount to anything.

"Well, it was worth a shot. Thanks, Cole." He eyes me up and down again, and then looks at the flowers resting on top of the donut box. "For the pretty blonde you were with last night?"

If he saw me with Lindsay, then he *was* there. I feel a little better knowing he's not lying about that.

"No, they're for my girlfriend." I can't help the smile that springs to my face from saying that word. Girlfriend. Ana and I have a lot to figure out, but we know we want to be together. And that's more than I could ask for.

"Oh, wow. By the way that chick was all over you, I would have sworn you were together." He winks then raises his eyebrows. "A man after my own heart. Mad props for that."

I don't react, but internally, I'm going back—again—and don't remember a single moment when Lindsay's hands were anywhere inappropriate. She hoped for more but was respectful. What is this guy talking about?

"Didn't I see you at the coffeehouse just a few minutes ago?"

"I think so. Wasn't sure if that was you or not. Figured I'd meet you here and—"

"How do you know where I live?"

"Gregory gave me your contact info. Right from his phone."

I take in a slow breath, still unsure about this guy. Gregory does have my address, phone number, and email saved in his phone. And he was pretty fucking shitfaced last night and could have easily shared all my info without actually meaning to.

"I thought you'd be headed home," the guy goes on. "You got to-go coffee, so I made an assumption. I thought I was wrong since you didn't answer the door. I was just about to leave when you showed up." He eyes the flowers again. "Now I see why I beat you here."

"Right. Have a good day."

Steven gives a nod and starts down the steps. I wait, watching him gain distance before I turn my back and balance everything in one hand while I dig my keys out of my pocket and let myself into the house.

It might not make sense, but something about the guy didn't sit right with me, and I'm starting to think it's the weird-as-fuck way he was looking at me. It was almost like desire, but for something other than romance.

Whatever.

I go in the house, and shut and lock the door behind me. I set the coffee, donuts, and flowers on the kitchen table and go up the back stairs to the master bedroom. Ana is still asleep, twisted up in the sheets. Her hair is over her face in a tangled mess. She looks so real and beautiful.

I sit on the edge of the bed and lose the battle of keeping my hands off her. Her flesh is warm and inviting. I want to strip out of my clothes and feel her up against me again. All day. Every day. For the rest of my life.

The thought jars me.

I'm nowhere near close to telling Ana that I love her. But I want to. I long to fall in love, to keep this going with no end in sight. It'll happen slowly, and it'll be beautiful.

Just like Ana.

Ana softly moans in her sleep as I rub her back, before rolling over, eyes fluttering away.

"Morning," she mumbles, eyes meeting mine. I smile down at her and kiss her forehead.

"Sorry to wake you up. I figured you'd want your coffee while it's hot."

"Yeah." She brings her arms out of the blankets and grabs me, tugging me to her. I move into the bed, curling my body around hers.

"This works too," I whisper and kiss her neck. We could stay like this all day and it wouldn't be enough. "I'm surprised the doorbell ringing didn't wake you up? You said you were a light sleeper."

"I think it would have, though the house is big enough maybe I wouldn't have heard it."

That weird feeling that something is wrong comes back. "No, you would have. The doorbell is wired to ring up here for that very reason. There's actually an intercom system throughout the house so you'd definitely hear it unless you're sound asleep."

"I guess you really wore me out." She smiles and runs her fingers along my back. "Who was at the door?"

"An author wanting to talk to me about his book."

"He just showed up? That seems extreme."

"It's not that uncommon, actually. I've heard some rather crazy stories from other editors and agents about authors getting borderline stalker to get their manuscript in their hands. It's a tough business, so I kind of get it. They think it gives them a leg up but it's fucking creepy and annoying."

She laughs. "What if I showed up on your front porch asking if you'd take a peek at my novel?"

The concern I felt before turns into lust. "I'd definitely take a peek. At your novel, of course."

"Just a peek? You wouldn't want more?" She moves the covers down, exposing her breasts.

"I almost forgot you were naked. You are so fucking hot." I slide my hand along her smooth thigh.

"Speaking of hot...coffee sounds amazing."

"Hot, and evil."

"I'm a she-devil. Best you find out now."

I laugh and kiss her, then help her to her feet. She throws on a shirt and panties and nothing else, which is almost hotter than being naked, and follows me into the kitchen.

"So this author," she starts and takes a seat, grabbing one of the to-go cups of coffee and popping the lid. She brings it to her nose and deeply inhales. "God, I love that smell. Anyway, what happened with the author?"

"I told him I don't accept unsolicited manuscripts and that was pretty much it. Thankfully. It's always awkward giving a rejection in person, though I suppose this wasn't a real rejection. And I was nicer than I had to be considering he showed up at my house on a Saturday."

"How'd he know where you live?"

"He said he got my info from Gregory at the party last night, which is entirely possible. Greg was drunk enough to not think straight and pass out my personal address to anyone, especially if he considered that person a friend." I start to say something else but stop, not seeing the point.

"What is it?" she asks and goes to open the donuts, but then notices the flowers. "Did you—are those..."

"Yeah, they're for you."

She gets up from where she's sitting and goes around the table, smiling broadly as she picks up the colorful bouquet. "They're beautiful. Thank you, Cole. Do you have a vase?"

"I do." I go to the kitchen sink and open the cabinet beneath, pulling out a plain, glass vase. I fill it with water and bring it back to the table. Ana undoes the string holding the flowers in a bunch and starts arranging them.

"You were about to say something," she reminds me.

"Oh. Right. It's nothing." I take a seat and open the box of donuts, stomach grumbling. I'm fucking starving.

"My mom used to tell me if it really was nothing then you wouldn't have said it in the first place. It always annoyed me when she'd say that. But now I kinda think it's true." She looks away from the flowers for a second to meet my eyes.

"I see merit in that. And I was going to say that the author was weird. But I can't put my finger on why, other than he just was."

"I know what you mean. People can give off vibes."

"Yeah, that's exactly it, and this Steven guy gave off a weird one."

Ana drops a flower and the blood drains from her face.

I stand, going over to her. "Ana?"

"You...you said this author's name was Steven?"

"That's what he told me."

"What did he look like?" She turns to me, face pale and eyes wide. "Cole, what did he look like?" she rushes out.

"Sandy blonde hair, kinda plain, a good half-foot shorter than me...I really didn't pay attention. I did notice a scar on his wrist, though, only because it went through a hideous tattoo of a snake."

My description makes everything worse, and Ana's hands tremble. She shakes her head from side to side, breath leaving in quick little huffs.

"Ana? What is going on? Do you know that guy?"

Her eyes fall shut for a few seconds as she gathers her composure. I wrap my arms around her and she leans into me. "Yes," she whispers and opens her eyes. "Steven is my ex-boyfriend."

chapter
three

ANA

*I*f it weren't for Cole's arms around me, I'm fairly certain I'd be on the floor right now. Anger surges through me, giving me the strength to stand. I fucking hate Steven for what he did to me. And I'm fucking pissed at myself for getting here. I don't want to be scared anymore. I don't want to be weak.

"Your ex that was arrested for fucking with you?" Cole asks. I can tell he's trying hard not to be pissed. Trying to stay calm. For my sake.

"Yes."

"What the fuck?" He lets go of me and starts to walk away. "I'm going to find him and—"

"Cole," I interrupt. "He's gone by now. Don't...don't go."

"Then we should call the cops."

"And say what? That an aspiring writer who happens to be my ex was hoping the head editor of the country's largest press would talk to him? We know how fucked up this is, but to anyone else, it's just a weird coincidence. You said it yourself...authors go to agents and editors all the time."

"Ana, I know how it sounds, and I've read enough crime

17

books to get that a lot of people think the police won't help. But you have a history. One that ended with an arrest. All you need is a smart cop who can see past the front he's putting up. The guy is obviously stalking you."

"He's never going to stop." The words leave my mouth and the realization makes a chill go over me. Cole comes back over and takes me in his arms again. I rest my head against his chest. "I'm sorry, Cole. You shouldn't have to deal with this. It's my baggage."

"Don't apologize. We all have baggage, trust me. I care about you, and I want to help. I really think you should call the police. At least find out if the guy is on probation. If he's breaking it, it might be easier than you think to get him arrested again."

I nod and close my eyes. It's not that easy. It was hard enough the first time to prove Steven was guilty. Cole doesn't get it. He's white, male, and wealthy. Things like this aren't an issue for him. I'm a female from a small town and don't have the luxury of hiring expensive lawyers.

"I'll call my mo—no, I don't want to worry her. She'll freak out if she knew Steven was here." I move away from Cole and let out a deep sigh. Anger floods my veins and I want to Hulk-smash everything in this fucking room. "I try so hard not to let him get to me because that's what he wants. But he makes me so fucking pissed." I ball my fists and close my eyes, imagining myself pummeling Steven. He's bigger than me and probably learned how to fight dirty in prison. My chances of surviving a physical fight with him are slim to none, as he proved before.

I'd kill for just an ounce of Wonder Woman's powers right now.

"I just want to move on with my life. I don't want to waste another second being angry or afraid. I want to put all this in the past...but I can't. He's ruining my life, and he's going to ruin yours too." The words break me and I drop my head, desperately trying to blink back tears.

"Ana," Cole says gently. He comes up behind me and slips his arms around my waist. Having him here, holding me, supporting me, is the only thing that's keeping me from coming undone.

Or from going crazy.

Because finding Steven and taking care of matters myself is getting more and more tempting.

"I'm no expert, but I do know there are laws in place to keep people from stalking. And my life is far from ruined. I'll take any type of mess if it means I get to be with you."

Cole's words bring tears to my eyes. *Inhale. Hold it. Exhale.* I turn around, and a tear rolls down my cheek. Cole catches it and wipes it away.

"You say that now. But just wait until he sinks in his claws. The guy is evil, Cole. Evil."

Cole's brown eyes fill with concern. "What did he do to you? No, don't answer that. Sorry. You don't have to talk about it."

I shake my head. "No, I do. You should know. If you're going to be involved with me, you're getting yourself involved with him, and I hate that. I hate it so much. It's not fair to you." My chest tightens and I feel like I've been plunged into ice water. Cole doesn't deserve to deal with this shit. Steven is my ex, my drama, my past.

Not his.

And yet being with me fucks everything up. I look into Cole's eyes and feel my heart break.

"I can't do this to you. I can't introduce you to my brand of crazy. It's my fault I went out with Steven in the first place, my fault I let him manipulate me for as long as he did. I'll get on the first flight I can and make sure he knows I'm leaving."

Cole tightens his embrace. "If you want to leave because you don't feel anything for me, then I won't stop you. But I don't think that's why."

More tears fall, and I angrily wipe them away. "He found out where you live. He knows I'm here with you and is trying to get to you. Or me. Probably us both. Steven's the kind of fucker who thinks if he can't have me, no one can. I...I don't want to risk you in any way. And it's because I do care about you that I want to leave."

"You're letting him win if you leave."

"That's true." I blink away the rest of my tears and shake my head. "I'm sorry I'm such a mess."

Cole gives me a half-smile. "Messy isn't bad, Ana."

I laugh. "You're so put together. Your life...your job... everything is where you want it to be."

Cole's expression softens. "It just looks that way. I promise you things aren't as picture-perfect as you think. But that doesn't matter right now. You matter, and I really think we should do something about this. Hell, I'll call Luke," he says as if that's the last thing he'd want to do, but will do anything for me. "He works with the police a lot, he might know what to do or where to go from here. I think he has a few friends on the police force."

I'm on the verge of a breakdown. "Can we just eat our donuts and drink our coffee and come back to this? I need a brain break for a couple of minutes."

"Of course."

We go back to the table, and I pick up a sprinkle-covered donut. "I wonder how hung over Gregory is today," I start and take a bite of my donut. It's soft, sweet, and so fucking good.

Cole chuckles. "He'll be feeling it, that's for sure. I'm keeping my fingers crossed he stays in retirement and doesn't decide to write another book."

"Will you have to edit it?"

"There's a chance I'll be—" He cuts off, and takes a drink of coffee. "If I'm available, yes. And it'll be put into his contract, once an offer was made. And we'd be stupid not to make an offer. Well, assuming he writes more epic fantasy."

My heart is still racing a million miles an hour and I'm trying hard not to think about the noises I heard last night and the fact that Steven showed up today. "I never realized how much drama goes on in the book world."

"This is nothing. Wait until you go to a book signing event with multiple authors. Especially the ones where cover models attend."

"Oh, that sounds fun!"

The smile is back on Cole's face. "That's one way to look at it. I've never seen it firsthand, but I've heard stories from authors."

"I've gone to small signings at bookstores. I got a book signed by Colleen Hoover last year, and paid more than I should have to get a signed set of Harry Potter from eBay."

"You're a Black Ink author now. If you want any signed books from the house, I can get them for you."

"If you're serious about that offer, I'd like at least a dozen by the end of the week. I need all of Emma Stark's books, including the last one. Preferably before it's out."

Cole laughs again and my heart slows. "You know Lexi edits those, right? She has the last one right now."

My eyes widen. "Seriously? Oh my God, I need it!"

We talk about books for a few more minutes, until I've eaten as many donuts as humanly possible. I finish my coffee, take a quick trip to the bathroom, and come back to find Cole cleaning up the kitchen. I get the feeling he likes things neat and tidy, which could cause some conflict if we stay together. Neat and tidy is not my forte. But artists thrive on chaos, right?

"So," Cole starts when I take a seat at the table again.

"So," I echo. "I can't put it off forever."

"We don't have to talk about this if you don't want to, but something has to be done, Ana. We can't let this guy walk."

I nod and start fiddling with a tangled curl. "Right. I don't suppose you've picked up on a few tips and tricks from all those crime books you've edited, have you? They say there's no such thing as the perfect murder, but I disagree. It all comes down to the details."

"We need to make it look like an accident. Or invest in a meat grinder and some pigs." He smiles, but his eyes don't shimmer like usual. No amount of humor can deflect the seriousness of the situation. Cole takes a seat at the table next to me and puts his hand on my thigh.

I pull on my hair and then take Cole's hand. "Steven is very manipulative," I begin. "I didn't realize it until I was in too deep for a quick getaway. He isolated me from my family and friends. Really messed with my head. Emotional abuse is what the therapist called it." I pause, risking a look at Cole. There is no judgment in his eyes. "He'd do things and twist it so it looked like it was for my benefit. Looking back now, I feel so stupid for believing him." I shake my head, feeling embarrassment rise inside. "And then he hit me. Hard. Broke my nose and cracked my cheekbone." Pain radiates through my face as I recall that nightmare. "And that night, when the bleeding wouldn't stop and the swelling got worse and worse, he wouldn't let me go to the ER. It was cold and snowing that night, which I remember perfectly because I had to walk in it. Steven would hide my car keys so I couldn't drive away."

My heart starts to thump and cramming all those donuts down my throat was a bad idea. "I drugged Steven and snuck out, walking to a neighbor down the street. We called the police, but it didn't end like you'd think. Steven denied everything, made it seem like I was the crazy one. It took months to get him held accountable for what he did. And his sentence was a joke."

Cole gives my hand a reassuring squeeze. I'm shaking, heart racing from reliving this. I focus on my breathing and find the courage to go on.

"But from the breakup to the actual arrest...he made it his mission to make my life hell. Stalking is putting it lightly. The few months between the breakup and his arrest were worse than the two years we were together, which sounds crazy, I know. But I guess I knew what to expect when we were together. When we weren't...there was no telling how far he'd go. And he was smart, I guess you'd call it, about what he did. The ways he watched me, how he'd just show up...it was very hard to prove it was stalking. We lived in a small town. There aren't a whole lot of places to go without running into someone you know. He knows how not to get caught. Which is why I'm so worried now. He knows we're together. He knows I'm here. There's no other reason for him to show up this morning if he didn't."

"The guy obviously has some mental issues," Cole says. "He shouldn't be allowed with the general public."

"Tell me about it. He put effort in his attempts to get to me. The things he did..." I shiver. "It was personal. Thought out. Planned." I pull my hand from Cole's and run it over my face, feeling the day-old makeup. "Shower with me?" I'm not in the mood for sex, but being alone in the shower brings on memories of *Psycho*, though the large glass door in Cole's shower make it impossible for someone to sneak up on me.

"You don't have to ask me twice."

Cole gets up and takes my hand again. He's tense. I don't think he's in the mood for sex either. We're just getting this relationship started and I'm already fucking it all up.

EMILY GOODWIN

~

"WHAT DO you want to do today?" I ask Cole, leaning away from the sink in the master bathroom as I brush through my wet hair. Little beads of water collect and splash onto the quartz countertop.

"We can order in and watch movies," he answers from inside the bedroom. I take a step back so I can see him. He's sitting on the edge of his bed, wearing just his boxers and looking at something on his phone.

"If *he* hadn't shown up, what would you want to do today?"

"Do you have a restraining order against him? It says here that two violations—"

"Cole," I interrupt. "Let's just go out and have fun. Steven is my loser ex-boyfriend, not a demon about to unleash the Four Horsemen. Though the latter might be easier. We can kill demons."

Cole puts his phone down and frowns. A beat passes between us and then he agrees. "All right. But...don't take this the wrong way or anything...I have a feeling he made you think you're overreacting. And you're not. Coming all the way from Kentucky to New York City—and then finding you amidst the millions of people here—is not something to let go."

"I know. Trust me, I do. But tonight...let's just go out. I brought a slutty dress and heels. Let me get dressed up and feel like a girl. Please?"

Cole smiles and nods, and I go back to the sink to finish brushing my hair. As much as I don't want to feel it, I do.

The feeling that this is all fleeting. That whatever Cole and I have going on is soon going to end. And taking the recent events into consideration, I don't think my concern is

24

without merit. Cole and I got over the hurdle of our tangled up and complicated feelings.

I like him.

He likes me.

We're seeing where the path takes us.

There will be bumps along the way, of course...everybody hits a few now and again. But a total roadblock? That can end the journey before it even starts.

chapter
four

COLE

I take Ana's hand and reel her in close, wrapping my other arm around her shoulders as I pull her in for a kiss. We're walking along a busy sidewalk inside Central Park, and the sun is starting to set. Brilliant orange melts into a gradually darkening blue, making the sky look as if it's on fire.

"Would it be totally cliché if I asked to go on one of those carriage rides?" Ana looks up at me, eyes shining, and smiles.

"It would, but for you, I'll do it."

"I kinda feel bad for the horses," she goes on, looking around the street for a horse-drawn carriage. "Where do they stay? Do they even have room to graze?"

"I'm not too sure on that, but I've been told there are some strict rules in place. Though it wouldn't surprise me if the living conditions were less than ideal."

Her nose wrinkles as she thinks, and it's fucking adorable. "I can't do it. If the horses are treated poorly, then paying to take a ride only enables the handlers. Kinda like how puppy mills work, if that makes sense."

"It does, and I've actually wondered the same thing. It

seems unnatural to have a horse inside the city like this, out on the street all day. You said you used to have horses, right?"

"Yeah. I showed at our county fair. I was never really into showing or being formal. It was more for fun. I lost my horse a few years ago, and his pasture mate got lonely—horses don't do well on their own—so we gave him to a children's equine therapy place."

"Do you miss it?" I ask carefully.

"Sometimes. My mom says she'll get more horses whenever she has grandkids. Which will probably be soon."

I don't mean to shoot Ana a shocked look, but I did.

"My sister," she clarifies with a laugh. "She's been with her boyfriend for a few years now. They live together and I'm pretty sure a proposal is happening this winter. She's had a grand scheme of how she wants to be asked in her head since we were kids, and it involves the giant Christmas tree our town puts up in front of the courthouse every holiday season." She sighs. "I never thought my little sister would be married before me. Funny, how things turn out, right?"

I laugh. "You're telling me. I never thought Luke would get married at all. Or at least not until he was a lot older. And now look at him." That bitterness is back, and I hate myself for it.

"You'll get your happy ending," Ana says softly, jarring me. It was only last night I confessed everything to her. Told her things I'd never told anyone. Things I hardly even let myself acknowledge.

Dark things.

Bad things.

Things that bring the truth to the surface. Things that prove I'll never be the hero. I don't have a heart of gold. I get jealous. I seek vengeance. Seeing other people find their happiness doesn't give me a sense of hope. It does the opposite and reminds me of what I don't have.

I'm a fucked-up soul, and it's only a matter of time before Ana gets swept up in my web of destruction. And now that I've witnessed the shit she went through before me, I think it's best she stays away.

But being selfish is just one of the reasons my soul is so fucked up, and I don't want to let her go.

"Now what?" Ana asks, swinging my hand in hers. The night has cooled off fast, and the smell of rain hangs in the air. So much has happened in the last twenty-four hours, enough to make my head spin, and this was all before Steven showed up.

"We can pick up dessert, wine, and go home? We could attempt to sit in the hot tub before it rains if you'd like."

Ana's green eyes sparkle in the fading gold sunlight. "I like that plan. Though I didn't pack a swimsuit."

"That's not a problem. If you did, it wouldn't stay on for long anyway."

~

I TRADE the wine glasses for heavy plastic tumblers and set them on a tray. The wind has picked up and the last thing I want to do is clean up glass from my patio. Being neat and orderly has been engrained in me. Sticking to my routine has kept me sane over the last few years. Straying from it feels odd.

And so fucking good.

"I suppose this will do," Ana says, coming down the stairs. The wine I was pouring sloshes out of the cup and onto the tray.

I blink. Swallow. Feel blood rush to my cock. "If not, you'll have to take it off," I choke out, staring at Ana, who's wearing nothing but a white bra with matching panties. I set the bottle of wine down, forgoing cleaning up the mess, and cross the kitchen. I take Ana in my arms, sliding my palms over her soft flesh. She hooks her arms over my shoulders and presses her hips against mine. I run my hands up her back, fingers moving along the groove of her spine.

Ana shivers and closes her eyes. I take my time looking her over. Her thick dark hair is pulled to the side in a messy braid, and she removed her makeup, not that she needed it in the first place. The pineapple charm hangs above her full breasts, and I can make out the outline of her nipples through the material of her bra. I'll be able to see through it in the water, and the thought of Ana standing in the hot tub, dripping wet, turns me on.

Feeling my dick harden against her, Ana bites her lip and runs one hand down my chest. Slowly. Tantalizing. Teasing. Her fingers hover over the button of my pants and she moves onto her toes to kiss me. The moment her lips press against mine—wet, warm, and tasting faintly like strawberry lip gloss—I know I can't wait until we get outside to fuck her. I don't want this feeling to go away. It's something I've never felt before, not even with Heather after she accepted my marriage proposal. The attraction I feel to Ana is bigger than anything I've felt before, and it's more than physical.

Ana is everything I could ever want in a person. A girlfriend. A wife. She's beautiful inside and out, and the fear that I'm going to fuck this all up hits me harder than ever.

I don't want to hurt her.

I don't want to lose her.

I won't.

I kiss Ana hard, tongue going into her mouth. My hand slides around her front, over her abdomen, and between her legs. I can feel the heat from her pussy through the thin material her panties are made of. I run a deft finger over her clit, and Ana moans.

God, I love that sound.

I push her panties aside and circle her entrance with my finger. Ana's head falls back and her eyes shut. I play with her clit for a minute before plunging my finger inside her pussy, finding her g-spot right away.

She moans again and slides her legs apart. Her breasts crush against my chest as her breathing quickens. I bend my head forward and kiss her neck, running my tongue across her collarbone. Down to her breasts.

Suddenly, I drop to my knees and bring her panties down with me. Her eyes open and she looks down at me, lips slightly parted. I wrap my arms around her legs, bringing my hands up to her ass-cheeks.

"Oh, fuck," she groans when I part her legs and put my open mouth to her. I lick her pussy, soft and slow, gradually building up pressure and speed. I twist my arm around her legs, sliding my hand along her inner thigh until my fingers brush against her core. I keep eating her pussy, waiting until she's close to coming to slip a finger inside again.

Ana's body tenses and she moans again as the pleasure builds inside, winding tight like a coil that's about ready to spring free. She throws one hand behind her, steadying herself against a barstool, and puts the other on my head, tangling my hair in her fingers.

Her thighs start to shake. Her pussy contracts and she screams my name as she comes, legs trembling. I don't move away just yet, and don't plan to do so until she's squirming and pushing against me.

"Oh...oh...don't you dare fucking stop," she breathes. "Make me come again."

That's a challenge I know I can win.

I break away for just a minute to push her ass onto the edge of the barstool. She leans back, cheeks and chest flushed, and puts both hands on my head. I'm back on my knees and throw one of her legs over my shoulder. I trail kisses along her thigh before I move back to the sweet spot again. She's so wound up, it doesn't take long before she's coming again, pulling my hair and moaning out loud.

When I move my head back, Ana's fingers are trembling. I hold onto her for a minute then pick her up and cross the kitchen, laying her on the living room couch.

"Fuck, you're good at that," she pants.

I flash her a cheeky grin. "I know."

Ana smiles and takes a deep breath. "Come here. But take your clothes off first. Strip for me? Magic Mike style."

"I know that's a movie, but it's one I haven't seen."

"We can have a Magic Mike, Fifty Shades, and The Notebook movie marathon day!"

I grimace. "Sounds fun."

Ana sits up and grabs the two belt loops on the front of my pants. "I wasn't serious, but because you're willing…" She brings me before her and unzips my pants, taking my cock into her hands. I push my pants and boxers down and step out of them. She licks her lips and brings her head down, taking my dick in her mouth. She sucks hard, sending a jolt through me. I rest one hand on her head, watching her bob up and down as she sucks me off. My heartbeat speeds up and this feels so fucking good. I don't want to stop her.

But I do.

Because I don't want to be done fucking Ana yet.

Slowly, I back away, pulling my cock from her mouth. Ana wipes her mouth with the back of her hand. I take her by the waist and turn her around. She's kneeling backward on the couch, holding onto the back for support. I get on behind her and guide my cock into her sweet pussy, slowly thrusting in and out.

I could come right now, but hold off for Ana's sake.

I slip a hand inside her bra, circling her pert nipple with my thumb. Ana tosses her head back, letting out a moan. I move forward and kiss the back of her neck. Her breathing quickens as she gets closer. I drop my hand, sweeping it over the tender flesh on her stomach, not stopping until my fingers find her warm, wet clit. I stroke it, bringing on another wave of pleasure for Ana.

I come right after she does, and we both fall onto the couch, hearts racing. I reach onto the floor, pick up my boxers, and give them to Ana to use to wipe herself up with.

"I'm never going to want to go back to Kentucky if you keep fucking me like this," she pants.

I pull her into my arms. "That's the plan." I kiss her forehead and hold her close for a few minutes before she gets up to use the bathroom. I go upstairs to get towels, trying to hurry and be back down before Ana is out of the bathroom. On my way down, I catch a glimpse of the sidewalk in front of the house.

It's not uncommon to see people out there at any hour of the night. But when I see a man just standing along the street, adrenaline pumps through me. A second later, he hails a cab.

Fuck.

I saw one guy standing on the street and assumed he was watching the house. I can only imagine how Ana feels. I shake my head and go back down. If Steven shows up again, I'll make sure he never does it again.

I won't let anyone hurt Ana.

"Oh, good," Ana says when she sees me holding the towel. "You didn't put pants on and you still want to go in the hot tub."

I chuckle. "No pants allowed."

She takes my hand and pulls me in for a kiss. It's been so long since I've felt this. My heart flutters in my chest, but for a different reason. We get the dessert and wine ready, and Ana helps me wrap my new tattoo before we get into the water.

The yard behind the large house is typical of one in the Upper East Side. Small, totally unnecessary, and filled with over-the-top landscaping. The hot tub is close to the house, made private by a fence and shrubbery. Though you can get a bird's eye view right down to it from one of the bedrooms upstairs. I unpleasantly discovered just how up close and personal the view is a time or two in high school when Luke brought girls over during the few years we lived with our grandparents.

The air cooled considerably, and the warm water is a welcome contrast. We split a piece of cheesecake and drink our wine before sitting back in the water to relax.

"I could get used to this," Ana says with a sigh, closing her eyes and resting her head against the side of the hot tub. "It's beautiful out here, and surprisingly private considering we're surrounded by hundreds of others."

I nod. "The price of real estate has gone up considerably since this place was purchased, but I'll never sell it." Technically, the house isn't mine to sell. My grandmother left the estate to both Luke and me, in an attempt to make us get the fuck along. I wish she could see us now. I raise my eyes to the sky. Somehow, I think she knows.

"You'd be a fool to let this go." Ana raises her leg, swishing the water around with her foot. "Though I'm sure you could get a million bucks for it."

"Millions," I say. "Sometimes I wonder what my grandparents would have thought if someone told them how much their house would be worth someday."

Ana turns and looks at the house. "Are there four stories?"

"Three, and a large attic that was used for the servants' sleeping quarters. The third story is filled with storage and doesn't have central air. It hasn't been updated at all, either, which is why it's closed off from the rest of the house. It's not like I need the space. The attic is pretty cool, though. There's

33

writing on the walls from the early 1900s of the servants' names and daily tasks. I can show it to you tomorrow if you'd like."

Ana smiles. "I would." She tips her head, looking into my eyes. "You know, I really like that you respect the history of this place."

"It has a lot of history, that's for sure."

We sit in silence for another moment, just enjoying each other's company.

"Cole?" Ana starts, looking at me for half a second. "I have a question, and it might be totally weird to ask. Or personal. It is personal. Really personal."

"Well, we were just pretty personal with each other, so go ahead and ask."

"I'm only asking for research. Book research."

I raise an eyebrow. "Now I'm curious. And as your editor, I think I need to know."

"Right." She shakes her head, almost looking embarrassed. "In pretty much every romance book I've read, guys love going down on their woman." She pauses and flicks her eyes to me. "Do you?"

"Very much so."

"But in the books, they also like the taste." She wrinkles her nose and shakes her head. "I can't imagine it tasting very, uh, good. But it sounds hot when you read it, I guess."

"What's the question?" I ask, amused.

"Do you like it? The way *it* tastes, I mean?"

I can't help but laugh. "If you made me a pussy-flavored cake, I wouldn't jump to eat it. But I do enjoy going down on you because you like it, if that makes sense. Seeing you get off turns me on. So I'm not licking your pussy because it tastes like candy, but because it's hot as fuck to feel you come against my face."

Ana's lips pull into a smile. "It's hot as fuck to hear you say that. It was very honest."

I smile back at her. "I have a hard time being anything but honest with you."

Water swirls around her as she moves closer, hooking her legs over mine. "So it's kind of like blow jobs for women then. We don't like—"

"All women love sucking a cock," I interrupt but can't stay serious. "Come on, Ana, don't squash my dreams on that one."

She rolls her eyes. "Right."

The wind blows and I pull her into my arms, sinking lower in the water. "But yes, it's the same, I'd imagine."

"So next research question," she starts. "If I spit afterward, is it that big of a deal? Women in books always swallow."

"At that point, I've already come, so I don't care what you do with it. As long as you don't spit it on me."

Ana laughs. "Good to know. Thanks for helping me with my research."

I raise my eyebrows. "Is there anything else you need help researching?"

Ana bites her lip and gives me a sultry smile. "Actually...yes." She spins around in the water and moves onto my lap, straddling me. My fingers slip easily over her wet skin as I bring my hands up over her back. It's crazy to think that this is happening. An amazing woman is naked and on top of me, wanting to have sex—again—after we just had an epic fuck not even two hours ago. We're comfortable enough with each other to ask personal questions and give personal answers. Ana isn't just the woman I'm dating. She's more than the woman I'm attracted to, she's my friend and I know she can easily become much more than that.

If I had to define perfection, it would be this moment right here.

chapter
five

ANA

"I'm not the best cook," I warn Cole, trying to flip the omelet in one piece. I fail, and it breaks apart. How the hell is anyone able to do it without breaking it? It has to be sorcery.

"That's okay," Cole says as he unloads the dishwasher. "I'm not either."

"It would help if you had decent food in this house," I joke. "I got all excited this morning when I looked in the pantry because I thought I saw chips and salsa. You have chips, but the salsa turned out to be pasta sauce."

Cole chuckles. "I suppose we could go food shopping later."

"Food shopping?" I look away from the eggs to stare down Cole. "You mean grocery shopping?"

"I guess. But I'll be buying food, so I call it food shopping. It's a New York thing, I've noticed from editing books written by people who aren't from here."

"You New Yorkers are weird."

"We are."

Smiling, I go back to the eggs and do my best to salvage

breakfast. After spending several hours in the hot tub last night, Cole and I came inside, showered, and passed out in bed, not waking until late this morning. We lounged around for a while before coming down here to lazily make breakfast.

An important conversation has to happen between the two of us, and I think we're both going on turtle-speed to delay the inevitable for as long as possible. Though the more time I spend with Cole, the less scary that inevitable talk seems.

Well, except for one topic we have to touch on. That's scary as hell and even more irritating. But I'm not going to waste a second thinking about Steven just yet. Not when we have crappy omelets and plain toast to feast on.

Cole makes a fresh pot of coffee and pours two mugs. He adds cream and sugar to his and leaves mine black, just the way I like it. I dish up the food, and we sit next to each other at the island counter.

The sun is out in full force today, and so is the wind. Despite the bright rays of light beaming down on the earth, I know the air is chilly, carrying with it the crispness of fall. It doesn't happen this early back home, and getting an early taste of the sweetness of autumn is exciting.

I fucking love Halloween.

"Tomorrow," Cole starts, and then takes a bite of food.

"What about tomorrow?" I ask, though I'm pretty sure I know where this is going. Cole has to work tomorrow. I don't. Well, I guess I do, but I can do my work from anywhere.

"I have to go into the office," he says after he finishes chewing. "Are you staying or, uh, not staying?"

For someone as well spoken and put together as Cole, it's damn adorable to see him get tongue-tied and flustered around me. It makes me feel good—I'd be lying if I didn't

37

admit that—to know that I'm able to undo the tight strings Cole keeps wrapped around his professionalism.

"I don't know," I respond. "I haven't booked a return flight or anything." I trade my fork for my coffee mug, knowing that Big Conversation #1 is coming. And now I'm nervous again. I want to stay in New York and spend more time with Cole. I'd like to get together with my agent again, and take Lexi up on her offer for dinner once more. There are a couple more touristy things I'd like to do and see, one being any show on Broadway.

But I don't want to come across as desperate or trying too hard. I don't want to let Cole know I'm willing to invest everything into this if he's not. The fear of getting hurt is so strong it mixes with the coffee and makes my stomach gurgle.

My mind flashes back to words my best friend spoke to me not that long ago, about how I used to be the type of woman who said what was on her mind and didn't give a shit about being judged. That version of myself is slowly rising to the surface again.

Finally.

"What would you like me to do?" I throw the question back at Cole, tipping my head and giving him a small smile.

"I want you to stay," he says with no hesitation. Cole's direct, gets right to the point, and knows what he wants.

I can only hope he wants me the same way I want him.

"But I'm worried about you being here alone," he goes on. "I'll be at the office all day, and you're welcome to stay here..."

"Right."

And now Big Conversation #2 has to happen. *Fucking Steven.*

"I'm not sure how to handle this," Cole admits. "I like you, Ana. I like spending time with you and getting to know each other. I like fucking you too, of course." He flashes a grin. "I don't want you to get hurt, but I don't want to make it seem like I'm trying to boss you around or anything and say you can't be alone, but thinking of you here all day when he's out there makes me uncomfortable."

"I understand." I bring my coffee to my lips and take a sip. "And I like being with you too."

Cole sets his fork down and takes my hand. "The last relationship I was in ended in a shitty way. After that, I thought I'd never find anyone who'd make me want to be in one again. But then I met you, Ana...you're the exception."

I gaze at Cole's handsome face. His jaw is set. Eyebrows pushed together. His words are sincere. I want to believe him. I want this to be true. For him to be the guy who comes in and proves them all wrong.

Love can exist. Not all men are jerks.

The sadness is there in Cole's eyes, hidden behind his confidence, and suddenly I see how scared he is to put this all out on the table. He was hurt too and has reservations about moving forward.

Yet he took the chance.

It's still hard for me to see the worth in myself. I'm trying my damn best here, but old habits die hard, no matter how hard I've tried to kill it. But Cole sees it. He sees it and decided it's worth the risk. Tears spring to my eyes. I take my hand away to wipe them. "Sorry."

"Don't be sorry," he says gently.

"I'm not an emotional person like this. But after everything that happened...I really lost faith. Not just in finding someone who makes me happy, but in people in general."

"I understand the feeling. Don't apologize for it, Ana." He gives my hand a squeeze. "So it *is* okay if I call you my girlfriend now, right?"

The word sends a shockwave through me, and suddenly

everything I want scares the shit out of me. I want to be Cole's girlfriend. I *want* to be in another relationship. The apprehension I feel is normal, right? After all the shit that happened with Steven, I'd be weird if I weren't nervous.

I smile at Cole. "I would very much like that."

Fear aside, Cole asking me to be his girlfriend solves the problem of not knowing what he wants with me. But—of fucking course—it opens up a whole bunch of other problems.

Do we have to be secretive? Cole didn't want word getting out in the office that we were sleeping together. Being an actual couple voids the stigma, I think. Or does it make it worse? And I know for sure being Cole's girlfriend brings about a list of things we need to talk about.

I don't live in New York, and I've never had a long-distance relationship before. There are things in my past that Cole should know about if we're more than just friends with benefits. I'm not the type of person to leave skeletons in the closet once I get close to someone. I'd rather pull out the old, dusty bones and bare it all. If not, the rattling and shaking of ones long since forgotten tend to fall out the moment that door is open, and it's always at the worst possible time.

After dealing with Steven and all his bullshit lies, the way he made me feel like something was wrong with me for wanting to be treated right, all the times he told me I was acting like a baby or a drama queen for getting upset when he outright insulted me…it messed with me, and I know it.

But something about Cole makes me think things can be different.

I've already met his family and friends. I've seen him at work. While I know there is definitely more to Cole, I feel like I have a good handle on getting to know him. Steven kept his personal life guarded from me, and then started to remove me from my own personal life.

He didn't want me to have friends.

He didn't want me to talk with my family.

He wanted me for himself, and at first, that notion seemed romantic. The thought alone is jarring, but when you spin it, when you tied it up with a pretty bow and a hell of a lot of manipulation, it works.

And now that it's happened to me, it makes me hyper sensitive to anything and everything that portrays possessiveness as romantic. Sneaking in to watch her sleep is not sexy. It's fucking creepy. Bossing a woman around isn't swoon-worthy. It makes you a jerk. I'll never understand the super-alpha male trend in romance because in the end, I want a nice guy who's not going to treat me like his property. Don't get me wrong; a confident man who knows his way around a woman's body and isn't afraid to show it is fucking sexy as hell.

Like Cole.

He's direct. Knows what he wants. Says it like it is and doesn't seem to give a fuck what others think. He takes charge during sex. He's smart, confident and knows it. But he respects me. He makes me feel good about myself.

So no matter how complicated things are, we should figure this shit out and give it all we have. But before I can go further into the issue and bring it up to Cole, my phone rings.

"It's my best friend," I tell Cole and pick up my phone to answer. "Hey, Jess," I say into the phone.

"I haven't heard from you in days. Are you still alive?"

"Nope. You're talking to a ghost. I'm making my way across the state line to haunt you right now." I take the last bite of my food and grab my coffee.

"You're hilarious, Ana. How are things? I'm guessing you've been so busy fucking your editor's brains out you haven't had a chance to call, right?"

I press the phone against my ear, hoping to muffle her voice enough that Cole can't hear. God, she's so loud.

"Maybe," I say.

"Ohhhh, he's next to you, isn't he?"

"Yes."

"Naked?"

"Jess!"

"Sorry," she laughs. "How are things, though?"

Cole takes the dishes to the sink and starts washing the frying pan. Keeping my coffee in my hand, I walk across the kitchen and look out the window. Another large house is right next to us, though this one has been divided into upscale apartments.

The water is running in the sink, and I don't think Cole can hear me, but I don't want to take chances. I'm not gossiping about him or anything, but it's awkward to have someone listening to your conversation regardless. I go through the kitchen and into the dining room.

"Steven showed up." The words ricochet through me, and I feel paralyzing fear all over again.

"What?"

"Friday night…at that book party I told you about. I thought I saw him there but then thought I just imagined it because it was a closed party and I didn't think he'd be able to get in. And then Saturday morning, he came up to Cole pretending to be an author."

"What…the…fuck. Ana—fuck. I don't even know what to say."

I close my eyes and let out a breath. "I don't either."

"Did you tell Cole about him?"

"Yes."

"And?"

"He thinks I should call the police."

"You should!" Jess exclaims. "You haven't yet, have you? Ana, do you remember what—"

"Of course I do. I just...I...I'm scared, Jess."

"I know," she says gently. "But you're also brave. Really brave."

The tears are back in my eyes again. "I don't feel like I am."

"You are. You're in New York now. You put your book out there and landed a deal. That took a lot of courage. Hell, just writing the damn thing took guts."

"Thanks, Jess." I set the coffee down on the dining room table and lean against the wall. "I'll be lucky if Cole still wants to be with me after this. The beginnings of relationships are supposed to be the best part. And we're dealing with the leftovers from my last."

"It could be a good thing."

"How in the world can it be good?"

"You know that saying 'if you can't handle me at my worst, you don't deserve me at my best'? Well, it's kind of like that in a sense. If Cole will stick by you through all this, and you haven't even been together that long, I think it proves his devotion. If you can get through this together, then you guys probably have a real shot at things in the long run."

I take a minute to let the words sink in. "I think you're right."

"I'm always right, Ana. Don't forget that."

"If I do, you'll remind me."

"Damn right I will. Now, Ana, please contact the police."

I turn around, looking through the dining room. I can see Cole's shadow as he moves about the kitchen. "I will."

"Promise me."

"Promise." I let out a breath and sink down into a chair at the dining table. "Is this ever going to stop?"

Jess hesitates, and that second is all I need to know that

she's unsure. Because there is something seriously wrong with Steven. He's not going to just forget about me and move on. The only way this will stop is if he's locked up forever. I'm miles away from home and he's here.

He found me.

Hundreds of miles away.

My stomach flip-flops and I have to close my eyes, concentrate on my breathing. Everything I tried to downplay in my mind is hitting me hard in the gut right now. The severity of Steven's stalking is rising to the surface and I can't ignore it any longer, can't brush it aside with a "it's happened before."

He's sick.

He needs help.

He needs to be locked the fuck up.

"Yes," Jess says. "Someday it will. Going to the police could speed things along. If you can get a restraining order against him this time and he keeps showing up, he'll be arrested again, I'm sure. He hurt you, and that's on record. He won't get away with this forever."

"Right." I swallow hard and wish I had her confidence. "Cole's done washing dishes. The running water was my cover to talk about this to you," I say quietly.

"I thought you said he knew?"

"He knows enough. And if he asks, I'll tell more. It's not the most pleasant thing to talk about."

"I know, hun. I'm sorry. Have fun and be safe."

"I will. Love you, Jess."

"Love you too, Ana."

I hang up and open Facebook, needing a distraction until my heart stops racing. But that backfires, and I have a glaring friend request from Steven to my Scarlett Levine page. My heart rate increases even more with the fear that he could fuck up my career. The publicist did tell me over and over how important social media is nowadays for authors. What if Steven starts rumors or leaves comments or—

"Ana?"

I whirl around, startled at Cole's voice.

"Sorry."

He raises an eyebrow. "Why are you sorry?"

I shake my head. "I don't know."

Cole comes over and takes a seat next to me, sliding his hand across the table. His fingers weave through mine. "Is everything okay?"

"In theory. Jess thinks I should call the police too. About you know who."

Cole's brown eyes turn serious. "You should, Ana. I wish I could say I knew what would happen, but I don't. Though I am sure an official report filed will help if there is another incident. Keeping a record of all the shit this guy is doing will benefit you in court if it comes to that."

My head moves up and down, and I start to feel like I'm leaving my body. My heart is racing even faster now.

"I just want this over, and I'm so sorry you got dragged into this mess."

"I'm not."

I flick my gaze to his.

"I like you, Ana. A lot. I meant it when I said you were an exception. I've never felt this way about anyone before. You give me hope…you make me want things I swore I didn't. I want to be with you. And if being with you means dealing with your asshole ex-boyfriend, then I want to help."

My brain can't form words. I can only smile and blink back tears. "Thanks," I choke out. "Still, I know this is the last thing you want to deal with."

"Only in the sense that it's causing you to be upset. We all have baggage, Ana. My ex was no saint, either. She did some shitty things that damaged a lot of relationships."

I pick up my coffee, needing a moment again. "So I guess we should get dressed and go to the police station?"

"If that's what you want, then yes. And I strongly encourage you to go."

I put my hand on Cole's. "Yeah. You're right. There needs to be a record of Steven being a piece of shit. Then we can go 'food shopping' like a normal couple."

Cole chuckles. "I like that. Being a couple, I mean."

I smile. "Me too."

~

"YOU'RE RIGHT," I say, looking around the store. "This isn't as exciting as I thought. And there are so many people."

"Sunday is a bad day to go food shopping," Cole tells me and eyeballs the cart, which is filling fast. "Is there anything else you want?"

"Cheese. I'm trying hard not to be appalled that you don't have a good stash of cheese in your house."

Cole laughs. "I don't eat it fast enough and then it goes bad. I hate wasting food."

"I've never had cheese long enough to go bad. I love cheese. I eat it when I'm stressed and it makes me feel better."

Cole raises an eyebrow. "That's a little strange," he teases.

"Hey, when you think about all the other things I could do when I'm stressed, eating cheese is totally innocuous."

"You're right." He directs me to the dairy section of the store.

"Should we invite Luke and Lexi over for dinner?" I ask Cole, putting a block of cheese into the grocery cart. We left the police station and went right to the grocery store. The cop I talked to pulled up Steven's record and assured me that I wasn't overreacting. The fact that Steven found me states

46

away only shows how fucking crazy he is. If he shows up again, I'm to call 911 right away.

"We can," Cole replies, though he doesn't sound too excited about it. He mentioned only a few minutes ago that it'd be fun for us all to get together. Just days ago, Cole confessed to me that he was jealous of Luke for getting married and having a family. The confession was refreshing, admitting something that we all feel but never say out loud.

Sometimes seeing others succeed—in life, school, careers —makes it seem like you won't succeed yourself. Like there is only one spot left at the happiness table, and they got it instead of you.

It's not true at all, and it's salient to me, but I do know that feeling. I've felt it from time to time. And it fucking sucks to see someone else have everything you want when you're scraping yourself off the pavement, just trying to make it through the day.

Jealousy is normal.

Envy, however, is not.

Cole didn't go any further into things, but I get the feeling he and Luke didn't always get along and it had something to do with all that.

"I'll text Luke and ask." Cole pulls out his phone, texting as we browse for junk food. A minute later, he gets a reply, shaking his head after he reads it.

"What?"

He looks at me. "I'm going to say something brutally honest," he warns.

"Your honesty is one of the things I admire most about you," I assure him.

"Luke asked if we wanted to go over to their house instead for dinner. It's a school night and they have kids."

"And?"

"It's annoying how people with kids try to dictate what

people without kids do. Like I'm being punished for not having a child."

I laugh. "It is a little annoying. I mean, I get it. It's a bit of a drive from here to their house, and packing up the kids is probably a hassle. But it's a hassle for the other people as well. People without children can be just as busy as people who do have kids."

"Exactly." He looks at me. "What do you want to do? Go over anyway?"

"I don't mind. I would like to see Lexi again." I debate bringing up how Lexi didn't drink anything at the party but decide against it. I don't want to come across as a gossip. I don't like gossip. Let me rephrase that: I don't like being the one to gossip. I'll listen to others gossip all day long as long as I'm not an actual part of it. "But you do have to work in the morning."

"We can go. Luke said he's making lasagna for dinner. Our grandpa's recipe. It's one of my favorites."

I laugh. "You're willing to go out of your way for food you like. I knew there was a reason you and I got along so well."

chapter
six

COLE

"*D*o you mind?" Ana asks, reaching for the radio dial. We just got in the car and are on our way to Luke and Lexi's house.

"No, not at all."

Ana flips through the satellite stations, stopping on a country music station.

"Really?" I ask with a laugh. "I guess I shouldn't be surprised, right?"

Ana laughs. "What's wrong with country music? And yeah...most of our local stations are country. Only one is strong enough to even come in when I'm in the barn, which is where I spent a lot of time as a child. I can change it if you hate it that much, though. I usually alternate between country and the 90s channel."

I take my eyes off the road to look into her eyes for a second. "You're serious?"

"Yeah," she admits and looks a little embarrassed. "It's a little weird, I guess."

"It is, and that's what I listen to, too. I go between that and podcasts. The 90s channel is number one in my saved stations."

Ana smiles, and she's so fucking beautiful when she's smiling. "I'm starting to think you're the best boyfriend I've ever had."

I reach over and take her hand, smiling as well. "No pressure or anything, right?"

"Oh, I'm definitely putting tons and tons of pressure on you. I'm thinking of doing a performance review at the end of the week too."

"Should I pull the car over and earn bonus points?"

Ana takes my hand and pushes it down in her lap, slowly widening her legs. "Are you trying to bribe me, Mr. Winchester?"

"Is it working?" I inch up the hem of her black dress until I can feel her warm flesh. Soft and tender against my fingertips, it's enough to get me hard right now.

Fuck.

"It just might be."

I give her thigh a squeeze and flatten my palm against her skin before taking my hand back and gripping the steering wheel as tightly as I can.

"If I keep touching you, I might run us off the road."

"I don't feel like dying today, so…" She brings one leg up, pulling her dress up with it, exposing her leg.

"You're killing me, Ana."

She bites her lip and drops her gaze to my lap. "I can tell. Maybe we can sneak away after dinner. Because I really want you right now."

God, this woman is hot. And she's mine.

~

"Uncle Cole!" Paige exclaims when I step into the house.

Lexi holds her dog back, who's trying everything he can to break free and run to me. The dog loves everyone and thinks everyone loves him just as much. "Come look what I set up!" She takes my hand and drags me forward before I have a chance to take my shoes off.

Harper toddles around the corner and gets knocked over by the dog, who Lexi just let go of. Pluto runs to Ana, sniffing her curiously and wagging his tail. Harper cries, and Lexi almost trips over Pluto to pick the one-and-a-half-year-old up. As soon as Harper's on her feet again, Pluto takes off the other direction after a calico cat and knocks her over again. She goes down hard this time, head hitting the tile floor beneath her. Lexi scoops up Harper, concern on her face, and checks her baby's head.

It's instant chaos.

There was a time when this would frustrate me just as fast, but now I kind of like it. Not the part where Harper got hurt, of course, but the hustle of bustle of a house filled with life. This is the first time the noise felt welcome, and I'm sure it has to do with Ana standing behind me.

This is the first time I've walked into this house and not been alone.

"Welcome," Lexi says, cradling Harper to her chest. The little girl clings to Lexi, pressing her face into Lexi's neck. "How was the drive?"

"It was fine," I say, kicking off my shoes. Paige is still tugging on my hand, eager to show me whatever she set up.

"Paige, honey," Lexi says, raising her eyebrows, giving Paige the subtle mom-look that says she's serious. "Remember what we talked about? Take a deep breath and calm down. Let Uncle Cole get in the house first, okay?"

Paige drops my hand and inhales deeply before huffing it out. "Okay."

"She just gets so excited about things," Lexi whispers to us. "Anyway...it's great to see you again, Ana."

"You too. And thanks for having us over," Ana says. We move into the kitchen. Luke is bent over the table, helping Grace with her homework. Dinner is in the oven behind him and smells a-fucking-mazing. Our grandfather was a chef and owned his own restaurant until he retired and sold the place. He was an incredible cook and when Luke was younger, he and our grandpa spent a lot of time together in the kitchen. I thought it was lame then, and wouldn't want word getting out that teenage-me took cooking lessons.

But Luke never cared what people thought, and now he's a good fucking cook, having learned it all from our grandpa. I regret not spending time with my grandparents because I thought it wasn't cool. They aged quickly and now I'd do anything to take it back. Family is everything to me now, and the desire to have my own—to help my own son or daughter with homework while cooking a sit-down meal to have together—burns inside.

But instead of hurting, it's warming my chest. Because for the first time, I feel like things might work out. That I might get this too: a family.

My family.

"Hey," Luke says, looking up from a textbook. He gives Grace a pat on the back and tells her she can take a break. She gets up and goes to Lexi and Ana. Paige drops my hand and follows her sister, saying she wants to show Ana the new shelves Luke just put up in her room. They all go upstairs.

"Thanks for coming over," Luke says and checks on the food. "Sundays are hectic. The girls just got back from their dad's and of course didn't do a single fucking minute of homework over the weekend. We'll be lucky to get it done before bedtime."

Shit. I forgot about that. Grace and Paige spend every

other weekend with their biological father, who's a fucking asshole. I distantly wonder if reminding Ana that Lexi has a crazy ex too would make her feel better or not.

"No problem," I tell Luke, feeling bad now for getting annoyed with him asking us to come over. Not only do they have to pack up a bag full of stuff for Harper, they have to deal with the older girls coming home and then homework. I know from hearing others in the office talk that kids are assigned a shit-load of homework nowadays. "I can help with homework."

Luke closes the oven and turns to me. "What?" he asks, though I know he heard me.

"I'll help," I offer again.

"How's your geography skills? I don't remember all the states let alone their capitals."

I laugh. "They don't teach the song anymore?"

"There's a song about the states?"

"Yeah, but I'm not singing it now."

Luke chuckles and pushes his messy hair back out of his eyes. He's wearing a button-up shirt over a Chicago Cubs tee. The sleeves are rolled up, showing off the tattoos covering his arms. The casual I-just-rolled-out-of-bed look works for Luke, which fits his personality. We're polar opposites.

Luke looks across the room at Ana, and then back at me. "How are things?"

"Good," I tell him, unable to keep the glimmer out of my eyes.

"You told her, then, right?" He lowers his voice. "You told her you like her more than a fuck buddy?"

"Yes. She's my girlfriend now."

"It's about fucking time. You won't be a dick anymore, right?"

"Fuck you."

Luke raises his eyebrows. "I think you'd rather fuck her."

53

"I would. And I will."

"Really, man, it's great. Lexi and I like Ana. And I know our approval is necessary for your happiness."

He's joking, but it's honestly a fucking bonus to have a girlfriend who gets along with Luke and Lexi. Ana went upstairs with Lexi and the girls, leaving me alone with my brother.

Though it's not as awkward as it usually was.

"How your tattoo?" Luke asks, opening the fridge and pulling out a salad.

"Looks great, though it's starting to itch like mad."

"That's normal. It'll peel next. Don't pick at it."

I make a face. "I won't, don't worry."

"You're such a nerd for getting a Harry Potter tattoo."

I look down at my shoulder, though I can't see the ink through my shirt. I got the Deathly Hallows symbol tattooed on my bicep, but it might have been more fitting to get the Dark Mark. "You're an even bigger nerd for not having one. Though don't act like you don't like it. I know Lexi made you watch the movies and read the books."

"It's a good series. The girls really like them."

"Need help with anything?"

"You can set the table. We'll eat in here and not the dining room. Lexi cleaned this morning so I want to keep it clean. She's not feeling very well and I don't want her to have to clean again."

"You could clean after dinner." The words come out of my mouth before I have a chance to think about it. It's something normal to hassle Luke about, but I still feel like I'm just an inch away from being exiled. Again.

"I work tonight," he says in a level tone. "I need to get a few hours of sleep before I go in."

"Oh, right. Lexi's sick?"

"She's tired. Been staying up late working," he rushes out. "Have you talked to Mom lately?"

"No, why?"

"She wants to come out for Halloween."

I raise an eyebrow. "That's not usually a holiday worth traveling for, unless I'm missing something."

"You are, but that's another problem in itself. She wants to go Trick-or-Treating with the girls."

"I didn't even think of that."

Luke shrugs. "I wouldn't have either until I had kids. So that means Mom and Dad are coming out in October, November, and then December. Are you ready for that?"

"They could stay with you."

"But you have that big house all to yourself. Unless Ana is going to stay indefinitely."

I grab a stack of plates and take them to the table. The fact that Ana doesn't live in New York constantly nags at me, and I feel like our time together is fleeting. I've never done a long distance relationship before, and the thought of not seeing her for more than a day causes pain to ripple through my chest.

What the fuck?

There's really no use denying it anymore. I'm falling for this woman, and I'm plummeting fast.

"I'm not sure what the plans are," I say honestly. "We haven't talked about it yet."

"Make sure you do," Luke tells me and his advice is fucking annoying. He means well, I know, but he's my *younger* brother. I should be the one dishing out relationship advice and worldly wisdom, dammit. "I know I told you before, but keeping secrets and not telling the whole truth caused a lot of problems for Lexi and me in the beginning. Learn from our mistakes."

"Mm-hmm," I mumble, unable to bring myself to actually

agree with him, even though he's right. The darkness inside of me wants to surface, and I'm doing everything I can to keep it at bay. Luke is a good guy. Better than me. And that's exactly why I'm feeling like this.

I don't take feeling inferior well, even though he's not meaning to make me feel that way. Sometimes I wonder if it's in my own damn mind, if the guilt of what I did got to me and made me neurotic. Lexi told me I need to stop punishing myself. Maybe she's right. Or maybe I just need to be a better person.

Ana makes me a better person. I'm not sure how, but she does. I don't want to be anything but fucking perfect for her.

"So you're okay with a long-distance relationship?" Luke asks.

"I'd rather it not be long distance, but with her...yeah."

Luke grins. "I know that look."

"What look?"

"That look on your face now. You really like this chick. Don't fuck it up."

"Way to be supportive, asshole."

"Just looking out for you, brother."

~

"How long are you staying in New York?" Luke asks Ana. We just sat down for dinner, and I know he's asking because I said I hadn't yet. I'm not sure whether to be thankful or annoyed.

"Um, I'm not too sure," Ana tells him, flicking her eyes to me. "I like it here, and I'm kind of enjoying the fall weather. I'm from Kentucky, and the weather doesn't change this soon. It's still hot where I live."

"Ever think about moving here?" Luke asks and digs into

his food. The question is casual, yet still seems obvious to me.

"Actually, yes," Ana says, surprising me. "I always wanted to get away from my hometown. I like it, don't get me wrong, but it's just small and filled with a lot of, well...how should I put this nicely...narrow-minded people. I'll admit I thought I'd go somewhere warm, like San Diego, but I'm really enjoying the city here."

"I love New York," Lexi says. "I was born and raised in Brooklyn and couldn't imagine living somewhere else."

"You all are from the city, right?" Ana asks, looking around the table.

"Those two are Upper East Siders." Lexi narrows her eyes with playful judgment. "I converted Luke at least."

"All I know about the different neighborhoods is what I've seen on TV," Ana admits with a laugh.

"Manhattan is nice," Lexi goes on. "The girls like going to Central Park."

"Uncle Cole's house has a ghost," Paige announces, cutting up her lasagna. She says it matter of fact, like she's commenting on the weather.

Silence falls over the table. I look across at my niece. "That's news to me."

"Paige, honey, why do you think Uncle Cole's house has a ghost?" Lexi asks calmly.

"I've seen him," Paige answers.

"I told her ghosts aren't real," Grace huffs, rolling her eyes.

"Yes, they are!" Paige insists. "I saw him last time we were there. He came out of the basement and his clothes were all bloody. I told him to go away and he listened. He's a good ghost."

"I'll be sleeping with the lights on," Lexi mutters and shakes her head. We laugh and go about our meal.

"Are you going into the office tomorrow?" I ask Lexi.

"No. I'll be in Wednesday and Thursday this week."

I nod, trying to think of a way to get her to invite Ana over without being obvious—to both Lexi and to Ana—that I'm worried about Ana being alone at my house with her creepy-as-fuck ex walking around out there. I don't know what I'll do if he comes up to me again, but I know it won't end well for him.

"I'll be in the city Tuesday. Do you want to meet for lunch?" Lexi asks Ana and my blood pressure goes down. Just a bit. Now, just to make it through tomorrow and everything will be fine.

The thought is jarring.

Because things are fine. Better than fine.

It's been years since I've been able to say this, and even longer since I've felt it.

Life is fucking good.

~

"COLE."

I stop dead in my tracks, nerves instantly shot. It's all I can do not to turn around with a grimace.

"Yes, Caitlin?" I say pleasantly, turning around. It's early Monday morning, and I just refilled my coffee.

"Lindsay had a great time Friday. She can't stop talking about it."

"That's great," I say, having to remind myself who Lindsay is for a moment. She's Caitlin's niece, and I was set up to take her as my date to the book release party on Friday. It was a harmless, strictly professional date, yet I had reservations.

"She's still in town, you know."

"I hope she's enjoying the city." Is Caitlin for fucking real right now? She's not really trying to set me up with her niece —again—is she?

"I think it's safe to say that she is." Caitlin's thin lips press into a smile. Fuck. I think she is. "There's a meeting tonight with us publishers about adding a new imprint. I'd like you both to sit in on it and weigh in."

Fuck, that's huge. "I'll be there."

"It'll be catered, so don't bother leaving for dinner. I'll email you the details."

There's a moment before she turns and walks away. A moment, and I don't say anything. Ana is at my house, alone and probably bored. I miss her terribly, and I'm still freaked the fuck out over her being by herself with her ex out there. She texted me not that long ago, saying she just got up and is eating breakfast. The alarm is on at the house, and the motion sensors are on by all the doors. I showed her how to use the security camera system, and she said she had no plans to leave the house today. I'm fairly certain she's safe.

But until I'm completely certain, I should go home. I *want* to go home. Home to my girlfriend. My incredibly hot girl-friend who I cannot wait to fuck again.

And I also want to go to that meeting. If any of the other board members have reservations about promoting me, this will be a good fucking time to show them that they have nothing to worry about. I'm perfect for the job.

I go into my office and get my cell out, laying it on the desk and contemplating exactly what to say to Ana when I call her. She's a grown-ass woman and certainly doesn't need me taking care of her. But I'm worried about her, and that worry intensifies along with my feelings for her.

Forgoing my usual preparations, I call Ana with nothing in particular to say in mind. She answers right away.

"Hey, babe."

"Ana. Hey. How are things at the house?"

EMILY GOODWIN

"Good. All is quiet here. Though I have to admit, after hearing Paige say a bloody ghost came out of the basement, I am a little freaked out. If you come home and find salt lines in front of every door, don't be mad."

I laugh. "There are white candles in the living room if you need them."

"Great! Can you pick up a sage smudge stick and some holy water on your way home too? Best to cover all our bases."

I laugh. "Is it sad I actually know of a place not far from here that sells that sort of stuff?"

"Not sad. Awesome. Totally awesome. Though I do wonder why you know about it."

"I actually went there to research something for a book."

"You're a very thorough editor."

Why do her innocent words seem seductive? Damn, I miss her. "I am."

"I should confess to you that I am looking through the cabinets right now for salt."

"Open the cabinet next to the oven. There's a big canister on the middle shelf."

"Oh, and it's organic," she says and I hear the cabinet shut. "Isn't all salt organic? It's not grown, so how can it *not* be? I don't think anything is sprayed on it like plants, right?"

"There aren't any regulations for salt like there are for meat and produce. It's a marketing ploy."

"And you fell for it when you were 'food shopping', you sucker."

Not only is Ana unbelievably sexy, she makes me laugh. I don't want to go to that meeting anymore. Which reminds me...I need to fucking tell her.

"I did. Hook, line, and sinker, they got me with the promise that pure sodium can be healthy when labeled organic," I say, and an alert beeps on my computer, letting me know I received an email. I absent-mindedly click on it, and see that the agent I was supposed to meet for lunch has to cancel. That frees up an hour and a half.

"I have some good and bad news," I start. "What do you want first?"

"What do I *want?* Hmm...I think you know exactly what I want."

Now I know she meant to be seductive that time.

"But give me the bad first."

"There's a meeting tonight about starting a new imprint. I have to go," I tell her. "It shouldn't take too long. Everyone is eager to leave at the end of the day."

"That sounds exciting. And important. That's not the good news mixed in, is it?"

"No, the good news has nothing to do with books."

"What is it?"

"I'm coming home for lunch."

"I'll make sure to have something ready for you," she says, and I can tell she's smiling. "Make sure you're hungry."

I lean back in my chair, counting down the hours until I can leave. Everything is going so right, falling into place exactly how it should be. It's what I've wanted for years, and now that it's finally happening, I'm happy. Really fucking happy.

The last time I felt like this, everything blew up in my face. I know history isn't damned to repeat itself, but if we don't learn from our mistakes, the fallout is ten times worse the second time around. I can't go back to that dark place again.

If I do, I know I won't come out alive.

chapter
seven

ANA

I push the chips and salsa away, licking the salt from my lips. I brush the crumbs off my hands and slide my laptop across the dining room table and open it up. I've wasted a good part of the morning walking around the house. I told myself I was 'investigating' because it sounds better than snooping.

It's not like I'm going through Cole's underwear drawer or anything, though. But this house is big with lots of rooms, and apparently a whole other floor plus the attic that I haven't seen yet, so walking around and getting familiar makes sense. Plus, it kept my mind off the very obvious fact that I'm alone and Steven is creeping around out there.

I open my writing program and reread the last page I wrote, trying to mentally get back in the story. I haven't written for several days, and that's the first time I've gone so long without writing in a while. I've been a bit distracted, though I'm not complaining. Cole is the best distraction I could ever have.

My fingers inch away from the keyboard and I find

BATTLE SCARS: BOOK FOUR IN THE LOVE IS MESSY SERI...

myself deep in thought about him, feeling what I can only describe as the butterflies in your stomach you get from a school-girl crush.

I'd been single throughout college, only dating casually but never getting a spark with anyone to pursue things more. And then I met Steven, and we dated on and off for a while before becoming serious. I realize now it was his way of gauging me, making sure I was a good fit for him and his manipulative ways. Being a kind, caring and trusting person who had a bad habit of wearing my heart on my sleeve, I was exactly the kind of woman he was looking for.

I never felt like this with Steven. There was no passion between us. No real connection. What I thought was love was him creating a psychological dependence, one I thought I needed because I wasn't good enough on my own. I feel the exact opposite with Cole, and it hits me right then and there how big of a difference there is between being needed and wanted.

Too distracted to focus and write, I get up and start making lunch. I have forty-five minutes until Cole gets in, and I'd like to have his food ready to eat so we have time for sex. Speaking of which...I should probably change out of my PJs. I preheat the oven so I can stick bacon in for BLTs later, and go upstairs for a quick shower before I get dressed.

I take the tablet that shows the security cameras up with me, doing a quick check of all the exterior doors before I undress. I throw my pineapple print pajama pants on the floor and pull my tank top over my head, turn on the water, and wait a minute for it to warm up. The moment I step inside and let the water rush over me, the doorbell rings. Just like Cole said, the tone plays through a speaker up here, loud and clear.

Despite the scalding water pouring down on me, I'm

freezing. My mind goes to a dark place, and I want to grab something—anything—heavy, and hit Steven in the face with it. Hard. Harder than he hit me. Though I refuse to sink to his level, and really, I'm a woman and I'm not as strong—

"No," I tell myself, quieting his voice that still echoes in my mind. I shut off the water and wrap a fluffy gray towel around myself. I left the tablet that shows the security camera footage laying on the bed. Not wasting time to dry off, I hurry into the room. Cold air hits my wet skin, and I shiver. My heart is racing by the time I get to the large bed and grab the device. I wake up the screen just in time to see a young woman leaving the porch.

It looks like she left something there, but I can't make out what it is. Then another woman walks up to the door, carrying a vacuum cleaner. Right. Cole has housekeepers that come once a week. Still, I quickly text him just to be sure.

Me: **Are the housekeepers supposed to come today? They're at the door.**

Luckily, Cole answers right away.

Cole: **Shit, I forgot about them. Sorry. They'll let themselves in, so you don't have to answer the door if you don't want to.**

Me: **I'll hide upstairs in the attic and make ghost noises.**

Cole: **Don't scare them away! They do a good job and I'd like to keep them.**

Me: **So much for fucking you on your lunch break.**

Cole: **I'll be joining you in the attic then ;)**

I send a bunch of eggplant emojis, then grab the dress I intended on wearing and pull it over my head as I walk. It would be awkward for both them and me to not answer the door and then have them stumble upon me just hanging around upstairs.

I trot down the front stairs and punch in the code to disarm the system.

"Hi," I say when I answer the door, suddenly feeling awkward. I don't know the etiquette here. Should I offer them something to eat or drink? Help them carry their stuff inside? Oh, shit. I turned the oven on and I'm pretty sure they have to clean it.

Both women look at me with surprise. They're the same two ladies I saw before, and the older of the two told me she was happy to see Cole with someone. Her words struck me, leaving me curious to just how solitary Cole had been before we started dating.

"What a pleasant surprise," the older woman says to me, smiling.

I reach forward and pick up a bucket full of cleaning supplies, unable to help the manners my parents instilled in me. *Be a good enough person so if someone talked shit about you, no one would believe it.* My father used to tell that to Sophia and me, and while he was less than poetic, the message stayed with me.

Be a good person.

Don't fuck people over.

It's not that hard.

"You don't have to do that, honey," the woman says.

"It's no problem." I step aside and let them in. "I'm Ana, by the way."

"It's very nice to meet you. I'm Misha."

"Courtney," the younger woman says.

Misha places the vacuum inside the foyer and takes the bucket from me. "You're from out of town?" she asks. "I noticed the suitcase last time."

"Yes. I'm, uh, visiting again."

Misha smiles. "It's nice to see that Mr. Winchester isn't alone. Are you staying in town long?"

We walk into the house together. "Yes," I say without thinking about it. I turn around, eyeing the unlocked door behind us. Should I warn them about Steven? On the one hand, it makes sense. On the other, they might not be happy that I'm the one finally filling the empty spot in Cole's life after they hear that I have a batshit crazy lunatic for an ex. "I'll be here until the end of the week, most likely."

"Enjoy your stay."

"I have been," I reply and then realize how dirty that came off. "I, uh, turned the oven on but I can turn it off. I wanted to let you know so you didn't get burned or anything."

"You can cook if you need to. We can work around it."

"Oh, it's okay. I'm not much of a cook anyway. I was going to make BLTs, but the microwave works just fine for bacon."

"Go ahead and make yourself lunch. We'll get started upstairs."

I clean up all the crap I got out in the kitchen and then stick bacon on a plate, cover it with a paper towel, and pop it in the microwave. I could open my computer and work on building my social media presence, but I can't seem to look away from the unlocked front door.

Courtney and Misha are upstairs. They wouldn't notice if I locked the door, right? Would it even matter? It's not like they're locked in and can't get out. This street is rather busy. I assume most people keep their front doors locked at all times. You never know who could lurk around and try the door to see if it's locked.

It could be a sick-in-the-head ex-boyfriend.

I pace around the kitchen, unease growing inside of me. The unease turns to anger, at both myself and Steven by the time the microwave beeps. I open the door and inhale the delicious scent of bacon before carefully peeling back the paper towel. I nuke them for another minute and a half before it's crunchy enough for me.

I make two sandwiches and then wipe down the grease that inevitably spatters on the sides of the microwave every time I make bacon the lazy way. I set both sandwiches on the table and fill up glasses with water.

Steven used to demand I had meals ready and waiting on the table for him. He worked, after all, and was hungry when he came home. Having a snack until dinner was ready wouldn't cut it because he was 'too hungry' for a snack. I loathed cooking for him and is probably the reason today why I hate making dinner. It harbors bad memories. Plus, I'm really that bad of a chef.

I pick at the bacon on my sandwich until Cole comes home. My heart flutters the moment I see him, and I can't help but smile.

This is how relationships are supposed to be. Being with Cole makes me happy, makes me feel like my life is being enhanced.

"Hey, Ana," he calls as he comes into the kitchen. I'm sitting at the table 'working' and stealing more bacon. I stand and go to him, needing to feel his arms around me.

"Hey, babe." I stand on my toes to kiss him, that giddy feeling bubbling inside again. Cole's hands land on my waist, slowly sliding down over my ass.

"Are you not wearing underwear?"

"No, I'm not."

Cole just looks at me and blinks. Then he opens his mouth only to close it again, laughing. "You're trying to kill me, right?"

"I am. I've heard that blue balls can lead to death. Though first I need to marry you so I can get your life insurance. And this house. The ghosts and I want to have a party."

Cole puts his lips to my neck and pulls up the back of my

dress, grabbing my bare ass-cheek. "As long as I get to fuck you first, I'm fine with that."

"Good. I'm glad I have your blessing for your murder." He sucks at my skin and I melt against him, cursing the fact that we're not alone. "I had just gotten in the shower when the doorbell rang. I threw my dress on thinking I'd go back upstairs, but they're up there now."

"It worked out in my favor."

I hook my arms around his shoulders, bringing my head back just enough so I can look into his eyes. "Is it terrible I'll seriously take you up on your offer to have sex in the attic?"

"I was wondering the same thing. It is my house…I can do whatever the hell I want. And I want to fuck you right now."

"Yeah, but…it's weird," I whisper and wrinkle my nose. I move closer and kiss him. "I think you're going to have to wait until tonight."

"The day is going to go so fucking slow knowing this is what I'm leaving."

"I'll send you naughty pictures."

"Please do." He pulls me close again before we break apart and sit down to eat.

"So, this meeting," I start, picking up my sandwich which is mysteriously missing all the bacon on one side. "What do you have to do?"

"Usually go over numbers and discuss how feasible things are before moving forward with anything. A new imprint will mean more work for everyone, and Caitlin has been cheap with hiring additional employees to Black Ink in the past. But I'm hoping that since I'm being consid—" He cuts off, and for a second I think the housekeepers came down the stairs and he stopped talking so they wouldn't hear him, like the news of a new imprint is actually top secret or something.

But they don't come down the stairs, and Cole takes a big

bite of his sandwich to keep from talking right away. It's a bit odd, I suppose, having noted that Cole's direct personality leads him to say pretty much whatever is on his mind. He's not one to start and then stop something, especially not when it comes to me. I've never been good at reading people, and I try to see the good in everyone even when there's not much good there to begin with. But I thought I had a good understanding of Cole, and one thing I know is that he's honest, and that very trait is really fucking important to me.

"I'm hoping," he starts again after he's done chewing. "I'm hoping she'll see the light on this one. New digital-only imprints are becoming very popular among the other publishing houses. It's the best way we can keep up with Amazon, and there's been a huge shift in the market the last few years for ebooks over print."

"Right," I say, wondering if it was just me or if Cole snapped into business-Cole again, abandoning the openness we've established with each other and falling back into dishing out facts, of keeping everything strictly professional.

Except, I know for a fact he wants to have sex.

What the hell? And people say women are complicated.

"Well, I hope it gets sorted out and I hope you're not there long at all. Are you going to be home for dinner?"

"They have a caterer set up to bring dinner, so I'm guessing no. I'm sorry."

"It's okay," I say with a shrug. "If we want to be a normal couple, we're going to run into things like this. Real life, boring stuff. People work different hours and shifts and sometimes don't see each other that much."

Cole chuckles. "Write a book about that. Two people in a relationship just going about their lives, working and watching TV. Yet things are fine, right?"

"Better than fine. But where's the fun in that? I need some drama and angst in my books." I nudge his foot with mine and take another bite of my BLT. I actually got bacon that time.

We chat about work as we eat, and by the time we're done, the housekeepers have already come downstairs. This is a big house, but there probably isn't much to clean, besides doing a quick dust and vacuum. Cole seems to be pretty neat on his own. He says hello to Misha and Courtney, and introduces me as his girlfriend to them.

chapter eight

COLE

"*I* didn't get a chance to say thank you," Lindsay tells me, leaning in close. We're in a conference room, and she took a seat right next to me, scooting the rolling leather chair as close as she could without bumping into mine. Friday night seems so fucking long ago, and I think back, going over everything quickly in my mind.

Lindsay asked me if I had a girlfriend that night. At the time, I didn't, so I told her no. The whole situation is complicated, and just when things settled over the weekend—albeit they were made complicated from another issue entirely—a happily ever after was in sight. Ana is my girlfriend. I like her, she likes me. We have each other and the rest will fall into place.

Sitting here, surrounded by the big-wigs who run Black Ink, I feel like a fucking fool for thinking things will work out for me.

I'm fucking an author. *My* author. And I'm here at this big table, under the microscope and being inspected by every single person around me.

"It was a hectic night," I reply.

"Yeah, that was. I heard the full extent of Gregory's antics when I got home. I had no idea that stuff happens in real life."

I laugh. "Luckily, it doesn't very often. Most release parties we throw run smoothly and the authors are professional and incredibly grateful."

"I bet you're grateful Gregory is done writing."

"He's ready to enjoy some time off," I say carefully. I don't want to so much as look at Gregory Lawrence ever again, but I won't say it. I keep my trash-talking thoughts to myself.

And to Ana.

Fuck.

Was it a mistake to trust her? I've spilled my guts to her on more than one occasion. She has dirt on me and if she went to any of the people at this table she could—*stop.* Ana isn't going to run with an envelope full of drama and tattle on me.

I trust Ana, and I don't hand out trust easily. Being betrayed by the woman I intended to spend the rest of my life with, to create and raise children with, kind of fucked with my head. But with Ana...it's different. I told her she was an exception, and it couldn't be truer. Everything about her exceeds my expectations. She's the kind of woman I've dreamed about in the rare instances I let my mind and heart wander hand-in-hand together.

Strong.

Smart.

Kind.

Funny.

Caring.

Adventur—

"Let's get started," Caitlin's voice cuts into my thoughts, pulling me back to the here and now. I didn't realize I'd gotten so lost in my own mind that quickly, but I guess falling in love can do that to a person.

Whoa. Wait. Back the fuck up.

Did I really just think I was falling in love with Ana?

I did.

Because I am.

"I'm going to cut right to it," Caitlin goes on. "You all know I'm retiring at the end of the year. Which means I only have three more months until I'm done. And you all know there are only a select few who are qualified to take my place. One of them is here with us today, and I'm going to let him take over." Her eyes settle on me, and there's no denying the thrill I feel at being handed the power to make this kind of decision. Caitlin mumbles something indiscernible about not wanting to be here and takes a seat away from the table, sitting near the door and pulling out an iPad from her over-sized bag.

"You're being considered for a publisher?" Lindsay whispers to me.

"Yeah." I let myself smile and feel just a brief second of excitement. She's the only one—besides those on the board—who knows. It feels fucking good to say it, to celebrate the possibility of my promotion.

"That's awesome! You'd be great at it too."

"Thanks."

"We should go out for drinks to celebrate," she suggests.

Shit. No. I don't want to go out with anyone after this. I want to go home to Ana. Before I can come up with an excuse of why I can't go out, Randal Meyers, one of the publishers, hands out iPads to us all and tells us to open the doc he prepared with info on this new imprint. For the next hour, we go over everything. My decisions count, and my input is valued. As the head editor at Black Ink, I always had weight on things like this; we can't add a new imprint if there's no one to edit the books, but being able to be more, to have power to create an entire new line of books, is fucking exciting.

I leave on a bit of a high. I didn't want to tell anyone in case things didn't pan out, but there's no way I can keep this from Ana. She'll be excited, and even though becoming a publisher will complicate the hell out of our relationship, I know we can work it out. Somehow, we'll figure out a way to make it work. As a publisher, I won't edit for her anymore, which takes that direct line of communication away. That's a good thing, really. And when it comes to future deals...well, I'll deal with her agent and not her.

The thoughts are jarring and almost stop me dead in my tracks. I get into the elevator along with Lindsay and two other board members. I'm plotting and planning for the future and imagining Ana in it with me.

I want her in it with me.

"My aunt is roping me into dessert and drinks at her place," Lindsay says apologetically when we get off on the main floor. "Rain check?"

"Yeah, sounds good," I say, mentally telling myself that whenever she comes to cash in that raincheck, I'll take Ana with me. "Have a good night."

"I will. Bye, Cole."

We go our separate ways and I step out of the building, getting hit with chilly fall air. I look to the street, still busy and full of life, for a taxi to take home. And then I see him, sitting on a bench down the street.

To anyone else, he's not out of place. They'd pass him by and not think twice. It's chilly, so the hood pulled down to his eyes is fitting. His head is down and he's listening to music, holding his phone in front of him and looking busy, as if he's waiting for someone to get out of a nearby office.

But the screen on his phone is dark.

He's not innocently passing time. He's watching. He's waiting.

For me.

My blood pumps through me, full of rage. I ball my fingers into fists and spin around, marching over to him. I have no plan in mind other than to hit him in the face. Hard. And more than once.

I come to a sudden stop at the edge of the sidewalk, narrowly avoiding walking into oncoming traffic. A bus rumbles by, and by the time it passes, he's gone. I look around, heart hammering so loud I can hear the blood pumping through my body.

People mill about the sidewalk, and a steady flow of traffic obstructs my vision. But he was there. Right fucking there.

Steven.

Not taking my eyes off the spot he last sat, I pull my phone from my pocket, panic rising inside. I look down for a second to unlock my screen and call Ana. The phone rings once. Twice. Three times. My heart beats faster and faster and scenes from that thriller I've been editing flash through my mind.

"Hey, baby," her voice comes through the phone. I close my eyes in a long blink and exhale. "Cole?" she asks. "Are you there?"

"Yeah. I just left the office."

"Oh, good. I made cookies."

I hold out my hand to hail a cab. "That sounds amazing."

"And I'm naked."

I slide into the cab and shut the door. "Stay that way."

"What are you going to do if I put my clothes back on?"

I flick my eyes to the driver and give him the address.

"Ohhh," Ana coos. "You're in the taxi. Talk dirty to me once you get home."

"I can do that." I look at the passing street, wondering where the fuck Steven went. "How was the rest of your day?"

"Rather uneventful, but good. I got fifty-two hundred words written after lunch."

"That's impressive."

"Once I get really into a storyline, I can't stop. Seriously, I want to keep writing. My poor characters are suffering greatly though. And I'm laughing at their pain."

"Spoken like a true writer." I want to probe further on her day, ask if she saw anything unusual. She's not familiar with the neighborhood though. Unless something was outrageous, she wouldn't be able to tell.

"I'm starting to feel like one. Remember how I said I don't feel worthy of even being called an author?"

"I do. That was the first time I ever saw you. I had no idea what you looked like before that, by the way."

"Were you pleasantly surprised?"

"Very much so."

"Good answer. Anyway, I meant what I said. But now that I'm almost done with another book, I really do feel like a real writer. The fact that I'm in New York and am sleeping with my editor adds just enough drama to my life to make me feel like I could be on a cool show about publishing too."

I laugh. "I'm glad I can help with that." She sounds so happy right now. I don't want to tell her that I saw Steven outside the office. I think back to the man. It was him, wasn't it? I didn't see his face directly, but I knew it was him. I've never been one to claim I have anything remotely like a sixth sense, but as soon as I laid eyes on that guy, something hit me. Almost like a chill but instead of shivering from the cold, red-hot anger filled me and I wanted to hit him in the face until he was nothing more than a swollen pile of torn flesh over blood and bone.

"Do you think you could help me with something else

when you get home? I need some inspiration for a sex scene. I feel like there are only so many ways to describe a blow job."

"So, you're saying that you're going to..." I trail off, only alluding to my hope that she's going to suck my dick. The cabbie is listening, after all.

"Yes. I need to try out a few positions if you don't mind. I spent a good portion of this evening looking at porn on Tumblr and want to try it before I write it. Someone did tell me that the rather extreme sex scenes should be tried out, after all."

"You're in luck. As your editor, I'm legally obligated to try them all out. I had your agent amend the contract to include that."

"I'm going to hold you to it. Don't make me report you for a breach of contract, mister."

I smile, getting turned on at the thought of her. "You have nothing to worry about."

"I'm glad you're always professional, Mr. Editor. So I'll see you soon, right?"

"Yeah, I'll be home in just a few minutes. Leave the house armed." Dammit. I shouldn't have said that.

"I planned to."

"Good." I let out a breath, glad she didn't ask why. I'm not lying to her, but *not* telling her that I'm pretty damn sure her ex was sitting outside my office building feels like one. I was the one who encouraged her to go to the police after all. Steven knows we're together. Maybe he was expecting her to be with me?

He's a shitty stalker if he missed that detail, and as much as I'd like him to be, I know from the few things Ana told me about the fucker, he's not. He knew Ana wasn't in the building.

So what the fuck did he want?

~

"HONEY, I'M HOME," I say when I step into the house. I disarm the system only to arm it again as soon as the door is shut and locked. I came through the front, and kick off my shoes by the door, forgoing putting them away like I usually do. Being neat and orderly brings me a weird sense of satisfaction, but it also gave me something to do.

After the breakup with Heather, my life took a shit. I hated Luke and had to deal with canceling everything we had planned for the wedding. Calling the venues and the travel agent to say the honeymoon was off was one of the lower points of my life. The shit I did after that was my lowest.

Ana doesn't answer and for a moment, my heart stops. There's no way something could have happened. I spoke to her only minutes ago and the house was still armed when I got here.

"I'm in the kitchen," she calls and I let out a breath. She's here, and she's all right. God, if I'm feeling this much fucking anxiety, I can only imagine how she felt.

And still feels.

"Those cookies smell—" I cut off as soon as I step into the kitchen. My eyes widen and my lips part. "Amazing."

I can't get over to Ana fast enough. She's standing at the counter, wearing nothing but a short bathrobe that's hanging off her shoulders. Her hair is twisted into a messy bun at the nape of her neck, and she's dropping spoonfuls of chocolate chip cookie dough onto a baking sheet.

"Hungry?" she asks as my arms go around her. She spins around in my embrace, holding up a spoonful of cookie dough.

"Fucking starving."

She smiles coyly and puts the spoon in her mouth. "Want some?"

"Later," I growl and put my mouth to her neck. I kiss her hard, sucking on her skin. Ana drops the spoon onto the counter, and the metal clatters against the granite. She leans back, pushing her hips into mine. I slide my hands over her body and she puts her hand over my cock.

"I love feeling you get hard," she purrs. "Hard for me."

"You are so fucking hot."

"Do you want me?"

"You know I do. I want you so fucking bad."

Suddenly, she puts both hands on my chest and shoves me away. "Take off your clothes," she orders.

It almost hurts to peel my hands off her body, but I do what I'm told. I've never had a woman take charge like this, and it's getting me so fucking hard. I look right into her eyes and slowly untuck my shirt before moving my fingers to the buttons. She licks her lips and a slight flush comes over her cheeks.

Slowly, I undo one button at a time. I start to lose patience myself and move onto my pants, taking my belt off first. Ana steps forward and grabs it, pulling it free from the loops and letting it fall to the floor.

And now we're tangled together again, lips pressed against one another's. I push my tongue into her mouth and dip her backward, holding her steady with one arm while I try to undo the tie on her robe with the other. It takes a few tries, but I get it free. The fabric billows its way to the floor, and Ana is naked before me. I run my eyes over her and am overcome with lust all over again.

She cups her hands around my face. "Hang on a second," she says softly.

"Is everything okay?"

"Yeah. It's perfect. I just want to remember this."

"Remember what?"

"The way you're looking at me. I don't want you to stop. I want you to always look at me this way."

"I will. Always."

Three words. Three little words. When separate, they don't mean much. Together, even, they could carry different meanings. But right then and there, Ana and I are on the same wavelength. I know what she wants, and she knows what I want.

It's the same thing: each other.

And not just for tonight.

Not just for tomorrow.

We want something serious, something that lasts.

Always.

I don't want to be with anyone else. It's Ana or no one, because as hard as I tried not to, I fell for her. I pull Ana to me and kiss her. I don't say it, but I think she already knows.

I am in love with her.

chapter
nine

ANA

*C*ole's hand slips down the smooth flesh on my back. He rolls over in his sleep but keeps his arm around me. After having sex and then filling up on cookies, we came upstairs to shower and sleep. I was tired in the shower. Tired when I lay down to go to bed. But my fucking characters wouldn't shut up.

Cole fell asleep quickly, and his deep, rhythmic breathing is comforting. And, oddly, inspiring. Lying there next to him, naked, warm, and really fucking happy, is making me want to give my characters their own happy ending. But they have to go through some dark shit first.

And I like writing the dark shit. How fucked up is that? Maybe it's because I know how the story ends that it doesn't bother me. I'll put them through hell now, knowing I'll make things come full circle later and let them get married and have a baby or two.

Slowly, I sneak out of bed, picking my bathrobe up off the floor. I slip my arms in and shiver. Tiptoeing, I go to my suitcase and pull out a clean pair of PJ pants. I've kept everything in the suitcase so far. I'm just visiting, plus I'm lazy. If I'm going to be here for more than a few days, I should probably unpack, though I'm not sure where to put my stuff. Is it too soon to worry about getting my own drawer?

Whatever…it doesn't matter.

I grab socks and go to the bathroom to pee and get dressed. Then I head downstairs and fire up my computer. There's still coffee in the pot from a few hours ago. I pour myself a small mug and microwave it since the pot was turned off and the liquid energy has gone cold. I sit at the island counter, snacking on cookies while sipping my coffee, and pound out two thousand more words. This book is going to be slightly longer than the last, which I like for some reason. Though when I imagine the paperback copies of the books, I want them to be similar in thickness. I roll my eyes at myself. That doesn't matter as long as I'm telling the story these characters want me to tell.

I rub my eyes, feeling exhilarated yet exhausted. It's going on three a.m., and Cole is going to get up in just a few short hours. I save my novel, finish one last cookie, then go upstairs to brush my teeth again and snuggle with Cole.

I pass out the moment my head hits the pillow and don't even wake up when Cole's alarm goes off in the morning. I would have stayed asleep if he didn't gently kiss me and whisper a goodbye in the morning before he left.

Once he's out the door, I stretch out and get comfy. I hear the distant beeps of Cole arming the alarm system. I lay in bed half awake, too tired and too lazy to get up. I grab my phone and do a quick mindless social media check, and then log onto Pinterest to look at domestic household projects that I'll never actually do but pin anyway. I set my phone down and close my eyes, drifting back to sleep and not waking for three more hours. This whole working from home thing is a dream come true.

I get up, get dressed, and sit in the kitchen filling up on

junk food as I write until Lexi texts me and says she's on her way and wants to know if I care to join her as she runs errands or just wants to meet for lunch.

Wanting to get out and do something, I tell her I'll gladly accompany her on her shopping trips today. I get another thousand words in my book and then log onto Instagram, shocked to see over a hundred new followers.

New York Times Bestselling author Quinn Harlow—who I know is good friends with Lexi—tagged me in a post saying she just finishing reading my debut novel and—oh my fucking God—loved it! She ended her post by saying, "If you haven't added Scarlett Levine to your TBR list yet, you need to!"

"Holy. Fucking. Shit," I whisper to myself, unable to keep the smile off my face. The first thing that hits me is how incredibly amazing Quinn is and how big of a following she has. All she did was make one post about a book she read—a mere twenty minutes ago—and I already have a hundred and thirty new Instagram followers. I click on the links she posted, which takes me to Goodreads, a book review site I've been warned about by my agent, Lexi, and now the Black Ink publicist to stay away from, and see that *All I Need* has been added to a ton of new readers' *to-be-read* lists.

I do a little happy dance in my seat and grab my phone to call my mom. I want to tell Cole, but I know he's busy at work. He told me last night that he's a bit behind on edits due to all the crap he's had to deal with at work lately. And I know he's been distracted with me, though I don't really feel bad about it. I like to think I'm a good distraction.

"Hi, honey!" Mom answers on the third ring. "How are you?"

"Great!" I start. "You'll never guess who read and loved my book!"

Mom, who's also a fan of Quinn Harlow's raunchy

romances, is just as excited as I am. We talk about books for a few minutes, and then Mom inevitably turns the conversation back to me and my personal life.

"You're still at your editor's house, right?"

"Yeah," I say, cradling the phone to my ear with my shoulder. "Though technically, I'm at my boyfriend's house now."

A few seconds pass before she says, "Wow, honey."

"Don't sound too thrilled, Mom."

"I'm not *not* thrilled," she says quickly. "I'm incredibly thrilled. This is making me a bit emotional, to be honest."

"Mom," I start, knowing exactly where this is going.

"I want you to be happy. You're such a good person. Your father...he'd be so proud." She breaks off, voice tight. Tears fill my eyes and my bottom lip quivers. Neither of us speaks for a few seconds. If we do, our words will turn into sobs. My heart aches and I miss my dad so damn much.

I dedicated my book to him. He taught me to never give up, to keep going despite the odds. That sometimes the harder things are, the more worthwhile they are in the end. He was the one who wanted to name me after a superhero, though he reminded me time and time again that it doesn't take supernatural powers to do amazing things.

"Tell me about Cole," Mom says, clearing her throat. "He is the boyfriend, right?"

"Yes, Mom," I reply with a laugh. "Cole is officially my boyfriend now. He's just great, Mom." I lean back in the chair and smile. "He's kind and handsome and has this sexy confidence but isn't arrogant...and he makes me feel good about myself. Which I believe is how relationships are supposed to make you feel."

"When do I get to meet him?"

Her question doesn't throw me because I've actually thought about it. If Cole wants to be serious, he's going to have to meet my family. "I don't know. He lives here."

"And you live here. So do I. I'm sure his mother will get to meet you sooner than later."

"Probably not, Mom. He said his parents live in Orlando. But his brother lives here and I met him. My first editor, Lexi, is Cole's sister-in-law, remember?"

"Yes, I remember you told me. I'm glad you're getting along out there. It's nice knowing you're with someone you can trust."

Now *that* throws me. And it's not about Cole's trust. It's that my mom doesn't know Steven is here. She's resting easy thinking that I'm out of that psycho's grasp. I close my eyes and all the giddy feelings that were bubbling inside of me are gone.

Just like that, Steven can ruin my day without even trying.

"It's nice being here with him," I say back. "I'm actually going out with Lexi. She should be here soon, so I should probably get ready."

"Okay, honey. Be safe. Love you!"

"Love you too, Mom." I hang up and go back to Instagram, needing that high again.

∼

"CAN I ASK YOU SOMETHING?" I look at Lexi, who's holding her daughter, Harper. We walked a few blocks and the one-and-a-half-year-old toddled along the sidewalk, happily jibber-jabbering to herself and trying to pick up every little piece of garbage on the sidewalk that she spotted. Which was a lot, by the way. Now she's passed out in Lexi's arms, her little lips squished together in a resting duck-face against Lexi's shoulder. Seeing her like that, all sweet and innocent—and quiet—makes me feel the slightest inkling of baby fever. Then I remind myself that before I can get a cute toddler like

Harper, I have to go through being pregnant and taking care of a newborn.

"Of course." Lexi gently shifts Harper to her other side. Our pace has slowed a bit and we're getting passed by other walkers. We're in Manhattan and are headed to lunch.

"It might sound weird," I preface.

"I like weird."

"Good. Because I'm a bit weird. Anyway…I was wondering if I'm the only one who feels this way because it makes no sense. And maybe I'm being presumptuous to even assume you feel this way. I'm only asking because I know you were in a serious relationship before." As soon as the words leave my mouth, I feel like I've insulted Lexi. She's my only friend in New York City besides Cole, and I don't want to lose her. I really like Lexi.

"Yeah."

"I was too, before Cole. And it ended badly. Now I'm so scared of things going wrong again. I feel like if I let myself be happy and enjoy this, I'm damning it all to hell. Is that crazy?"

"Not at all," she says without hesitation. "And I know what you mean. When Luke and I first started dating, I was so sure he'd turn out to be a loser like my ex or that he'd get tired of me and dump me the first chance he got, I almost let it ruin us. My insecurities made me jump to conclusions and assume the worst about Luke without talking to him first. And that wasn't fair to him. It's almost like a self-fulfilling prophecy and I looked for things I could pick apart. I wanted to find the bad before the bad found me, but there wasn't anything there. At all. Looking for things that can go wrong is a sure way to not find them, but create them."

"I never thought of it that way. But you're right. You're so right." Cole told me that Lexi's ex-husband is a huge asshole. I saw a bit of it firsthand when he showed up uninvited at

Lexi's middle daughter's birthday party. He demanded to see the girls and then called Harper ugly, which couldn't be farther from the truth. The baby is freaking adorable. "Can I ask you something else? Something a bit personal?"

"Go for it. I'm pretty much an open book. After having three kids, I don't really have shame anymore."

"How did you get over it? Your last relationship, I mean?"

Lexi's green eyes meet mine for a second, full of empathy. "I stopped having feelings for Russ like the day after our wedding. I never had the *right* feelings, and I know how hard it is to decide what is right or wrong when it comes to the heart. There really isn't a right way to love someone, after all...but there is a wrong way. Hurting someone isn't love, and that's what Russ did."

She hikes Harper up higher on her hip and lets out a breath. She looks tired, and I wonder if that has anything to do with the fact that she's pregnant. Or at least I think she is based on her not drinking at the release party this weekend.

"I was in denial for a long time," she goes on. "I got pregnant just three months after the wedding, and once the kids were here, it made things a million times more complicated. I stayed with Russell way longer than I should have just for the girls. But that doesn't really answer your question, and I don't really have a good answer other than I just did. It got to the point where being with Russ was more painful than being alone." She looks at me again, and it's like she's reading my mind. "But you're not talking about feelings for your ex, right? You're talking about moving on as a whole. About trusting again after the person you thought you knew turned out to be the biggest *Jersey Shore* wannabe loser in the entire fucking world, right?"

"Yeah," I say quietly. "Opening up...trusting...it's hard." I momentarily consider telling Lexi everything about Steven. He's not your run-of-the-mill jerk ex-boyfriend. He's a psycho stalker who sent me a box full of dead pinky mice the month after I broke up with him.

"It is. And if it helps," she starts, "I've known Cole for a long time. Deep down, he's a good person with a big heart. We've had our differences in the past, but I trust him. I let him babysit, and that's saying something," she tells me with a smile. "I don't let many people watch the girls."

"If he's good enough for that, then he's good enough for me, right?"

Lexi laughs. "I am pretty picky." She looks at Harper. "But how can I not be? This kid is a monster. She figured out that she can push her kid chair up to the counter and climb up there. That was fun to turn around and see last night." She shakes her head. "I need to con—I mean ask—Cole to watch the girls again so Luke and I can go out."

I laugh and swallow the questions that want to come out word-vomit style. They're questions I should ask Cole but border on that fine line of legitimate things couples should discuss but can't be asked too soon.

Does he want to get married?

Have children?

Where would we live?

Would he be okay with visiting my family in Kentucky if things got serious? How would we decide whose family to be with at holidays?

Like I said…those are definitely things we need to know before a big commitment. We've only started this relationship and are still testing out the waters. Yet after going through hell before, I want to put it all out on the table now.

I want to know exactly how deep this water is before I dive in, eyes closed and holding my breath.

"Your stay is open-ended?" Lexi asks as we come to a stop at a crosswalk.

"Yeah. I packed enough stuff to last a week, so I'll either go home, start repeating outfits, or go shopping."

Lexi smiles, green eyes sparkling. "Luke and I are both really happy to see you and Cole together. I can tell you make him really happy."

At first, her words bring a smile to my face. And then I remember that the housekeeper said something similar.

"You're the second person who's said something like that. Am I missing something?"

"His last relationship ended badly and I don't think he's dated much or at all since then. He hasn't had a girlfriend since I've gotten to know him on a personal level." We move with a crowd of people and cross the street. "He's been my boss for years, but we really didn't talk much or anything until Luke and I started dating."

"And you met Luke randomly, right?"

"Yeah. He, uh, he was supposed to be a one-night stand," she admits. "Obviously, one night with me was all he needed."

We laugh and keep talking about how they met and fell in love until we reach the restaurant. Harper wakes up not long after we give our order and refuses to sit in the highchair. Between wrangling the toddler who keeps wandering away and trying to eat the appetizer we ordered, Lexi asks me about my book, remembering everything with impressive detail.

"I'm totally taking the series back from Cole as soon as I can," she says. "I cannot stand Caitlin Black. I probably shouldn't tell you this because it's not professional for an editor to shit-talk their boss to a signed author, but I feel like you've already crossed that line and I can dish the dirt."

I laugh. "Cole's already told me how much he hates her."

"Everyone does. I've heard rumors that she's retiring, though I've been hearing that for the last four years now and it never pans out. She looks the same as she did when I first started at Black Ink, like she never aged. When I was a kid, I won a goldfish at a fair, and all but one died. The thing lived forever and was the ugliest, meanest fish ever. It lost an eye and was always covered in this white fungus that we couldn't get rid of. And it ate anything I tried to put in the tank with it. Caitlin Black is the fish. Old and mean, making everyone wait for it to die so you can stop looking at it. Only I don't want her to actually die. Just get the hell out of the building."

"I had a mouse like that. Goldie. She lost all her fur and had literal fat rolls. I'd never seen that on a mouse before."

"Grace really wants a pet mouse. But I have a slight fear of rodents because there was a rat family living under my porch at our old house. They got really big and even my dog was scared of them."

"So the New York sewer rat thing isn't just a myth?"

"I wish."

I laugh again, and it hits me that sitting here talking to Lexi feels so natural. Harper comes over to me and holds up her hands. I pick her up and she curiously looks at my face before poking the pineapple charm on my necklace. I'm not a shy person, but I'm not the most outgoing either. Not anymore, at least.

I border the line between introvert and extrovert. Making new friends isn't daunting, but I'm not exactly a social butterfly either. Which is what makes this whole thing with Lexi so striking.

And puts a pit in my stomach.

It's fucked up, I know, to feel this dread when things are going right. I should enjoy the ride, not constantly fear the rug coming out from beneath me and everything crashing down around me, burying me in the wreckage.

Do normal people feel this? Are they able to just enjoy a good thing without the lingering and constant nagging that it's temporary? I'm not sure I completely believe that a good thing can last in the long run.

Luck runs out, after all. All good things come to an end.

I remind myself of what Lexi said. When you expect the bad to happen, it will. Not because it was going to, but because you make it happen. I have weird theories on the power of thought and transforming energy into actions, and those theories tend to come out quite passionately if I've been drinking.

The rest of lunch goes by quickly. Lexi and I are alike in many ways, and the fact that we're both getting freaky with Winchester brothers is oddly bonding. Harper spills Lexi's iced tea right before we get up to leave. It sloshes down the table and all over Lexi's lap as well as soaking the cute dress Harper's wearing.

"Motherfucker," Lexi mumbles, shaking her head. I help her clean it up the best we can. "I have a change of clothes for Harper in the diaper bag, but she's all sticky now."

"Want to take her to Cole's and give her a bath? I have a key and we're not far."

"That's a great idea, actually."

Lexi takes her own coat off and wraps it around Harper, not wanting to get Harper's jacket wet. She'll need it on the drive home, after all. Lexi didn't think twice about stepping into the chilly October air jacketless and seeing that sort of unconditional love pulls on my heart and gives me another inkling of baby fever.

What the hell is wrong with me? I should at least get to my six-month anniversary with Cole before I want to pop out his babies. I always thought that shit people said about a woman's biological clock was sexist bullcrap, but maybe there's some fact behind it. Because that's all this is. I don't really want a baby. I'm not really in love with Cole enough to start daydreaming about a family. And I'm certainly not imagining him resting on the couch with our little baby snuggled up against his muscular chest.

Nope.

Definitely not.

Fuck. I'm a bad liar.

≈

"I'm so glad you suggested this," Lexi says as she turns on the water. We're back at Cole's house, upstairs in one of the bathrooms to give Harper a bath. Lexi pulled spare clothes out of a dresser from a guest room. She told me it was Luke's room when he lived here with Cole a few years ago and thankfully, he was too lazy to bring all his shit home once he moved in with Lexi and the girls.

"And you are too, aren't you, baby?" she coos to Harper, taking off the toddler's sticky clothes. "Oh, shit, I left the diaper bag downstairs."

"Shhh-ttt," Harper repeats.

"Fuck," Lexi mutters. "Wait, no. Dammit. I mean crap. Don't say that, baby." She sighs heavily and I laugh. "Whatever, right?"

"In all fairness, it's kind of cute. Totally in a it's-not-my-kid-so-I-can-laugh sort of way."

"I laugh too," she confesses. "I probably shouldn't. And I still forget she's talking and repeating stuff. Though I think it's more denial. You're growing way too fast, baby."

"I'll get the bag. Where is it?"

"By the door."

Lexi lifts Harper up and into the tub. I leave the bathroom and go down the main staircase, which empties into the foyer by the front door. The diaper bag is sitting right next to it. I reach for it, fingers brushing the nylon straps.

And then something clatters behind me.

I jump back, nearly knocking into the entryway table that houses candles and an expensive-looking vase. The door is locked, but I didn't turn the alarm system back on. I freeze, all the hairs on the back of my neck standing on end. I don't know where the noise came from for certain, but it sounded like the basement.

Of course, it's the fucking creepy-ass basement.

I wrap my fingers around the straps of the diaper bag and force myself to turn around. Wishing the noise did indeed come from the bloody ghost Paige claims lives in the basement, I look down the hall.

There's nothing there.

But I heard something. I know I fucking did.

I let out a breath. Inhale. Hold it. Exhale. Nothing. It's all in my head. Every little bump or creak in this old house is nothing to freak out ov—

Something clatters to the floor, echoing throughout the house. It's the distinct sound of metal falling to concrete. My heart rate spikes and my nerves are on fire. I grab the diaper bag and high-tail it up the stairs.

The bathroom Lexi and Harper are in is off a bedroom. I go into the bedroom first, shut and lock the door behind me, and then race into the bathroom, doing the same with that door. The water isn't running anymore, and the only sounds that fill the room are Harper's gentle splashes.

Lexi turns, wondering why the hell I shut the door behind me. The amusement on her face disappears the moment she sees me.

"What's wrong?"

"I think someone is in the house."

"What?" she asks, though I know she heard me. She reaches for Harper, pulling the little girl out of the water.

"I heard a noise. Like something fell in the basement. I

never re-armed the house once we got in. We came in the front and I locked that door, so I thought it was okay."

Lexi wraps a towel around Harper, who's starting to fuss and reach for the water, wanting back in. Lexi grabs her phone, unlocks it and gives it to Harper, which I think is odd at first, and then realize she's doing it to keep the kid quiet.

Harper watches videos of her and her sisters dancing, keeping quiet as Lexi madly reaches into the diaper bag, getting a diaper and clothes for her.

"Are you sure?" she asks me, hands shaking.

"Yes. I heard a thump and dismissed it. Then I heard something fall and it sounded like murder-tools hitting the cement floor."

"Murder tools?"

"Yeah. Like a big-ass knife or a heavy metal something that he'll use to hit us over the heads with."

"Do you have your phone?"

"Yeah."

"Call Cole. Ask him to look on the cameras."

I nod and pull up Cole's number, pressing the 'call' button. I put it to my ear as it rings. Lexi dresses Harper and dries off her arms before taking the baby into her lap. Lexi told me that she gets scared easily. I can see she's fucking terrified, and having her baby to protect probably makes things ten times worse.

"Voicemail."

"Shit," Lexi mumbles. "I'll call Jillian."

We trade phones, distracting Harper with photos on mine while Lexi calls her editor friend and Black Ink.

"Jillian, thank fucking God," Lexi breathes. "I need you to get Cole. Now. Yeah, it's important enough to interrupt a meeting."

Shit. I know what I heard, though I can't help but worry I'm overreacting.

Being a drama queen.

Emotional.

Childish.

Acting like a teenage girl.

All the things Steven told me when I'd get upset.

I close my eyes and shake my head. I heard a noise—twice —and the police officer I spoke to not that long ago told me to trust my gut. And my gut is telling me that two locked doors aren't enough to stop him if he wanted to hurt us.

"Hey, Cole," Lexi says after a minute. "I'm at your house with Ana. We're upstairs in Luke's old room and thought we heard something coming from the basement. Can you check the cameras and see if there's a ghost wandering around or something?" A few seconds pass before she speaks again. "No, I don't think you need to—fine. Oh, okay." Another pause. "We're in the bathroom, and I'm not sure." She looks up at me. "You locked the bedroom door, right?"

"Yeah, I did."

"She did. Okay, here she is."

Lexi holds out the phone to me. I take it, and she cradles Harper to her chest, kissing the toddler's wet hair.

"Are you okay?" Cole rushes out. "I'm on my way."

"No, don't leave work. Please, stay. And yes, I'm fine," I whisper. "Harper spilled a drink on herself at lunch so we came back here to give her a bath. I locked the door but didn't think to arm the house again. I went downstairs to get the diaper bag and heard two loud noises. The first was like a thud, the second sounded like metal falling to the floor."

"Do you think it's Steven?" Cole asks, getting right to the point.

A chill comes over me, followed by guilt. If Steven is in the house, then I put not only Lexi, but Harper, in danger. I close my eyes, trying hard not to cry. Though if I do, I can always blame it on the fear. There was a time in my life when having people think I was weak for expressing my emotions physically—crying, screaming, clenching my jaw—was one of the worst things.

But I'm human, and humans experience emotions. A wide range of them to be exact. The problem isn't in how you express them. How you let them out. Let them be known. Control them to an extent, but allow yourself to feel.

Anger.

Sadness.

Joy.

Love.

No, the problem isn't in experiencing emotions. The problem is not feeling anything at all.

No guilt. No shame. No regret or sense of common decency. Void of all emotions that make us human.

"That's my fear," I say softly.

"I just logged on," he tells me. "And I'm looking through the cameras. I don't see anything now. You locked the front door?"

"Yes, I checked it."

"That's clear…so's the back…and the side…the basement looks fine, but there's just that one camera by the windows. Wait," he says and my heart falls onto the floor. "There's a lot of dust in the air like something's been down there. I'm alerting the security team," he says, and I know he means the people who work for the alarm company. "They'll be there along with the police in five minutes or less. Keep the door locked."

"It's probably nothing," I blurt, emotions switching from fear to embarrassment at an impressive rate.

"It's better to get it checked out. I'm hoping it's nothing. That the bats are back or something."

"Bats live in attics," I correct, though I know Cole's just trying to ease my mind. "Though it could be the giant sewer rats. I just learned they're real. I thought it was an urban legend."

"It very well could be," Cole goes on. "I don't go down there as often as I should to check on things."

"Right. You were in a meeting?"

"Of sorts. I was on the phone with an agent."

"Sorry."

"Don't be. We were having a difficult time coming to an agreement on terms. The break will do us both good."

"Well then, I don't feel as bad. Sometimes a little break like that is all you need to come back with a clear head."

"That's what I'm hoping. And by a clear head, I mean she realizes that she's being ridiculous and agrees with me or the deal is off."

I laugh and feel the knot in my chest loosen. "What's the book about?" I ask just to fill the time. Cole tells me, and a few minutes later, Lexi's phone beeps, letting me know another call is coming through. I pull it away from my ear to see who's calling. Luke's name—surrounded by heart emojis—flashes across the screen. "Luke is calling Lexi," I tell Cole. "I'll call you from my phone if I can get it away from Harper."

"All right," he says. "Hurry."

"I will." I hand the phone to Lexi, who looks instantly relieved when she hears her husband's voice.

"Da-da," Harper says and reaches for Lexi's phone. I sneak my phone out of her hands to call Cole back, listening to Lexi explain what's going on to Luke. It sounds like he got an alert from the security company and couldn't get a hold of Cole to see what happened, so he tried Lexi to see if she knew anything.

Hearing Lexi recant everything—that we came here to give Harper a quick bath and that I heard a noise—makes me feel utterly stupid again.

Stupid and weak.

I ran up here and hid. I didn't grab a chair and push it up against the basement door to keep whoever was down there at bay. I didn't get the tablet and take a look at the security system myself. Didn't grab a knife or anything to defend myself with.

I just ran.

I close my eyes, exhale, and look at Lexi and Harper.

No more.

No more running.

No more being afraid.

If Steven is here, it's time to settle this once and for all.

COLE

*M*y heart hammers against the confines of my chest. Adrenaline surges through me, and I tap my foot against the floor, waiting for the minutes to tick by. I can't take my eyes off the security cameras. I look back and forth between the two near the stairs. If anyone came from the basement and went onto the second story, I'd see them.

Ana told me to stay here, and I know she's wrestling with feeling silly and being fucking terrified. After what feels like an hour, Ana calls me. I answer my cell right away, needing to hear her voice. I'm sure this will turn out to be nothing like Ana said. I've had animals in the basement before. The house is well maintained, but it's old. I have no idea how the fuck squirrels get in, but they have. Once when I was a teenager and Luke and I were home alone—our mother worked the nightshift as a nurse and my grandparents were on a holiday—a raccoon got in and sounded like a gang tearing the place apart.

Not being there to protect Ana is killing me. She's tough

as nails and won't take shit from anyone. I'm fairly certain she can hold her own in a fight, but that's not something I want to risk. Not now. Not ever.

I love her, and if anything happened to her, it would destroy me.

"I don't hear anything," Ana says. "I'm standing by the bedroom door and don't hear a thing. How's it looking on the cameras?"

I tap my fingers on my desk, about ready to jump out of my fucking skin. I can't sit here and do nothing but monitor the motherfucking screen. I'll run home if I have to. And if Steven is there, the only way he's leaving is in a body bag.

"Still clear. I can see both staircases, so if anyone were to get up them, I'd know."

"About that…" Ana says. "The back stairs. Do the people at the security place check in every now and then?"

A smile pulls up my lips. Only Ana could make me smile, could make the anxiety momentarily go away in a time like this. "They could, I suppose, but aren't supposed to. For privacy reasons, but I guess there's nothing stopping them and no way of me knowing."

"Unless someone pulled out their phone for a home video."

"If that happens, I'll make sure to get us the proper royalties."

Ana softly laughs. "I'm going to go downstairs and check things out."

"No, Ana," I say, and hear Lexi echo me in the background. "The cops should arrive at any minute."

"Exactly. I'll be fine."

I stand, unable to sit here any longer. "Ana, if someone is in the house, just—"

"Oh, good," Erica, my assistant says the second I walk out

of my office. "I was just coming to get you. Some author is here for a meeting, but I don't see his name on the schedule."

"Hang on a second," I tell Ana and turn my attention to Erica. "I don't have any meetings today. Maybe he got the date wrong."

"Probably. Do you want me to tell him to come back?" She leans in. "He's kinda creepy, to be honest. He touched my hair. I don't know why people think it's okay to touch my hair, but it's not."

"Did he give his name?"

She nods. "Steven."

"Call security," I tell her, and her eyes widen.

"Cole?" Ana's voice comes through the phone. "What's going on?"

I don't fucking know what's going on. If Steven is here, then he can't be at the house. "I'm not sure," I say, walking briskly through the office. "Please stay in the room, okay?"

"Sure," she agrees with a sigh. "The doorbell just rang. I'm going into the hall to look downstairs."

I listen to the door open and Ana's quiet breathing as she moves through the hall. "It's the police. I see a car on the street in front of the house. I'm going to go downstairs and let them in."

"Okay. Call me back as soon as you can." I hang up and emerge into the lobby. There's a tour going on today, and over a dozen elementary-aged children mill about, chattering and talking. Half look bored out of their fucking minds and the other half are excited to be inside the country's largest publishing house.

And right now, they're in my fucking way.

"That's odd," Erica mumbles. "I told him to wait here."

I move my phone down and stride to the front desk. "Hilary," I say a little too loud to the secretary. She's talking to a teacher and whirls around, startled. "Oh, Cole, great timing! This is Cole Winchester, the editor-in-chief. He's in charge of the—"

"There was a man here," I interrupt. "Dark blonde hair, light blue eyes. Said his name was Steven and had a meeting with me."

"Yeah, he's sitting...well, I don't know now. He was right there."

I move closer so the students on the field trip don't hear me. "You didn't see where he went?"

"He left," the teacher Hilary was talking to informs me. "He almost took out one of my students on his way out, which is why I remember. Just a minute ago. I saw him get in the elevator."

"Is everything all right?" Hilary asks, looking paled.

"Get security up here. Have them look for him."

Hilary nods and reaches for the phone, not taking her eyes off me. Luckily, we've only dealt with security issues a few times over the years I've been here, and nothing has ever been that bad.

I take off, passing up the elevator and going to the stairs. I push open the heavy door and step into the rarely-used stairwell. It's muggy in here and smells like stale cigarettes and sweat. Going as fast as I can, I race down the stairs, not stopping until I'm on the main floor. There's only one way in and out of this building without the proper clearance to get in through the back.

It's lunchtime, so the lobby is full of people coming and going. Heart racing and breathing hard, I look around, scanning the doors. Did I miss him? The elevators rarely go straight down. It takes a fucking while to go from the floor Black Ink is on to this main one, having to stop every few floors to let someone on or off.

I stand there, looking abso-fucking-lutely crazy, watching

for Steven. Spinning back and forth from the elevators to the doors. Over and over. A minute passes. Then another. And another.

He's gone, hidden inside the building or having snuck out onto the street.

"Mr. Winchester?"

I whirl around and see one of the building's security guards coming over. I let out a breath.

"I got a report about a man entering your office," Henry, the guard goes on. "White male, late twenties, with dark blonde hair and light-colored eyes. Goes by the name Steven."

"Yes."

"You have a history with him?"

"Not personally. He's the ex-boyfriend of an author we recently signed. She flew out to the office for paperwork and he followed."

"A stalker?"

"Yes," I say, not sure if I should be relieved how easy it was to tell the truth and still keep the fact that Ana and I are together a secret. It doesn't matter in this case. Steven is a fucking loser.

"Is that author here now?"

"No, but I'm assuming the guy was looking for her."

Henry nods and takes down a few notes. "But he asked for you, correct?"

"I'm the editor for the new author. She'd been in a meeting with me recently. To discuss her book and the details of her contract," I add, then regret it. None of that matters. None of that is relevant. I meet with authors—male and female—all the time and no one questions it. I guess I have a bit of a guilty conscious about this, and I don't want word to get out that I'm fucking Ana.

Or that I'm in love with her.

Not yet. Not when so much is on the line right now.

"All right. I'll take a look at the camera footage and get the word out about this guy. You have nothing to worry about."

Oh, but I do.

~

"YOU DIDN'T HAVE to leave work," Ana says for the third time. "I feel so bad. I told you it was nothing."

I pull her into my arms and kiss her forehead. The police checked out the house. A few things had been knocked off a table downstairs—which was the noise Ana heard, but there was no sign of forced entry. Ana joked that it was the ghost Paige had seen, but the cops think it's more likely to have been an animal. Rats and even cats have been able to sneak into old houses like this through very small openings.

I already called pest control to come out and have a look for rodents. The last thing I need is mice chewing up my shit and spreading their diseases all over the fucking place. People can get really sick from rodent droppings, and my nieces come over here.

"It was something, and we have a reason to be on edge," I assure her.

Ana hooks her arms around me and rests her head against my chest. Things are falling back into place, though it feels a bit like suspended animation. Everything is hovering in midair, temporarily whole until we get hit with a blast that sends everything flying.

"And, like I said, my day was giving me a headache. I'm glad to be home early." I kiss Ana again, debating on telling her about Steven.

That's twice in a row I'm fairly certain he's showed up. Neither times I saw his face for the actual proof, but I'm not one to believe in coincidences like that.

"I'm glad you are too." She stands on her toes to kiss me. I pull her close, dipping her back as my tongue enters her mouth. "Wanna fuck me on the stairs again?" she whispers with a smile. "Put on a little show? The people monitoring your house might be on high alert after that little scare."

"You know I'll take you up on that offer anyway."

She laughs. "I would be disappointed if you didn't."

I take her hand and lead her into the family room. We sit on the couch, and I turn on the TV just for the background noise. Lexi left shortly after I got here, needing to be home in time for her kids to get off the bus. She suggested we join them this weekend. She and Luke are going to dinner and a movie with her sister and her husband. Ana agreed, saying it would be fun.

She has to go home eventually, and I know we need to talk about it. I want her to stay, and worry that once she goes home she'll realize she doesn't want to be with me anymore. It's been a while since I've been in a relationship, and I've never felt like I was very good at the maintaining part. Though I'm sure that was largely because I was with someone who wanted someone else. No amount of maintenance could have kept that ship from sinking. As much as I try to keep the thought out of my head, I can't help the dark thoughts that creep in, making me wonder if Ana is going to get sick of me, decide that she's had enough, or that I'm not bringing enough to the table for her to stay all in.

Because I'm not sure if I do, and I'm not sure if I'll ever feel good enough for her. Though in all fairness, there probably isn't anyone in the whole fucking world who is good enough for Ana.

"Thanks again, Cole," she says softly, looking up at me. I hook my arms around her and she settles against me, propping her legs up on the cushioned ottoman in front of the couch. "You didn't have to go through all that trouble for me."

"Of course I did," I promise. "And it really wasn't trouble."

"Are you sure?"

I can tell she feels bad and is still embarrassed that she got freaked out. Being cautious when you have a stalker who's hit you so hard he's broken fucking bones is no reason to be embarrassed. He made her feel that way, told her that she was overreacting by feeling perfectly normal emotions in response to his actions. Fuck, I want to break *his* bones.

"Positive. It's not any trouble when...when..." When you love someone. Because I'd walk through hell and back for her. She's the most incredible woman I've ever met, who's been through so much and came out stronger. She didn't let her past turn her bitter, didn't turn her life upside down to get back at Steven. She picked herself up off the floor and did her best to move on.

I'll never meet anyone like her ever again, and I don't want to go a day of my life without her being in it in some way.

"...When it's your girlfriend," I finish.

"Well, good," she says, smiling up at me. "Want to watch *Fixer Upper*? I can attempt to make dinner after that."

"I like the sound of that." I tighten my grip on her and kiss the nape of her neck. Maybe if I keep holding her like this, she'll never leave.

THE REST of the week passed by uneventfully. Ana spent the week writing, mostly staying at the house, and sometimes going to the coffee house to set up and write for the day. We were both on edge Wednesday, but were able to quickly fall back into the routine we're starting to establish.

She's more of a night person than I am, but that's mostly due to me having to get up early for work. The last two mornings she's gotten up and eaten breakfast with me, going back to bed once I leave for work and texts me when she's up. We text back and forth throughout the day, not talking about anything in particular.

Now it's Friday night, and since we have plans to go out tomorrow with Luke and Lexi, we're ordering takeout and staying home. We're sitting in the living room, salad, pizza, and breadsticks out in front of us on the coffee table, eating and debating what to watch, when Ana's phone rings.

"It's my sister," she says. "FaceTiming me. That's odd." She answers and waits a second for the call to connect. "Did you call me by accident?" she asks.

"Hello to you too," her sister says. Her voice is similar to Ana's. "What are you doing?"

"Eating and looking for a movie to watch."

"Are you alone?"

Ana raises an eyebrow. "No. I'm with Cole."

"Ohhhh, the sexy editor?"

Ana looks over her shoulder at me. "My family might have Googled you before I flew out to New York."

I laugh. "I usually research any new author I work with, so I can't blame you there."

"Let me say hi!" Ana's sister calls.

"Are you drunk?" Ana asks her and scoots closer to me, leaning against my chest. I slip my arm around her and move closer to her face so I can be seen through the phone. Ana's sister looks a lot like her, but with shorter hair.

"I might have had one or two drinks. Hi!" she says to me. "I'm Sophia."

"Nice to meet you, Sophia."

"Mom," Sophia says, turning her head. "Come here!"

"Oh my God, Soph, stop. What are you doing? Why are

you drinking and why are you FaceTiming me? I'd think someone died but you're way too chipper for that. It's weird, actually. Did you smoke something?"

"No!" she laughs. "I'm celebrating, and that's why I called." She holds up her left hand. "Jason proposed!"

Ana instantly smiles and congratulates her younger sister. I believe her to be genuinely happy for her, but I wonder if she's feeling just the slightest like I did when Luke got engaged. Not jealous because I wanted Lexi for myself, but reminded just how fucking single I was at the time. Times have changed, but I like things happening in a predictable order. I'm the older brother. I should have been married first simply based on math.

"Tell me how he asked!" Ana gushes. I play with the bottom of her shirt, sweeping my fingers over her soft skin, only half paying attention to her sister talking.

"Mom and Aunt Alberta want to throw a party this weekend. It's nothing fancy, of course, but I really want you to be there. We need to start planning stuff and I need my sister to help me pick out a dress. And then plan the *official* engagement party."

"This weekend?" Ana shakes her head. "That's short notice, Soph."

"But you live here. Just come home."

Her sister, direct in her drunken state, is right. Ana doesn't live here.

"I want my shoes back, anyway," she goes on. "I need to wear them."

"I don't even know if I can get a flight this fast," Ana says.

"Oh please," her sister says, waving her hand in the air. She catches sight of her ring and swoons over it. "I can't imagine the planes to Salt Creek book that fast."

"They don't book at all. Salt Creek doesn't have an airport, dummy."

"You know what I mean."

I look down at Ana, who's biting her lip. She doesn't want to go home, and I can only hope it's because she'll miss me.

I know I'll fucking miss her.

"I'm inviting you too, Cole," Sophia slurs. "Mom told me that you told her you two are a couple now. You have no reason to—where are you?" Sophia narrows her eyes and moves closer to the phone.

"I'm at Cole's house," Ana says slowly, eyebrows going up. "Is Mom around? Or Jason? I think you've had too much to drink." Ana turns to me again. "She hardly ever drinks. One glass of wine makes her drunk. I've held her hair back more times than I care to remember."

"I'm not that drunk. Everything looks fancy."

"Oh," Ana says and sits up, switching the camera view so her sister can see the rest of the family room. "This house is fancy. It's a century-old Victorian townhouse in the Upper East Side."

"Are you serious?"

"Very. See for yourself."

"That looks like a movie set. Or Bruce Bane's house."

"Bruce Wayne," Ana corrects with a laugh. Bane is—never mind. But yes, Cole's house is amazing. I feel fancy being here."

"Stop making this about you," Sophia says and Ana laughs. "Anyway…I'll see you tomorrow, right?"

"Soph, I don't—"

The phone cuts off, and I'm not sure if her sister hung up on purpose or by accident. Ana shakes her head with a sigh. "So, that's my sister."

"She seems nice."

"She is. I've accused her of being a bit dull in the past, but she's a good sister. And I knew Jason was going to pop the question soon."

"I remember you saying that. Do you want to go home?"

Ana blinks and looks down for a second before moving her gaze back to my eyes. "Yeah, I'd like to go to her engagement party. And I'd like for you to come with me. But it's weird...it doesn't feel like home anymore."

chapter eleven

ANA

*C*ole takes my hand in his, lacing his fingers through mine. He's pulling my suitcase behind him, and I have his. Mine's twice as big and three times as heavy. He's a light packer, and we're only here for a little over twenty-four hours. We got on the earliest fight we could, landing in Kentucky a little after eight a.m.

I'm fucking tired and ready for a nap.

"My mom's here," I tell Cole with a yawn. She's picking us up from the airport and taking us to her house, where my car is. I told her I could pay for a cab to take us to her house, but she insisted. That's just how she is, and I know she's excited to meet Cole. "Thanks for coming." I give his hand a squeeze.

"You're my girlfriend. You don't have to thank me. Didn't you say that being together means doing boring couple stuff?"

I laugh. "Yeah. I did."

"See? No need to feel bad. And I don't think this weekend will be boring."

"I hope not. Though my family can be a little overbearing."

"Please. You haven't met my mother yet."

I like talking with Cole like this, like we both have our sights set on the future and we're both in it. It feels good. It feels right.

It's fucking terrifying.

"My family likes to drink wine and then they get loud."

"They sound fun. Please tell me there will be drunken barn parties."

"Sophia is way too posh for that. Well, she likes to act like she is. But don't let that fool you. She was my partner the year we won the hog wrestling competition at the county fair."

Cole laughs. "That's something I'd like to see."

"Just mention it to my mother," I say dryly, "and she'll pull out the videos." I roll my eyes. "She's oddly proud of us for winning. Of all the things to be proud of, right?"

"Well, you haven't really accomplished anything else."

"You're right. Catching a pig in a big puddle of mud is much more impressive than landing an agent and getting a publishing deal with my first novel."

"Don't forget getting the industry's best editor to work with you."

"But Lexi had to give up the project," I tease.

Cole laughs and gives my hand a gentle tug, pulling me close to him. He kisses my forehead and steps forward to hold open a door. We step out of the airport and move down the sidewalk until I see my mom's truck. She gets out, waving wildly.

"Oh geez," I mutter.

"Ana!" Mom calls, still waving.

"Hi, Mom," I call back so she knows we see her. "I hope you don't mind being hugged," I warn Cole but it's too late. Mom's here and throws her arms around me. I hug her back, setting the suitcase down. "Mom, this is Cole. Cole, this is my mother."

"Nice to meet you," Cole says, holding out his hand to shake. "You're lucky, Ana. You look just like your mother."

Mom laughs and hugs him, fawning all over Cole for a few seconds. We toss our luggage in the back of the truck and get in the old Chevy. It was Dad's truck, and he always said it was a lucky charm, and that the angels were partial to American-made Chevrolets and kept a closer watch on him when he was driving.

Cole sits in the back next to me, and I reach up and push the passenger seat forward to give him more leg room.

"It's a bit tight back there," Mom says, looking over her shoulder. She starts the rumbling engine. "You can sit up here, Cole."

"Nah," I say. "We like making you feel like you're the limo driver."

Mom shakes her head, eyeballing me in the rearview mirror. "How was your flight?"

"Early," I say the same time Cole says, "Fine."

"Ana's never been much of a morning person," Mom says.

"I've noticed," Cole agrees with a laugh, and then looks at me with wide eyes.

"She knows I'm staying with you," I say quietly, knowing that's what he was wondering. "I'm a big girl. I can do what I want," I add with a wink.

I yawn again and rest my head on Cole's shoulder. He and Mom talk, mostly getting-to-know-you shit, and I doze off for over an hour after failed attempts to converse along with them. When I wake, the sun is out in full force and my heart lurches at the familiar sights of my hometown.

A funny feeling comes over me. I'm back where it all started. Where I was born. Raised. Where we buried Dad.

Where I met Steven. Broke up with Steven. Wrote my book. Where I lived.

And it still doesn't feel like home anymore.

The funny feeling starts to turn into guilt, and my stomach gurgles unhappily. I'm the type of person whose guilt sometimes manifests physically, and nine times out of ten, it's with some sort of stomach issue.

I look around at the hills and farmland and feel out of place. It's so fucking weird.

"Morning, sunshine," Cole says softly.

"I could sleep for at least two more hours," I grumble, rubbing my eyes. "It's going to take me a week to recover from this."

"I'm glad to see you're still as dramatic as ever," Mom jokes. "Good thing you don't have to get up and go to work."

"I'm lucky, I know," I say.

"If you went to bed before two a.m. you wouldn't be so tired," Cole says, and I give him a look, shaking my head.

"It's not a problem when I get up after ten. I like the night."

"A lot of authors say that," Cole tells us. "And there's been research on creative people working better at night."

"And being messy, right?"

"Nice try," Mom quips, turning around. "Though I have heard that too. Artists thrive in chaos."

I watch the landscape pass by, becoming more and more familiar the closer we get to Salt Creek. It's not that I don't like this place anymore. I do. It'll always have a special place in my heart, and I think I'll always feel a little protective of this place and the people in it. I had a good life here, surrounded by good friends. My good memories outweigh the bad by the thousands, yet I feel like I'm done with it.

Is it possible to outgrow a town?

"Hey," I say to Cole. "Cows."

"There's so many," he says, looking out the window.

"Cole was born and raised in Manhattan," I explain to my mother, who's giving him a weird look. "This is going to be a culture shock for him."

"I've left the city," Cole tells me, raising an eyebrow. "I've traveled a lot."

"Yeah, but isn't most of your travel for work?"

"It is."

"And you go to other big cities around the world, in office buildings."

He can't help but laugh. "Fine. Though I have gone to Gregory Lawrence's farm before." He grimaces. "Think of the release party and multiply it by ten. That's how drunk he was."

"Celebrity 'farms' are a lot different than a backyard barn and free-range chickens all over the lawn," I say with a laugh. "I've seen pictures of Gregory's estate and it's super impressive. But don't worry, I won't have you feed the chickens or the goats."

～

"I LIKE YOUR FAMILY," Cole tells me. Sophia and Jason's engagement party is winding down, and those remaining have moved outside and are crowded around a bonfire, drinking beer and laughing. Cole and I are on the back-porch swing, covered with a thick fleece blanket. I'm on my third glass of wine, and it's making me sleepy.

"I'm glad." I snuggle closer to Cole. "They're good people."

"They seem like it. And you turned out all right."

"Just all right?"

"Yeah. You like country music." We both laugh and he leans forward to kiss me. "You don't see the stars like this in the city." He lifts his eyes to the sky and pushes off the porch with his foot, making the swing rock back and forth.

"No, definitely not."

"It's quiet here. Is it offensive if I say it's kind of creepy? It would be all too easy for some crazy inbred hillbilly family to kidnap us and keep us as entertainment in their basement."

"Funny you should say that. Salt Creek has been the inspiration for every B-grade, made-for-TV horror movie, you know."

"I knew it."

I close my eyes, the rocking of the swing lulling me to sleep. "But, no, it's not offensive at all. It's true, too. Not so much about the inbreeding, though a kid I graduated with did marry his cousin. But we're very...rural."

"Tired?"

"Just a little."

Cole pulls the blanket up over my shoulders. "Want to go inside?"

"Will you come with me?"

"Of course."

"Then yes, but you have to help me up."

Cole puts his feet down, stopping the swing, and helps me to my feet. Taking the blanket with me, we go inside and up to my old bedroom where our suitcases are. "I didn't intend to stay here," I remind Cole. "I have my apartment in town."

"You said it's a bit of a drive, right?"

"Yeah, like forty minutes, but it's okay. We don't have to stay with my mom."

"I don't mind," Cole says. "You're tired."

"I am," I mumble.

He sits on the bed and pulls me down with him. I kick off my shoes and snuggle up against his chest. I hear Cole's shoes fall onto the floor at the foot of the bed and he brings the blanket up over me.

"Thanks for coming," I whisper.

"I'm glad I came. It's fun talking to people who know you."

"Yeah, I guess it is. You can get the dirt on me."

Cole kisses my forehead and I close my eyes. He runs his fingers up and down my arm and right there, squished together on my childhood bed, snuggled under a My Little Pony bedspread, is the best place in the world.

Wherever he is, is where I want to be.

~

SUNLIGHT STREAMS THROUGH MY WINDOW, strong and bright, and much too hot for my liking for October. I'm already missing the cooler air on the east coast. Cole is still cuddled up close to me, stripped down to just his boxers. Thor is sleeping on the pillow above him, paws outstretched so he's touching Cole's hair.

"So you approve?" I whisper to my old cat.

Thor responds by blinking and looking away, which is either a 'yes' or a 'fuck you' in cat language, though it doesn't really matter. Seeing my asshole cat kind of loving on my boyfriend is pretty much as sweet as all those photos of muscular men holding babies, if not sweeter. I smile and slowly get up, grabbing my toothbrush and face wash from my suitcase, and go into the bathroom.

Cole is still sound asleep when I get back, and Thor has moved into his coveted spot—my pillow—so I go downstairs to find something to eat. I can hear my mom and sister talking and want to get as much as possible out of this visit since I'm going back to New York with Cole this afternoon.

"Hey," I say, coming into the kitchen.

"You passed out early," Sophia quips, raising her eyebrows. "Have enough to drink?"

"I always have enough," I shoot back and go to the fridge, getting out orange juice. "How much later were you guys up?"

"Just like an hour or so. Cole's still sleeping?"

"Yeah, and Thor was loving on him. I didn't have the heart to wake either of them up."

Mom slides a pan of cinnamon rolls into the oven. "He came down here after you fell asleep."

I look up from the glass of orange juice I was pouring. "Oh. Why?"

"To help us pick up. He washed all the dishes."

A smile pulls up my lips. "That was very nice of him."

"It was!" Mom beams. "I really like him, Ana."

"So do I," Sophia says. "Jason didn't even help pick up. He's still passed out on the couch." She rolls her eyes. I've always liked Jason. He's a good guy, a little nerdy but it's fitting for my sister. I know he doesn't drink often, so when he does, it hits him hard. Lightweight.

"Good, because I like him too."

"Don't sound too happy," Sophia mumbles.

"What?" I raise an eyebrow. "I am happy."

Sophia looks at Mom and then at me.

"What?" I ask.

"Last night," Mom starts, "Cole told us how much he cares for you."

"And that's a bad thing?"

"Oh, no. Of course not. But he lives in New York and you…you don't."

I take a drink. "I know. And I think it's pretty safe to say Cole knows. Though if he didn't before, he does now. You know, since he's here and all."

"Diana," Mom says softly. "We all know you can be a bit impulsive and that's gotten you into trouble before."

The trouble she's referring to is the shit-storm with Steven. And a handful of other things I did out of impulse.

"I'm not going to move in with him anytime soon if that's what you're wondering. I've been staying with him, but it's only because a hotel is pointless when we're...well...you know."

Mom rolls her eyes. "I'll pretend I have no idea what you're talking about. But that's not what I'm worried about."

"Then what are you worried about?" I take another few sips of my orange juice, feeling a headache coming on. I didn't drink *that* much last night, and waking up slightly hung over is making me feel old as fuck.

"That you'll end up going in the complete opposite direction."

I look down at the counter, not knowing what to say to that, which says something in itself. It's rare when I don't have a witty comeback or am able to deflect things with humor. But right now...I got nothing.

Because it's true, and it's making me feel like there's something wrong with me. I'm either one end of the spectrum or the other. I go in too hard, too fast, and end up falling on my ass, looking stupid and hurting *bad*. Or I play it so safe I don't even try.

"I don't want to see you give up on something that I think will turn out to be great in the end. I know I've only met Cole once and it was for a short amount of time, but he came down here to help. He made an effort to talk to us and get to know us when he very well could have stayed upstairs. I can tell he really cares."

I nod, not trusting myself to look up and make eye contact.

"Ana," Sophia begins. "After meeting Cole for like five minutes, I told Jason he needs to step up his game, and he just freaking proposed."

"Cole is pretty great."

"He is," Mom and Sophia say at the same time.

"Which is why I think you should spend more time in New York," Mom tells me, and once again, I'm speechless. "This last year you haven't been living. I know what happened isn't something you'll ever get over, and I can't blame you for becoming guarded. Heck, even I am when I meet new people. I worry about you girls constantly and locking you both in a tall tower, safe and away from danger still seems tempting."

"The witch in the Rapunzel stories always dies in the end," Sophia reminds Mom.

"I won't make the same mistakes she did." Mom winks. "But your father always reminded me..." She trails off, tears filling her eyes. The waterworks will go around; it's hard for any of us to talk about Dad without getting emotional. "He always said there was a difference between living and surviving. That having a life isn't the same as being alive. Getting away from here...away from him...it's good for you. And I think you've landed a good guy along the way."

I blink and a tear escapes, falling onto the counter. Mom is right, and my father's words ring true in my head. The sicker he got, the more optimistic he became. It pissed me off at first. He was dying. His time was limited. Why the fuck was he so full of life? So determined to make the most of the shitty situation and act like everything was okay.

Then he told me that he knew how shitty everything was. That it sucked more than anything to know he would be leaving us, that we'd have to see him as he deteriorated. Take care of him. Bathe him. Feed him. Watch him die. He didn't want to be a burden, but until that time came, he could inspire us and make sure we lived the life he wished he had.

Dad was right. Living in fear, constantly guarding my heart to keep it from breaking is not really living at all. Cole and I have a good thing going, and it would be downright stupid to call it quits out of fear.

But Mom was wrong about one thing. I can't go to New York and be away from Steven. No matter where I go, he follows, and that's not fair to Cole. It's not fair to anyone. Maybe I'm wrong, but my gut tells me if I really care about Cole and the people in his life, I won't get them involved with Steven, which is bound to happen in a matter of time.

Lexi.

The girls.

The other people at Black Ink.

All are fair game to Steven if he knows I have any sort of emotional attachment to them.

And *that* is a reason to walk away. Not to protect my heart, but to protect Cole's.

chapter
twelve

COLE

"*T*hat's the third cup this morning," Lexi says when I walk into the break room Monday morning. She's sitting at the table with Jillian, her best friend and fellow editor.

I pull the coffee pot from the base and raise an eyebrow. "I'll refrain from commenting on the number of donuts you've had."

"Four. I have no shame when it comes to donuts."

I laugh. "You and me both."

"What happened to the fresh fruit and healthy shit we used to have?" she mumbles, breaking her donut apart.

"Donuts are cheaper."

"Cheaper and tastier."

"They're too tempting," Jillian says, shaking her head. I don't know Jillian well, but she's always well put together, organized, and on time. I think she's a bit of a health nut and follows a lot of those trendy diets. She's a great editor too, which is really all I care about. "Bring back the fruit."

"I'll see what I can do." I add creamer to my coffee, thinking that if I do become a publisher, that's something I can actually do. Little things that boost morale can add up and make a difference. I turn and see Lexi yawning. "You look like you could use some more coffee too. Girls keep you up?"

"No," she starts and then looks like she just said something she wasn't supposed to. "I was editing for Quinn. She asked me to co-write a book with her, actually."

"I told her she should do it," Jillian says. "I know how much Quinn makes from a release. You could take that fat wad of cash and go on a relaxing vacation with Luke before-"

Lexi gives Jillian a look, making her shut up right away. Clearly, I'm missing something. On a different day, I might try to figure it out. Or at least be curious. But right now, I'm too fucking tired to give a shit about anything.

Except Ana.

We didn't get in until after one a.m. last night. The flight was delayed at first due to weather. And then there was a mechanical issue that took "ten minutes to fix" five separate times. After that, we got stuck in traffic.

So, yeah…I'm fucking tired. I'm off my game today and I know it. I had to look at my schedule three times within twenty minutes because I couldn't remember what the fuck I had to do this morning.

But this is worth it. So fucking worth it.

My feelings for Ana continue to grow, and meeting her family and seeing the place she grew up made me feel that much closer to her. It's not just about sex, even though the sex is fucking amazing. What we have is real. What we have can turn into something more.

I believe in us, and I'm not one to believe in fucking anything.

～

"I THINK it's safe to say I'm officially the world's worst cook." Ana dumps a bowl of boiling noodles into a strainer in the sink. "Spaghetti is supposed to be foolproof. And I burned the noodles."

"How do you burn noodles? Aren't they in water?" I loosen my tie and uncuff my sleeves.

"Half were sticking out when I put them in the pot. I thought they'd just like slide down in when the bottom half got all soft and cooked. But that didn't happen, and I must have had the heat up too high and the flames got the parts of the noodles that were sticking out."

I look at Ana, blink, and then laugh. "I can honestly say I didn't think that was possible."

"I'm sorry I ruined dinner."

I come over to her, slip my arm around her waist and look at the noodles. "It's not ruined. We can cut off the burned parts. You didn't burn the sauce, did you?"

"Ha, no. But it might have splattered all over the microwave." She makes a face, shaking her head. "I'm kidding. Well, it did, but I cleaned it up."

"You didn't have to make anything, you know."

"Well, I'm here all day tending the house and doing chores while you go out and earn a living for the family. It's the least I can do, sir."

I laugh and put my lips to her neck. "I expect dinner on the table when I get home and the kids in bed by seven, then."

"I'm already off to a late start." She turns around in my arms and puts her hands on my shoulders, looking up at me with big eyes. "How ever can I make it up to you?" She takes her lip between her teeth and lets one hand slowly drop from my shoulder to my waist, fingers slipping around my belt.

"You know," she starts and moves her other hand down. "There is something about a man in a suit I find irresistible. It's even better when it's my own boyfriend."

I can't be bothered with talking anymore—even dirty talk. Ana unbuckles my belt and I take her by the waist, lifting her up and onto the counter. Her legs wrap around me and she inhales, breasts rising into my face.

"Should we eat?" Ana asks, raking her nails across my back.

"It can wait."

~

"Are you going to tell me what that security issue was about or am I going to have to beat it out of you?" Melissa, the head of the marketing department, asks me Tuesday afternoon. We're sitting in her office going over schedules and releases, making notes on the books we anticipate will be the biggest sellers. Ana's book is on the list, and got bumped up after Quinn Harlow's endorsement. Still, I'm mentally reminding myself to treat her like any other author and not give her special treatment.

"Scarlett Levine, the new author I took on," I start.

"You mean were forced to take on, right?" Melissa asks quietly, raising her eyebrows. "We all know you don't edit romance. It had to be Caitlin, right? She's getting ready to finally leave this place and wants to boss everyone around."

"That's Caitlin at her finest," I respond. Melissa has worked here for as long as I have, and I like and trust her, but I still don't like to say anything bad about anyone at work. One can never be too careful and all that shit. At least I have Lexi to shit-talk others with now.

"She's doing it to me too." Melissa shakes her head. "The woman knows nothing about marketing yet is questioning everything I do. I cannot wait until she's gone, and I just hope whoever takes her place isn't as big of an asshole."

"You and me both," I muse.

"Anyway, the security issue is about Scarlett Levine?"

"Sort of," I start, choosing my words carefully. Obviously, the issue with Steven can't be ignored, but I want to keep as much private for Ana's sake as I can. "She came here for a meeting to discuss the book and stayed in the city for a while. The guy who came in the building looking for her is her ex-boyfriend. I don't know the details," I lie. "But I guess things ended badly and he's still hung up on her."

"Wow, that's crazy. But you know what they say. Real life is stranger than fiction. Poor girl. She was so nice and easy to work with, too. Find out details for me! I'm nosey and curious," she says with a laugh. "You're her editor, she'll talk to you."

"Maybe," I say back with a laugh. It's not unusual for editors and authors to develop friendships during the course of an edit. Writing a novel, after all, can be a rather intimate process, and sometimes the root of a story needs to be explained and understood to better edit the thing.

"So, did he ever find her?"

"No," I say, but in the back of my mind, I'm thinking *not yet* because I have this bad feeling something is going to happen. My pulse increases just thinking about it, and knowing that Ana is home alone and plans to go out later to write at a coffee house.

"Speaking of Scarlett..." Melissa starts and I look up, eyes widening. "She got a great endorsement from Quinn Harlow, and that gave her a good boost on social media. I'm getting some giveaways set up for Scarlett all over the place to keep this momentum going."

I let out a breath and nod, happily going back to work. There's no way anyone in the office besides Lexi knows that I'm dating Ana. And it has to stay that way for just a couple more months, until Caitlin leaves and I take her place. Once my promotion is secure, I won't worry. Well, not as much.

It'll still be in the back of my mind that someone will throw a fit that an author is fucking a publisher, though really, there's nothing anyone can fucking do about it.

Especially if Ana's first book does well *before* it gets out that we're together. Fuck. That's even longer to wait. I distantly listen to Melissa going over marketing shit while I contemplate everything in my head, coming to the conclusion that until Caitlin is out of here, no one can know about my relationship with Ana. Caitlin's hellbent on making things difficult before she's gone, and won't hesitate to yank any or all marketing funds away from Ana if she thinks I'm giving her special treatment.

"Cole?"

I blink, realize Melissa has said my name more than once and shake myself.

"Sorry. Got lost in thought."

"Happens to the best of us," she says slowly. It's out of character for me, and she knows it. Fuck. I can't be distracted, not now when so much is on the line.

"Do you have an estimate on when Scarlett will finish her second book?"

"The last time we spoke she told me she was ahead of schedule. I'll email her today and get a word count."

"Great. I'm thinking if we can get something lined up ahead of time, a rapid release will work great in her favor and we can time it between Quinn's releases. She only has two with us this year instead of her normal four." Melissa sighs. "I can't blame her for going indie with her other books, but damn, I miss seeing those numbers rolling in."

"You and me both."

"You're close to Lexi now, right?" Melissa starts. "She's your sister-in-law and everything."

"Yeah."

"You couldn't suggest to her to try to convince Quinn to

come back, could you?" Melissa is half joking, but also half serious. We'd all love to have Quinn back at the press exclusively.

"I'll see what I can do," I agree, just to move on. And then I remember that Lexi said Quinn wants her to co-write a book for her. There's nothing stopping Lexi from doing that, but it could easily piss off people here. And she didn't seem afraid of a conflict of interest. Am I the only one who worries about this shit?

I drive myself fucking crazy.

Melissa and I go over several more books and an hour later, I go back to my office and start responding to emails and approving files. Ana texts me, telling me she's at a cafe not far from the office and plans to stay there the rest of the afternoon. She's nearing the halfway mark of her book, which puts her *way* ahead of schedule. I smile and reply, telling her I'll meet her there after work.

Thinking of food reminds me that I skipped lunch—again —to have a conference call with an editor from a different branch of Black Ink. I get up and go into the break room to take whatever leftover donuts are remaining. On my way there, I go past Lexi's office and see her hunched over her desk.

"Lexi?" I call, coming to a stop. "Are you all right?"

She looks up and forces a smile. Her face is pale and there are dark circles under her eyes. "I don't feel well, but I'm fine."

"Are you sick?" I resist the urge to step back. I hate being sick and don't want to catch anything. I don't have time for that.

"Uh, maybe. I'm fine though. Just feeling that afternoon slump. It's hitting me hard and I can hardly keep my eyes open."

"I'm going to the break room. Want a coffee?"

Lexi makes a face and shakes her head. "No, but thanks."

I check my watch. "There's only a couple hours left today. If you feel that bad, go home early."

"You don't mind?" Relief washes over her face.

"Not at all," I reply, not saying that part of me sending her home is to keep the germs at bay. "Are you okay to drive? You look pretty, uh…"

"I look like shit, you can say it. I don't even need a mirror to know how bad I look today. Trust me, I feel even worse," she snaps and then shakes her head. "Sorry. I'm just so fucking tired." Her eyes get glossy like she might cry. What the hell is going on with her?

I raise an eyebrow. "Do you want me to call Luke or something?"

"No. I'm mad at him right now."

"Really?" I take a step forward. "What did he do?" Dammit, I should not feel satisfaction knowing Luke fucked up. But I do. I try to rationalize it by saying that if Luke and Lexi fight, it makes things more real. Because real couples fight. Have issues. Disagree.

And then make up.

I've never gotten to the second part.

"He cleaned the house. Like, perfectly."

I raise an eyebrow. "And you're mad at him because of that?"

"Not because he cleaned the house. But he did it and it's like I can't do it."

What? I blink, look at my sister-in-law and shake my head. "I'm not following, Lexi."

She shakes her head and glares at me. "It was like a spite-cleaning."

"Okay. How dare he, right?"

She throws up a hand. "I know! I'm capable of cleaning,

and I keep things fucking nice and neat!" She lets out another breath. "You really won't mind if I leave?"

"No, but be careful driving, all right?"

"I will. I can snooze on the subway for a little bit before I get to my car and drive home. I'll be fine. Thanks, Cole." She shuts her computer and starts packing up. Mentally laughing, I go into the break room, grab a donut and another cup of coffee then head back to my desk. I spend the rest of the day working on a project, and check my email for the last time before I leave since I don't plan to do a single work-related thing once I leave the office.

I get a shit-ton of emails every day. From agents, other editors, and writers who think their novel is the best fucking thing in the world and is so mind-blowing they deserve to bypass the normal agent-to-editor submission process and in the end, I'll be thanking them for the chance to work on a literary masterpiece.

I cannot fucking stand entitled assholes.

My assistant helps filter through emails that come in to my Black Ink email account, moving any legitimate queries into a different folder for me to read later. I quickly browse through those, and get sucked into a submission for a paranormal series. It's geared more toward young adult readers, but is interesting as fuck. I make a note and forward it to another editor who works with books for younger crowds.

I switch over to my personal email and delete all the junk mail, and then email my mother back. I try to email her a few times a month, just letting her know how my life is going. And my emails are always the same. Things are fine. Yes, I'm still single, and no, please don't try and set me up with your gynecologist's daughter who lives in New Jersey. I hit send and pick up my coffee, finishing the last of it. Another email comes through, and I wonder if Mom replied that fast. I click over and see an email with a blank subject line. I'm about to delete it, assuming it's junk, when I notice the sender's email.

"Steven," I whisper and lean forward. "What the fuck do you want?"

I mouse over the email, hesitating for a moment. I'm no IT expert, but I know opening an email can trigger viruses and shit. Whatever. I'm too fucking curious and anxious to see what the fucker has to say. I open the email.

Cole-

Ana has always been a terrible cook. Just thought I'd let you know. I hope the spaghetti wasn't as bad as it looked. It didn't seem to ruin your night though.

-S

My fingers curl into my palms, digging into my flesh so hard it's almost breaking the skin. I close my eyes and stand, doing everything I can not to freak the fuck out and flip my desk and break shit.

He was watching us.

Last night.

Maybe the night before.

And before that.

Violating our privacy. Violating Ana. Watching her while she was alone in the house. Probably getting off on it, and who's to say he didn't pull out his phone and start recording us? Fuck…I slam my fist down on my desk.

"Goddammit," I say through clenched teeth, wanting nothing more than to find the fucker and hit him as hard as I possibly can.

Over and over.

Until he's fucking dead.

This is what he wanted, and I'm playing right into it. Sending an ominous email just to mess with me. And now I know exactly how Ana felt when I urged her to contact the police: helpless. Because what the fuck are they going to do over this? It's not threatening enough to warrant the paper-work needed to trace the IP address...is it? The guy has a history of violence and admitted to watching us. Though—fuck—there's no way to prove it. It's our word against his.

And then a whole new level of panic hits me. He was watching us last night. Was he still watching this morning? Did he follow Ana to the cafe? The fucker could be there now, waiting for her to get up and go to the bathroom or something. I whirl around and grab my phone, calling Ana. She answers right away.

"Hey, babe," she says and I feel calmer just hearing her voice. She's okay. Steven hasn't gotten to her. "Leaving the office?"

"I'm just about to." I force myself to slowly inhale. I don't want to freak her out now. Not until I'm there with her. "Still at the cafe?"

"Yeah. I got another chapter written. I'm loving this book. But I got another idea for a totally different book again."

Normally, I would have laughed and teased her about being a typical author. But shit isn't normal right now. "Stay there. I'll be there soon." My tone is flat, but it's either that or she'll know what's really going on. And there's no need to upset her yet.

"I planned to. Want me to order you anything? The line has been long and slow today, so if I get it now it should be out by the time you get here."

I'm not hungry; my appetite has been replaced with the need to cause physical harm to Steven. But having her stand in line means she'll stay there, around other people. Safe.

For now.

"Sure. Surprise me and order for me."

"All right. See you soon."

The call ends and I go back to my computer, reading his email again as if it contains a hidden message. To be able to see into the kitchen window, he'd have to climb the fire escape on the apartment next door. There are security cameras all around that place. If there is footage of Steven climbing the fire escape and watching us, he can get charged with something. The guy is a creep, but he's fucking stupid. Which will work in our favor. IP addresses can be traced. Trespassing is a crime. He'll be found and punished.

For the first time in my life, following the rules feels wrong. It's not enough. Steven's been arrested before. He got out early because he's related to someone with clout. It's not right. I've never wanted to take matters into my own hands before. But I do. I want to make sure Steven never hurts Ana ever again.

And there's only one way to be sure.

chapter
thirteen

ANA

I roll my shoulders and stretch my neck, back tense and tight from being hunched over my computer all afternoon. Maybe I should buy one of those posture braces to make me sit right. My mind flashes to my horse showing days when my trainer would make us ride with broomsticks behind our backs, slipped into place in the crook of our bent elbows. It was uncomfortable, and probably dangerous, now that I'm actually thinking about it but it made me sit up straight.

I order Cole's food, take my number, and go back to my table. I stick my ear buds back in my ears and pound out another five hundred and fifty-three words before the food comes. I close my computer, sneak a bite from Cole's plate and waste time on Instagram until Cole comes in. He smiles when our eyes meet, but he looks stressed.

"Bad day?" I ask, standing so he can embrace me. He pulls me tight against his chest and puts his lips to mine. The kiss is welcome but takes me by surprise. We're in the middle of a public place, after all. He pushes his tongue into my mouth and holds me tight against his chest, not letting up. I wrap my arms around him, taking solace in his kiss.

"It just got much better," Cole says, slowly breaking away. We take seats at the table and he picks up his fork but doesn't start eating. "How was your day?"

"Fine," I say with a shrug. "I didn't really do anything. I'm still not totally used to this being my job. I feel like I'm not doing anything productive and it's all fun," I admit with a laugh. "When will it feel like work?"

"Once your book is out," he tells me, forcing a smile. Something is up with him, and he doesn't seem to have any intention of telling me. "That's what I hear from a lot of authors. Or when you're chasing deadlines and the words aren't coming. That can get stressful, and will definitely feel like work then. Oh, I talked with Melissa from marketing today about your book. She'll be emailing you soon, probably tomorrow. She's impressed with Quinn Harlow's review."

"I'm still fan-girling over that. Like, is this real life? Seriously." I shake my head, thinking back to the late hours I kept while writing my first book. I always wanted to publish it, but found writing to be cathartic and helped me deal with all the shit that was going on.

Losing my dad.

Breaking free from Steven.

Dealing with the repercussions of that asshole.

Lost friendships.

Damaged self-esteem.

Writing my characters going through similar shit and getting out and becoming happy in the end gave me hope that I could do the same. Though I didn't really believe in it... until I met Cole.

"I'm glad I get to be part of it," Cole says, and his smile is genuine again. It makes me feel better almost instantly, and I realize just how much his honesty matters in this relationship. "Nothing out of the ordinary happened today?"

I reach over and take his hand, knowing what he's hinting at. "Nothing. And don't worry about me." He turns his hand over and laces his fingers through mine. "Cole, I know you don't like hearing this, but I've been through this before. And it taught me that I can't live my life scared because that's not living at all. And even my mom brought it up over the weekend."

"She did?"

"Yeah." I shake my head, feeling a bit of color rush to my cheeks. "She and my sister both really liked you, by the way. I'm not sure if that's important to you or not."

"Of course it is." The smile is on his face again, and his brown eyes are sparkling. Some of the stress leaves him and his shoulders relax. He's in need of a back rub. As soon as we get back to his place, I think a dip in the hot tub and a massage is just what the doctor ordered. "Family is important to me, and I know it is to you too. Having my girlfriend's mom and sister like me is a pretty big deal." He rubs his thumb in little circles on my wrist.

"What's even more impressive," I start, trying to sound serious, "is that Thor approves. He gets the final say, and if I'd listened to him before, I could have saved myself a lot of trouble."

"He slept on my chest and was purring. Does that mean I pass the test?"

"Shut up. No way."

"Yes, way. When I went to bed that night, after you'd already passed out, he very slowly came over and laid on my chest and let me pet him."

"No fair!" I laugh. "That asshole cat hardly lets me pet him."

"He must have exceptional taste." Cole laughs. "My mom

and stepdad are coming to town in two weeks. It'll soon be your turn to be judged," he jokes.

"Ha, I think I can pass this test. But shit—I'm actually nervous thinking about it."

Cole gives my hand a squeeze. "If anyone doesn't like you, there is something seriously fucking wrong with them." He looks into my eyes for a moment, and the things we don't say are louder than the words spoken. God, I'm falling so hard for this man.

"What did your mom say to you over the weekend?" he asks.

"Oh, uh," I start and shake my head. "Basically, that she can tell you make me happy." I bite my lip. "Because you do. And she knows that it's been a while since...since I was happy before because of all that happened." I stop and wave my hand in the air. "The past doesn't matter. I'm really liking the present right now."

Something flashes over Cole's face for a millisecond, but he recovers fast. "I like it too. I'm glad you had a good day."

"I got so much written. I'm going to have this thing done in a week if I can keep this pace up. I don't know why, but I write faster and faster the more I get into a book. Can I tell you a spoiler?"

Cole laughs, looking like himself again. "Yes, you're allowed to tell me spoilers. I actually like to know how a book ends before I start editing. The ending can impact things along the way. As a reader, it sucks. But it's important for editing since there are times when we have to talk through things."

"Great. Because I like revealing spoilers about my books."

Cole picks up his fork and starts eating as I talk about the book. The stress leaves him, and things seem back to normal again. Cole finishes dinner, I pack up my stuff, and we get up to leave. It's chilly but sunny outside, so we decide to walk instead of getting in a cab. Cole puts his arm around me, and I lean in, inhaling his cologne, wanting to remember everything about him. The way he smells, the way he feels against me…it's all so perfect.

Which fucking terrifies me as much as it excites me. Things don't typically go my way.

"Want to see a movie this weekend?" I ask Cole. "There's the new superhero one coming out Thursday."

"Yeah, I want to see it too. It's gotten great reviews."

"Should we invite Luke and Lexi?" I ask carefully, knowing how Cole feels about his brother from time to time. I love my alone time with Cole, of course, but the social part of me is coming back to the surface and a double date sounds fun.

"I think they have the girls this weekend, and when they do, they usually do something with them."

"I didn't even think of that. That must be weird for Harper to see her sisters leave like that, don't you think?"

"Yeah. I've wondered about that too. She's too young to really understand what's going on. Though I wouldn't be surprised if the weekend visits stopped happening as the girls get older. Lexi's ex-husband isn't very involved."

"I don't understand that. I can't even imagine being away from my children, and I don't even have any."

"I agree. My biological father was that way," Cole says softly. He mentioned his stepfather before but has never brought up anything else about his upbringing. "I haven't spoken to him in over twenty years. I have no idea where he is or if he's even alive."

His words hit me hard. "Wow. I'm so sorry."

He shrugs. "It's okay. Ed, my stepdad, is a great guy. He's been married to my mom for I think fifteen years now. Sixteen? I don't remember. Is that bad?"

I laugh. "No. I only remember my parents' anniversary

because it was three months before I was born. My mom still wore white. I imagine it was quite a scandal in our town. It was even smaller and more backwoods than it is now."

Cole chuckles. "The whole everyone-knows-everyone thing weirds me out. I like my privacy."

"God, you're telling me. Which is why I love it here so much. Yeah, there's a ton more people, but most people here don't seem to care about one another. Which sounds really bad when I say it like that."

"I know what you mean. It's easy to blend in here."

"Exactly."

"And I'll ask Luke," Cole says. "About the movie. If Grace and Paige are at their dad's, Lexi's mom or sister should be able to watch Harper. Though that means we might have to catch an early show so they can get back before it's too late."

"Oh, right. I keep forgetting that people with kids can't just leave like people without kids. That has to be such a huge adjustment." I shake my head and look up at Cole. Things are going well between us. I'm not expecting a proposal anytime soon, but I am debating on having a few of those Big Talks couples are supposed to have to know if things are compatible in the end or not. "Do you want kids someday?" I ask, biting the bullet and getting it out there.

"I do," he says. "Do you?"

"Yes. I always imagined myself getting married and having at least one baby. I always imagined a little girl, and she'd look just like me. That's probably weird, isn't it?"

"Nah. I imagined a boy who was like me, looks and personality. Only better," he adds quietly.

His words tug on my heart and I tighten my arm around him. "It's weird to think about, isn't it? How our traits get passed down. I hope my kids get all my good ones and none of my bad ones."

Cole raises an eyebrow. "You have bad traits?"

"Only one. Other than that, I'm practically perfect in every way." I smile and look up at Cole. "So, girls—or at least the ones in my class—would play these stupid games and pick out wedding shit and kid's names, and I was convinced Willow was the most beautiful name in the world. My best friend Jess and I would fight over who got to name their daughter Willow."

Cole laughs. "Is Willow still the most beautiful name in the world?"

"I do like it, but I think I'd go with something else now."

"Naming kids is stressful," he muses. "They're stuck with it for the rest of their lives."

"Having a name that can be shortened is nice. I've gone by Ana for pretty much my whole life. I got irritated with people asking me if I was named after Princess Diana." I shake my head. "Don't get me wrong, I love princesses, but not every little girl wants to be a princess, ya know?"

"I've wondered about that, actually. My nieces are all about the princesses right now. I think I told you my mom lives in Orlando and goes to Disney World all the time. She loves getting the girls princess related—"

Cole cuts off and comes to an abrupt stop. His jaw tenses and he narrows his eyes, looking across the street.

"Cole?" I ask, trying to follow his gaze. The street is busy, full of cars and people dodging them. "What is it?"

He shakes his head and let out a breath. "Nothing. I thought I saw...but it wasn't."

"Steven?" I ask and feel an instant chill. It's all I can do not to look around wildly, making sure he's not here.

"Yeah. Him. I'm on high alert after...fuck, Ana. I have to tell you something and I wanted to wait until we were back at the house."

My blood runs cold. "What is it?"

"He emailed me. On my personal email, which I guess

isn't that hard to find, but it's not like I have it advertised." Cole and I keep walking, trying to keep up with the steady flow of people on the busy sidewalk. I blink, watching the ground pass by beneath me. "He was watching us, Ana. Last night. He knew you burned the spaghetti."

All the happiness that was building inside me comes crashing down. Because of Steven. Suddenly I feel like I'm being sucked down into a dark spiral, below the street and into the sewers. I sway on my feet and feel giant sewer rats rip into my skin. It's been over a year, and this nightmare is still going on. I'm hyperaware of everything, and it's making me sick. The wind that's constantly blowing my hair in my face. The rumble of cars and buses on the street. The low, indiscernible chatter surrounding us. People bumping into my shoulders annoyed that I'm stopped in the middle of the sidewalk but not bothering to go around.

It's all too much.

Cole's arms wrap around me, steadying me. "Ana, are you okay?"

"No," I say, voice breathy. "I...I think I should go home."

"I'll get a cab. We're close."

"I don't mean your house. I mean I should go home to Kentucky."

Cole's brows furrow. "Why?"

"I can't keep doing this to you. It's not fair. I'll go home, Steven will follow me, and you can have a chance to live your life again without having to watch over your shoulder constantly."

"I am living my life," he says slowly. "With you. And it's the best my life has been in a really long fucking time. I'm happy with you."

"But you could be happier. I know what it's like, how disrupting it can be. Living every day wondering if he's watching, when he'll show up...it's no way to live. I'll go back to Kentucky for a while, let him follow me there and then…and then…"

"Then you'll be right back to where you started and I'll be without you," he tells me. "I'm not going to let him scare me off. He's not going to take you from me." Cole cups my face in his hands. "Ana. I told you, you're worth it. I'd walk through hell and back for you because…" His eyebrows push together and he looks at me with desperation. "Because I love you."

Everything around me fades, and I can breathe again. My heart floats to the top of my chest and I can't get close enough to Cole. I love him too. I've known it for a while, even as I tried to resist falling. He's everything I want in a man.

In a friend.

In a lover.

A partner.

Yet, I'm scared. Hearts are such fragile things. Taking it out of the safety of my chest and putting it in his hands is dangerous. Stupid, even. It's easy to break a heart.

I look into Cole's brown eyes and feel my own well with tears.

"I love you, too."

$$\sim$$

"You should go to bed," I tell Cole, eyeballing the clock. "You'll be tired tomorrow."

"You're right." Cole rests his head on my shoulder but doesn't make any attempt to get up. "How much of this episode is left?"

I pick up the remote to check. "Thirteen minutes."

"We can watch the end of it."

"And I thought you weren't into this show?" I tease, running my hand through Cole's hair.

"I wasn't," he says. "The first episode didn't grab me, but you were right. Now I can't stop watching."

I laugh and pull him into my arms. Cole yawns and comes toward me, resting his head in my lap. I keep running my fingers through his hair for the rest of the episode. Thinking he fell asleep, I go to turn the TV off.

"You can't stop it now," he says sleepily. "I need to see what happened."

"Pretty much every episode ends on a cliffhanger. Even the season finales."

"I knew I shouldn't have started this show."

I laugh again and lean over to kiss Cole. "I would say I'm sorry, but I'm not."

He rolls over and grabs me by the waist, kissing me before getting up. He stretches his arms over his head and then takes my hand. We go through the kitchen—all the blinds are down tonight—and take the back staircase to the master bedroom.

By the time we've showered, brushed our teeth, and gotten dressed for bed, we're both wide-awake again. I'm used to late nights since I get to sleep in. Poor Cole has to be up in a little over four hours.

"So, this Halloween party Black Ink puts on," I start, watching Cole pull the comforter back and toss all the fancy pillows on the ground. I love the way a made bed with lots of pillows looks, but it's so impractical. Why put half a dozen pillows on a bed every morning when you're just going to take them off a few hours later? Or in my case, when you stay in bed most the day anyway?

"Does everyone dress up at it?" I ask.

"Most people do. I never have."

"You're so lame. Dressing up is fun, and when it's a

costume party and you're not wearing a costume, you stick out, you know."

"Oh, I know. I get told that pretty much every year. I'm guessing you like dressing up?"

"Heck, yes. As an adult, there are only a select few times when it's appropriate for me to wear a costume. I tend to take advantage of it. If I wear a costume, will you?"

Cole makes a face and we get into bed. "I suppose so. Though I have no idea what to dress up as."

"Me neither. Not yet at least. I'll search Pinterest tomorrow. We can go as something together."

"Together? Like the ass and head of a horse?"

I laugh. "No, like a themed costume. Like Bonnie and Clyde, but not that because it's too overdone. Something kind of matching without being way too lame. A couple-costume."

Cole's face tightens. "Couple-costume?"

"Too lame?"

"Uh, a bit. You can look though, and run ideas by me. See if you can force me into a costume." He looks away, totally uncomfortable with this.

"I won't force you," I tell him. "But I'd be really happy if you dressed up with me. And I think I'll have to get a special costume for your eyes only."

That piques his interest. Cole moves closer and slips his arms around me. "I do like the sound of that."

"What's the overall feel? Do people dress slutty?"

"I've seen a few questionable costumes over the years, but most aren't too bad. Tasteful, I guess you could call them."

"Do they have a costume contest?"

"Yes," he says with a laugh. "There are awards for best costume. I don't think it's anything worth winning, though."

"The prize is getting to brag for the rest of the year that you had the best costume, duh. Just like that time I won the

144

hog wrestling contest. I got shit for it but love telling anyone who will listen that they are in the presence of a hog wrestling champion."

He laughs and puts his lips to my neck. "I've dreaded work parties for the last five years."

"Why?"

"That was the last time I had a date to one," he admits.

I roll over and hook a leg over him. I'm curious about Cole's past but don't want to push it. He told me he loves me and I don't want him to regret saying it.

"You didn't date anyone for five years?"

"No."

"So, before we got together, you hadn't had sex in five years?"

"No." He closes his eyes and a tremor of pain goes across his face.

"Can I ask what happened?"

Cole nods but doesn't open his eyes, and then I remember that it's late and he has to be exhausted. "It's a long story. One I'm not proud of."

"You don't have to tell me."

"I want to. As strange as that sounds. I don't want to hide anything from you." He looks at me for a moment before taking my hand and closing his eyes again. "I was with the same woman on and off since high school. I thought we were going to get married and everything. Then she broke up with me and said she was in love with someone else the whole time."

"I'm sorry, Cole," I whisper.

"Don't be," he whispers back. "Things were never that great with her, to be honest. I wanted it to work more than it was working. And I wouldn't have met you." His eyes open and he looks at me. "You have a part in your book where your characters talk about all the shit that happened in the past, and how it made them who they are today…it's true. There's more to that story, the parts I'm not proud of, the parts I wish I could take back. But it happened and no matter how much I regret it, it made me who I am now. Or maybe that's all bullshit we tell ourselves to feel better about the bad choices we've made."

"I've made a lot of those," I say with a slight laugh. "And I've been told the same thing: the past makes you who you are today. Which, I mean, of course it does. You can't get to today without going through the past first. And if you don't learn from your mistakes then…then…I don't know. You just live with regret and guilt your whole life and that's pretty miserable."

"It is. Especially when you think you deserve it."

I bite my lip and push up on the mattress to better look at Cole. "No one deserves it."

"I haven't told you the part I'm not proud of yet."

"I won't judge you."

He turns his head and meets my eyes. "I know."

My heart flutters and I slip my arm around his muscular chest.

"My ex broke up with me because she'd been in love with someone else for years. And that someone was Luke. My brother. She'd been in love with Luke since she met him in high school," Cole says slowly, fighting against the words. "When she broke up with me, she made me think it was so she and Luke could be together, and that it was under his urging for her to break up with me because he wanted to be with her too. But he didn't and had no idea she even liked him. I didn't know that then, and for years, I hated him for it."

I wait for him to go on, heart beating rapidly inside my chest. It aches for Cole, and now his feelings toward his brother make sense.

"And then Luke was hurt—badly hurt—in a fire. He was unconscious for days and the doctors didn't know if he had brain damage from smoke inhalation. The fact that my brother could die at any moment hit me hard and I thought I could move past all that happened before and start over fresh with him. He was living in Chicago at the time and when I got there...she was there too. Sitting at his bedside, holding his hand. It was the proof I needed that they'd been together the whole time, but really, she saw our mother post something on Facebook about Luke's accident and got to the hospital first. Fast forward a few months, and when Luke and Lexi started dating, I tried to break them up. I didn't think Luke deserved to be happy after what he'd done to me. Like I said, I'm not proud of it. Even after they forgave me... and made me the godfather of their baby...I couldn't forgive myself."

I don't know what to say because 'I'm sorry' doesn't seem like enough. A slew of emotions surges through me, and I think of the anger and pain it would cause me if someone I loved told me they'd been in love with my sister the whole time instead...and that Sophia was okay with it and wanted to be with them too. I'd probably beat the shit out of her and never talk to her again. It would feel like the ultimate betrayal.

And Cole hasn't forgiven himself. I'm not sure how long Luke and Lexi have been married, but going off the fact they have a daughter who's going on two years old, I'm guessing it's been at least two or three years. That's a long time for Cole to hold onto his feelings of guilt.

"You're not a bad person," I finally say, and bring my lips to his.

"I'm not good enough for you," he whispers, voice heavy with emotion.

Tears pool in my eyes. No one ever said that to me before.

147

Steven always told me how he was too good for me, and how thankful and grateful I should be to be with him. I would be nothing without him. Couldn't function on my own. He got into my head and made me think I wasn't worthy of love.

Cole is the opposite.

It's funny how things work out. From the outside looking in, I never thought a man like Cole would be the one. Handsome, rich, living in this huge house with a prestigious job, someone like Cole is the last person I thought I'd fall for. Ever. Let alone after all the shit that happened.

"You are." We kiss again and Cole pulls me on top of him. "It's kinda crazy when you think about stuff in reverse. Like everything that had to happen in order for us to meet."

"It is crazy because a lot of things did fall into place just right. We met because Lexi had one too many projects and had to give up her most recent one. And she had too many because she's only at Black Ink part time, which is because she has Harper at home. And she wouldn't have Harper if she and Luke hadn't met. Fuck, this is messing with my mind. And making me even more glad I didn't succeed at breaking them up."

"Weird how things have to happen to make another happen, isn't it?"

"Yeah, it is. I don't know if we would have met otherwise. I might have seen you at a company event, and thought you were hot of course, but actually conversing...I don't know."

"You'd be so taken by my beauty in whatever costume I decide to wear to this Halloween party you'd come up to me, drink in hand, stumbling over your words because you're so nervous to talk to me."

"That sounds about right." Cole slides his hands down my thighs and yawns again.

"Go to sleep," I instruct. "You'll be tired in the morning if you don't."

"Staying up with you is worth it."

"It's totally worth it, but I don't want you to be tired. Even more tired, I should say."

"You're right." He gets comfortable, keeping his arms around me. "I love you, Ana."

"I love you too."

chapter fourteen

COLE

"*Y*ou did good in there," Caitlin Black says to me.

"Thanks." Maybe on her last day, I'll correct her grammar. But until then, I'll bite my tongue.

"Barring a major disaster, I foresee a promotion in your not-so-distant future," she says quietly as we step out of the conference room. After an hour and a half of negotiations, I got a very popular author to sign with us instead of a competing publisher—with a smaller advance than they offered. We'd make it up in marketing dollars, giving his book a bigger release. If Caitlin were still around when the time came to invest into promotion, she'd find a way to pull dollars away and go back on everything we agreed upon, but do it in such a way it didn't breach the contract. She's slimy like that.

The book sounds great—a humorous thriller with a plot I've never read before—and I believe it can be one of our biggest sellers the year it releases. Assuming I'm a publisher then, I'll make sure we give it the attention it deserves.

"Let's both hope a major disaster doesn't happen," I say back.

"Right." We take a few steps down the hall. "You know this industry well, Cole. I stand by my decision to have you take my place. You'll put the company first. Me and you... we're not so different." She gives me a tight smile and walks toward the lobby. It takes until I get into my office for her words to sink in.

She thinks I'm still single and don't want a family. I've been married to Black Ink the last few years, and she's assuming it'll stay that way. That's why she wants to promote me, but it couldn't be further from the truth.

I love Ana.

I want to marry Ana.

I want to have children with Ana.

But none of that will happen anytime soon. Hell, I probably shouldn't have dropped the L-word already, but I couldn't help it. By the time I seriously consider a proposal, Caitlin will be long gone. It's just two more months, I remind myself. Two more months of pretending to be my old self, not interested in relationships or family.

I respond to Ana's text now that I'm out of the meeting. She's at the house working on her book and said she's feeling too lazy to get dressed and leave today, but is willing to put clothes on and meet me for lunch if I want her to. I tell her it's okay, and that I'll probably work through lunch in my office anyway. I have to get through three chapters of edits today or I'll fall behind.

I haven't been behind in years.

I order food to be delivered to the office and lean back, getting started on editing. I'm two pages in when someone knocks on my door.

"Come in," I call, not looking up from the computer. The

door slowly opens and I raise my gaze, hearing footsteps but not seeing anyone.

"Hiiiii."

A smile comes to my face and I recognize the little voice right away. I stand, now able to see Harper from behind the desk. She waves with both hands then turns around, reaching out.

"Daaaa! Da-da!"

"I'm right here," Luke says and steps in. Harper runs to him and he scoops her up. "She wanted to come visit her uncle," Luke tells me. "Listen to this: Harper, say 'Cole'."

Harper points at me and says, "Cowe."

"Good job, baby!" Luke tells her.

"That's pretty cute," I say. "And thanks for the visit, Harper. I'm guessing you guys are here to see Lexi?"

"Yeah, we came to surprise her. She doesn't know we're here yet. She's on the phone and her door is closed."

I take a step back. "Come in and stay out of sight. I'll call her in if you want."

"That'd be great. I said something I shouldn't have said this morning and want to make it up to her."

Harper toddles into the office and immediately starts climbing onto the leather chairs by my desk. "What did you say?"

"Grace gets defiant when she doesn't get her way and mouths off to Lexi. This morning was one of those where everyone was crabby, tired, and the dog and cat kept chasing each other and knocking shit over. I was frustrated and snapped at Lexi when I heard Grace talk back. I said she needs to be the mother and not the friend." Luke grabs Harper a second before she falls. "Lexi puts up with a lot, and it's because of the shit her ex put her through. He yelled a lot and told her she wasn't a good mom all the time, which is bullshit. She's great. I was irritated at the moment and should have worded things differently, and now I feel bad."

I nod and look at Luke. "Does Lexi talk about her ex much?" I ask, my mind going to Ana and her ex. Lexi still has to deal with Russell because they share children, and Ana still has to deal with Steven because he won't fucking leave her alone.

"Not unless she has to. I can tell she doesn't like talking about him. She thinks it makes me uncomfortable, but it doesn't, not in the way she's worried about, I mean. It's no secret I don't like the guy, but if they hadn't been married, Grace and Paige wouldn't be here and Lexi wouldn't have gone out that night and met me. I've had relationships in the past, and Lexi and I both know nothing compares to what we have now."

Talk about a chain of events. I wouldn't have met Ana if it weren't for Lexi being part time and all, and she wouldn't even be with Luke if she hadn't gotten divorced in the first place. Thinking about everything that had to perfectly fall into place for Ana to walk into my life at the exact moment makes my head hurt. "Right." How the fuck did my brother go from being the guy who literally runs away from his problems to the most well-adjusted person on the planet? "That makes sense."

Luke pulls a sippy cup from the diaper bag and gives it to Harper. "Is Ana still in town?"

"Yeah, she is."

"You're smiling."

"No, I'm not."

Luke smirks. "Fine. You're not. I take it things are good with her?"

"Very good." Dammit, I am smiling. I turn and look out the window, watching cars go by below.

"Is she ready to meet Mom and Dad next week?"

"Next week? I thought they were coming for Halloween."

"They are. They get in on Wednesday."

"But Halloween isn't for another—seriously? They're staying that long?"

Luke laughs. "Yep. They're staying with us this time, though. Lexi could use a bit of a break during the day and Mom is all about playing with the girls. And Lexi and I thought we'd give you and Ana some space. The beginning of relationships are the best, though the I-can't-stop-touching-you phase never went away between me and Lex."

"I've noticed. We've all noticed."

"Don't be jealous."

"I'm not." And really, I'm not. Not anymore. Because I have someone *I* can't stop touching. "Want me to call Lexi in now? It looks like she's off the phone. Her line is open."

Luke scoops up Harper and crouches down behind one of the big chairs. I go around to my desk and pick up the office phone. Out of habit, I look at the street below. The office is high up, but not so high I can't see people, though the fine details are too hard to make out. It's interesting to people watch from above, to see people frantically running about or lazily walking along the sidewalk in no hurry at all.

I'm too high up to make out the details, but the second I see him, dressed in a dark hoodie and sitting on the same bench as before, I know it's him. His head is turned up to the building.

Watching.

"Cole?" Luke asks.

I hesitate, considering telling Luke about Steven. It's smart to let someone else know about the fucker, just in case shit hits the fan, and Luke would offer a fresh perspective on the whole situation. But here's not the place. Besides, maybe it's better he doesn't know. Because when I beat the shit out of Steven, I don't want Luke involved.

I shake myself and dial Lexi's extension. "Can you come in here for a minute? I need to go over something with you," I say to her.

Lexi sighs but agrees. A minute later, she's walking through the door. Harper sees her mom and gets excited, running to Lexi with her arms in the air. Lexi smiles widely, picks Harper up and gives her a hug. Then she sees Luke, and tears fill her eyes.

"I'm sorry I was a jerk this morning," my brother says, and pulls Lexi into his arms. I turn back around, and the man who was sitting on the bench is gone. I blink and stare down at the street before turning away and rubbing my forehead. There's no way to be sure it was him. But...fuck...that's the same bench he was sitting on before.

This is crazy. I turn back to Luke and Lexi, who are borderline making out while Harper digs toys out of the diaper back, and clear my throat. They break apart and Lexi takes Luke's hand.

"Sorry. Want to join us for lunch?" she asks, and Luke looks annoyed.

"No, thanks. I need to get through a chapter over my lunch break or I'll fall behind."

"I know how that goes," Lexi says. "I'll see you later, then."

They leave and I close the door behind them, needing a minute to calm the fuck down before I get to work again. Right on cue, Ana sends me photos of the costume she just ordered to wear to the Halloween party. I open my texts to respond.

Me: **Very fitting. And I always thought Wonder Woman was sexy.**

Ana: **I got something for you too.**

Me: **Should I be worried?**

Ana: **Nah. You'll look good in spandex.**

Me: **You're joking, right?**

Ana: **I wouldn't joke about Superman's costume.**

I laugh and lean back in my chair, and the anger I was feeling minutes ago is gone. Ana has that way of making me feel better without even trying.

Me: **I'll wear it, just for you.**

Ana: **We can role play after ;-)**

Me: **I'm going to hold you to it. Wonder Woman has a lasso, right?**

Ana: **She does. And yes, I like to be tied up.**

I'm getting turned on, eager to go home and fuck Ana. I want to bury my head between her legs and feel her clit vibrating against my tongue as I make her come.

And then it hits me: if we dress like Wonder Woman and Superman at this party—this company party—people will assume we're together.

Fuck.

Ana is so excited about this and I don't want to let her down. I let out a sigh and shake my head. We have a while until the party. I'm sure I can figure something out before then. My phone vibrates in my hand as another text comes through.

Ana: **Left you speechless, eh?**

Me: **Slightly. The rest of the day is going to go by slow now.**

Ana: **Maybe this will help.**

A photo of her—naked—comes through.

Me: **You are so fucking hot. And cruel.**

Ana: **That's why you love me, right?**

Me: **Just one of the reasons.**

Another editor knocks on the door, needing help with a project, and it takes me a minute to put myself back into work mode. Ana is the best thing to ever happen to me but might be the worst for my career.

ANA

I dry my eyes with my sleeve, careful not to mess up my mascara. No one can know I was crying. They'll ask why, and I won't be able to come up with a lie. Not again. I take a deep breath, close my eyes, and breathe out through my mouth. I repeat the process again, internally cringing from the stench of this public bathroom.

I put on a smile, wash my hands, and leave, finding Steven leaning against the wall, looking bored.

"Did you fall in?" he asks. One could easily mistake his question as humor, but I know better. He was annoyed that I had to pee in the first place and told me to just wait, but I drank two glasses of iced tea at the restaurant before we got to the movie. Of course, I'd have to pee before the show started.

"No," I say back quietly.

"Are you going to mope around all night? Because if you are, I'm leaving and you can find your own way home."

"I'm not moping," I say slowly. "Not at all." I point to my face. "See? I'm smiling."

Steven rolls his eyes and lowers his voice so only I can hear him. "Whatever. I'm so fucking tired of your attitude all the time. You're miserable to be around sometimes, Ana. I don't even want to be here anymore. You took so long in there we won't get the good seats."

"I was in there for like a minute and—" I snap my mouth closed. There's no point in arguing with him. It's the same thing every time. I look up at the man who tells me he loves me and see the anger on his face. My heart starts to race and panic sets in.

I don't want him to be mad at me. He'll control his anger here but once we get home...

I need to fix this.

"Let's go see. I already bought the tickets online anyway."

"Great job, Ana. Waste your fucking money by missing the show."

I pull out my phone to check the time. "Steven, the show doesn't start for twenty more minutes."

"And I like to get there thirty minutes before to get the good seats."

"This theater had the option to buy tickets with assigned seats, so I did. Back row and right in the middle, just where you like to sit."

Steven looks at me, realizing his argument is invalid. "Fine."

"Do you want to go sit and I'll get popcorn?"

"You want fucking popcorn? We just ate? Did you not listen to what I just fucking said? You blow through money."

"It's just popcorn, and we don't go to the movies that often."

"Goddammit, Ana, why do you have to start a fight over every-thing? I don't know why I bother with you. I'm leaving." He marches forward.

"Wait," I say and reach out, trying to catch his wrist. Steven whirls around and knocks my phone from my hand.

"What?" he seethes.

Tears spring to my eyes and my fingers shake as I bend over and grab my phone. The screen has a fresh crack right down the *middle. Thank God we're still in the hallway by the bathroom. No one can see us.* "Please, let's stay."

"Quit your damn crying. You're a fucking adult and you cry like a baby."

"I'm not crying, and you broke my phone." *I hold it up so he can see.*

"You're the idiot who dropped it. You're so careless, Ana. You'd think you'd take better care of your things. I'm not buying you a new one."

"I didn't ask you to buy me one. I'll buy it myself—"

"We don't have money for a new iPhone right now. God, Ana." *He shakes his head, still seething.* "Great job ruining the night. I'm going home. Find your own way because I don't want to look at your face right now. I'm too fucking pissed to be around you."

"Steven, stop it!"

"Leave me alone."

I startle awake, heart racing. I can't catch my breath and I know I'm on the verge of a panic attack. My hands fly to my heart and I press down as if that will stop it from beating right out of my chest. Slowly, my eyes focus on everything around me, and it takes a good few seconds to remember where I am.

Cole's house.

I fell asleep on the couch after I spent the morning writing. It's been a week since Steven sent Cole that email, and we haven't seen or heard from him since. The last few days have been blissfully perfect, full of incredible sex, dinners out, and I nearly completed the first draft of my book. I spent hours on the phone with my mom and sister, planning wedding stuff and vetoing bridesmaid dresses I refuse to wear.

Life's been fun.

Life's been good.

Things are finally going my way.

Is that why I'm freaking the fuck out right now? I'm waiting for the inevitable fallout. I squeeze my eyes closed and try to take deep breaths. Steven isn't here. I'm not that girl anymore, the one who picked up her broken phone off the movie theater lobby and chased after a cruel and malicious man, begging him to love her.

Don't dwell on the past, but don't repress it either. My therapist's words ring in my head. Great shame and embarrassment weigh down on me when I think of the shit I put up with. Everything happened slowly; he didn't treat me like that on our first date. Or our second. He treated me well at first, just long enough to sink his claws in. Which wasn't hard to do, considering I hadn't been dealing with the loss of my father well.

I run my hands through my hair and the panic starts to turn into anger. Steven is a sick, manipulative fuck, taking advantage of me like that. I take another breath, hold it, and slowly exhale. I don't want to be scared, but I don't want to be angry either. I want to let this go. Move on. Enjoy my life with someone who actually loves me.

Someone like Cole.

Speaking of which...*fuck.* He's going to be home soon, and we're leaving right away to go to Luke and Lexi's for dinner, where I'll be meeting his parents for the first time. Shit.

Still feeling the effects of my nightmare, I do my best to shake it off and rush upstairs to shower. I strip out of my clothes, turn on the shower, and hesitate before I get in. The house is armed, and I brought the tablet that shows all the security cameras in with me. I do a quick check—they're all clear, of course—and get in the shower, ignoring my fears.

Steven is just a man. A sick, evil man, but a man nonetheless. He's not going to materialize inside the house, bypassing the locks and alarm system.

I quickly shower, do my makeup, and start drying my hair. Cole texts me and says he's running late, which works in my favor and allows me to not only dry but straighten my hair. I'm dressed and ready by the time he walks through the door.

"Hey, babe," I say, striding through the house. I'm eager to see him because he's my boyfriend and I love him, but I don't want to be alone anymore, as much as I don't want to admit it. I'm still scared.

"You look amazing," Cole takes off his jacket and steps forward, taking me into his arms.

"So do you. I told you how irresistible you are in a suit, right?"

"You did." He runs his hands down my back and squeezes my ass. "We have time for a quickie, right?"

I bite my lip and look into his eyes. "Not if we want to get to dinner on time."

"I can make you come in only minutes."

I swallow hard, warmth rushing through me. "Prove it then."

Cole flashes me a cocky grin and inches the hem of my black dress up. "I will."

And, fuck, he does.

chapter
sixteen

COLE

"Sorry we're late, I got held up at the office," I say to my mother as we step into Luke and Lexi's house. Their dog, Pluto, runs over and wildly greets us. I *did* get held up at the office, but that's not what made us this late. I delivered on my promise and had her coming in just minutes. And then again, and once more after that. Ana told me her legs were still shaking when we walked up the steps to Luke and Lexi's house.

"You work too much," Mom says, and gives me a hug.

"Mom, this is Ana. Ana, this is my mom and stepdad, Ed."

Ana smiles and holds out her hand. "Nice to meet you."

We go through introductions and make our way into the living room to wait until dinner is ready. Ed goes into the kitchen to help Luke, and Lexi and Ana start talking about some sort of drama an author started on Facebook. Harper brings me a book and climbs onto the couch next to me. I pull her into my lap and start to read, but all she wants to do is flip the pages and laugh at the same yellow bird that appears on every page.

"Ana is lovely," Mom says quietly, sitting down next to

me. Harper looks at her apprehensively and leans closer to me for a moment. I know this right here is a big part of why Mom is coming up to visit so often. She wants Harper to get to know her better.

"I think so, of course, but I'd say I'm biased."

"It's good to see you smile again." Mom takes Harper from me, smiling broadly herself. "You two seem pretty serious."

"We're getting there. It hasn't been that long yet."

"Time isn't an objective way to measure what you feel in your heart. It's not too soon to just consider your future together."

"Don't be too eager to marry me off, Mom."

"I'm not, well not entirely. You know I'd love to see you settled down with a little one of your own on the way. Don't think I forgot how eager you were to start a family before."

"If it happens, it won't be for a while." I sigh. "I'm in no rush this time."

"Good, but don't think you need to wait a certain amount of time to move forward. I was with your father for six years before we got married, and look how that turned out. Ed and I got married not even a year after we met."

"I know."

"My point is, don't wait because you think you should. Time isn't a good indicator. Go with your heart."

I look across the room at Ana. "I am this time."

Mom puts her hand on mine. "Good. I like seeing both my boys happy."

"I like being happy."

"How's work?" Mom asks. "Besides busy."

"It's been good," I start, and consider telling her about the possible promotion. I haven't told anyone in fear that it might not happen, but I'm feeling it tonight. Though instead of telling Mom now, I decide it's best to wait until we're all at the table together in order to save myself from repeating the story more than once. Efficiency is important too, after all.

Lexi goes upstairs, and Ana joins us on the couch, talking to Mom. They seem to get along just fine, and for the first time, I feel like we're all a normal, functional family.

It's fucking nice.

The pleasantries carry over to the table, and now I'm just waiting for a free moment to talk as we eat to share my news about becoming a publisher.

"It's almost time to start planning our summer Disney trip," Mom says, looking at Luke, and then turns her eyes to me. "You should come. Have you ever been, Ana?"

"Not since I was a little kid," Ana tells her. "I'd love to go back, though. Cole told me you go pretty frequently."

"We're annual pass holders for a reason. We love that place. It doesn't lose its magic as you get older."

"I've heard that it's quite fun to go as adults. Now I'm feeling the itch to go."

"I like the princesses," Paige tells us. "That's my favorite part."

"That would be fun! To have us all there. Wouldn't it, Ed?"

"That would be," my stepdad agrees. "We could get a villa and all stay together."

"Actually," Luke starts, and takes Lexi's hand. "We think we're going to skip this summer. It's hard to travel with a newborn."

Mom raises her eyebrows and looks at Harper. "But you took her last year and she was even young—" She cuts off abruptly, realizing what Luke said the same time I did. And then it hits me that Lexi isn't drinking wine. One look at my nieces' excited faces lets me know all I need.

"You're pregnant!" Mom exclaims.

"Yes," Lexi says, eyes getting a little misty. Luke slips his arm around her and kisses her neck.

Mom lets out a cry of excitement and goes around the table to hug Lexi. "Another baby! Oh, Ed! We get another grandbaby!" Mom wipes away tears and puts her arms around Lexi.

"Can we get it now?" Grace asks Luke and he nods. She races out of the room, returning with a framed photo of an ultrasound picture.

"Grandma, look!" she calls, waving around the frame. Mom smiles and puts her hand to her chest. This is a dream come true for her. Grace called her 'grandma' and Luke and Lexi are having another baby.

I see the letters that spell out 'brother' seconds before everyone else does, and my heart sinks. God dammit, I'm still the same asshole. I've accepted that Luke was the first to get married. The first to have children. The first to go on family vacations with Grandma and Grandpa.

But in the back of my mind—and I don't even know why I thought this—I had this image of my wife and I having a child and it being a boy. I'd get that first, at least. It's fucking petty, I know.

And I hate myself for it. God, I'll never change.

"You're having a boy?" Mom practically shouts.

"I won't be *that* outnumbered anymore," Luke jokes, and everyone laughs like it's the funniest thing in the fucking world.

"I'm surprised you found out what you were having this time around," Ed says. "I'm guessing Lexi got the final say this time?"

"Yes," she says. "Not knowing what we were having last time killed me." Lexi flicks her eyes to me and smiles. Oh, right. On the way to the hospital she confessed she knew she was having a girl the whole time, able to recognize from the ultrasound. I guess I'm the only one who still knows that secret. "Though we actually got all the chromosome testing done this time—and everything is fine—so we found out early. I'm not dealing with the constant morning sickness like I did with my last pregnancy, and was convinced something was wrong, but it turns out, being pregnant with girls just makes me incredibly nauseous for some reason. Though this time I've been a bit emotional."

"A bit?" Luke teases, and Lexi glares at him. That explains why she's been acting weird at work lately. "I mean, it's more than fine if you are. You're carrying my son, after all. You can be whatever you want. I love you, you know that, right? And you're beautiful."

"Good save." Lexi rolls her eyes and smiles. "It's going to be so weird. I don't know how to raise a boy." She turns to Luke, looking all misty-eyed. "But he'll have the best dad to do the job."

Ana leans in close. "Sorry if I gag," she whispers, and I smile. "But I have a feeling you're thinking the same, right?"

"I'm resisting the urge to vomit on the table." I put my hand on her thigh and give it a squeeze. She very well might think the over-show of affections is too much, or she might be saying so because she knows how I feel on all this. Either way, having her here is more than I can ask for.

I'm not going to have the first boy to carry on the Winchester name.

I'll wait to share my news about the promotion.

And it's all okay. Because I have Ana.

IS IT FRIDAY YET? I throw my pen down on my desk and lean forward, resting my head in my hands. It's not Friday. It's not even afternoon on Thursday. It's ten fucking a.m. and I have a headache. In need of caffeine, I stand and stretch before making my way to the break room for another fill up on coffee.

Ana and I left Luke's house not long after dinner; they had to put their kids to bed so we couldn't stay late anyway. I made the mistake of checking my email when I got home and gave myself an early preview to the shit-show that's going on with one of our subsidiaries.

Normally, this would stress me out but I'd be able to sit back and watch the head honchos deal with it. I have my own editing work to do, anyway. But Caitlin thought this would be a great fucking time to 'test the waters' and let me handle things. Really, she's too fucking lazy to do her job for the rest of the year. She's well aware of the bind this puts me in too. If I decline or say anything at all about it, she'll use that against me.

And I really want this fucking promotion.

I want it for myself, of course, but I want it for the company too. This place is part of me, and I know I can make it even better and bigger. Before I can get there, I have to jump through Caitlin's hoops. And in this case, go to Los Angeles to deal with the issues the subsidiary can't handle on their own.

And I have to leave in the morning.

I fill up my coffee, add extra cream and sugar to get me through the stress and go back to my office, shutting the door and hiding from the world for a few minutes. I settle in while I drink my coffee and read through another chapter of the current book I'm editing.

The stress still eats away at me but starts to get pushed back as I read, which is the best thing about books. For a moment—however brief—it offers an escape from reality, and right now, instead of worrying about leaving Ana alone, the impossible amount of work I need to complete before the day is over, and having to go into another office and basically yell at everyone, I'm fighting dragons on the mystical mountains of Atlantica.

I read the chapter, correcting typos as I go along, and then go back and start taking notes. Epic fantasy is my favorite genre for many reasons, like how big the worlds are. I keep extensive notes on each book, which provides the author with a 'book bible' of sorts to easily reference. It surprises me how many authors forget characteristics of their main characters over time.

I'm reaching the end of the chapter when Erica, my assistant, pages me.

"Diana Veti-ma-something is here to see you," she tells me. "She's an author, but I didn't see her name down for an appointment."

"It was a last minute thing," I say, trying hard to maintain my composure. Fuck. I never told Ana that we need to keep anonymity about our relationship. "She was in the city, meeting with her agent and—" Shit. I don't need to give Erica an explanation. "—We thought it would be good to discuss her book," I say quickly. "You can send her in."

"Okay."

I shake my head at myself and save the changes I made to the book, then put my computer into sleep-mode. I see Ana walking through the office and my heart softens. I want this promotion, but I don't want to hurt Ana. Ever. I'd never forgive myself if I did. She's too beautiful, too good for me. I feel like I'm at her mercy every time we're together, like I'm not worthy of her affection and certainly not of her love.

I need to tell her playing down our relationship is temporary, and in a few short months, we can let the world know. But until then, things have to appear platonic. Shit. I have to tell her I'm going to LA tomorrow too. I'm not sure what's the right thing to do, but giving her one bit of bad news at a time seems best.

"Hey, babe," she tells me, a smile on her pretty face. She's wearing tight jeans, a gray shirt with a pineapple printed on the front, and heeled boots. Her hair is in a messy braid over her shoulder and she's not wearing makeup. She's so fucking gorgeous and I want nothing more than to pull her close and kiss her hard. "I thought I'd surprise you with lunch." She holds up a bag of takeout and turns to shut the door.

"Leave it open," I blurt, making Ana look at me weird. "You didn't have to bring me lunch, but I'm glad you did." I get up and take the bag from her, stepping around and out of direct line of sight into my office before giving her a quick kiss. "I'm glad you're here, actually. We need to talk."

"That's never a good thing to hear."

"It's not," I agree and look out of the office again, worried someone saw us. "I have to go to California tomorrow and deal with a fuck-up one of our subsidiary publishers made."

"Oh. That's it? I thought you were going to say something worse." She lets out a breath. "Sorry. I tend to expect the worst sometimes. How long are you going to be there?"

"Hopefully just a day or two. I won't bore you with details, but each sub has its own line of imprints, and Black Ink is basically the mother of them all. Usually we function well on our own, but when something goes wrong with an imprint, it comes back to us."

"Sounds stressful."

I shrug. It is, but that's only because I have to play the role of junior publisher on top of head editor.

"They seem very unorganized. It's a new imprint aimed for the millennials, and they hired a bunch of younger people trying to appeal to that market and they're just not experienced enough. If we bring in someone who's been there and knows—sorry. I'm boring you with details, aren't I?"

She wrinkles her nose. "Just a bit. But it is kind of interesting to hear all this. From the outside looking in, I didn't know just how much went into a publishing house and all. It's giving me an idea for a book, actually. I haven't read any author-editor romances lately."

"An author writing about an author?"

Ana shrugs. "They say write what you know, right?"

"I guess, but I've also heard authors shouldn't write authors before, too."

Ana laughs. "I'm not one for rules. As you know." She bites her lip and leans forward, seductively gazing at me. Fuck, I want her. It's killing me to keep this distance between us.

"What's for lunch?" I say, turning away before my cock gets hard. Ana opens the bag and pulls out Chinese food. I take a seat at my desk again, leaving Ana to sit across from me. I feel like I'm brushing her off, but really, there's nowhere else to sit in here.

"When I leave tomorrow," I start, opening a box of fried rice.

"I'll be fine, Cole," Ana quips. "You don't have to babysit me, you know."

"I love you," I whisper, though there's no way anyone can hear us talking unless they were standing in the doorway. "So, I worry."

She gives me a half smile. "I love you too, and I get the worry. I'll be fine. I promise."

I smile back, not telling her there's no way she can promise she'll be fine. A number of bad things can happen, including those Steven could inflict.

"Actually, I could go back to Kentucky. My lease is up on my apartment soon and once it's out, I planned to move anyway. I only lived there to be close to my old job."

My heart thumps against my chest. "Where are you going to live?"

She sticks her fork into her noodles. "I haven't quite figured that out yet. There's limited real estate in Salt Creek."

"Do you want to go back there?" I ask, nerves buzzing.

"Not really, but my family's there so…I guess that's where I'll—"

"Stay with me."

Ana slowly looks up from her food, green eyes wide. Her full lips part and she stares at me for a beat. And then she smiles. "Okay." She blinks and shakes herself. "I mean, are you sure?"

"Yes. I love you, Ana. I love being around you. I love waking up next to you, and going to sleep kind of next to you," I say with a laugh since she stays up writing most nights. "I know it hasn't been that long, but I don't think that matters. I don't want to *not* be with you. And it just makes sense. Your lease is up and you need a place to live. I have a place where we can both live. And you like being close to work, and I am your editor, after all. And your publisher and agent are all in the city. From a career standpoint, it makes the most sense."

"That's very practical of you, Mr. Winchester," she says with a nod. "This is an offer I can't refuse."

"Don't feel pressured," I add quickly. "If you want your own place in New York, I won't be offended. And you could always stay with me while you look." I'm backpedaling, suddenly afraid she'll say no, which only drives home how much I want Ana.

She puts her food to the side and smiles, taking my hand. "I'd love to move in with you. I'm practically living with you already, anyway."

ANA

"*Y*ou know how my lease is up soon?" I say, holding the phone up to my ear with my shoulder while I dig food out of the fridge.

"At the end of the year, right?" Mom answers.

"Right."

"Don't tell me you want to renew it. That place is too dumpy for you now that you're a famous author."

I roll my eyes and laugh. "Mom, the book hasn't been published yet, remember?"

"But that other author liked it."

"Right," I say, not wanting to pick at this. "Anyway…I found a place."

"In New York?"

"Yeah." I grab stuff to make a salad and set it on the counter. "A really nice place."

"Did you have it inspected before you signed anything?"

"Uh, I didn't have to." I'm beating around the bush. "I'm going to live with Cole," I say, and Mom is silent. "Mom? Are you still there?"

"Yes, honey. That just threw me since you assured me you

were taking things slowly with him and you *weren't* going to move in together yet."

"Just like a week ago you were telling me how much you wanted me to stay in New York because it made me happy, and how much you like Cole."

"It's a big step, Ana, and you have a history of being impulsive. And I say that with love."

"Saying something 'with love' doesn't make it any less insulting, Mom."

"I want you to be happy."

"Being with Cole makes me happy. And I'm not signing anything or taking responsibility for the house or property or anything like that. Cole's the one taking the risk here. I could go in there and rob him blind. I know the code to his alarm system, after all."

"Ana, be serious please."

"I am serious, Mom. And, Cole and I are serious. He's not like anyone I've met before. He's so honest and open. I know I can trust him. And if you want to drill him with questions like we're teenagers and not adults, feel free. He's going to come with me to help me pack up my stuff in a few weeks."

"You might be an adult but you're still my daughter. I'll have the questions ready. And make sure you abide by your eleven p.m. curfew or else I'll have to take your phone away."

"Hilarious, Mom."

"You get your sense of humor from me, don't forget. How is everything else in New York? Are you writing?"

I prepare my lunch and fill Mom in on everything—except that Steven's been here, sniffing around like a rabid dog who just can't stay away. After getting off the phone with Mom, I take my lunch into the family room and eat while watching TV.

Being alone in the house during the day is nothing new. Being alone here at night…yeah…that'll be a little creepy. I can't deny that. I look around the house, feeling the sheer size of it closing in on me. There are so many places to hide, and there's a good chance there's a ghost in the basement. Maybe I should invest in a gun.

"Are guns even legal here?" I ask myself and do a Google search. Cole texts me, and his message shows up through iMessage on my computer.

Cole: **It's a shit storm over here and I feel like I stepped into a high school cafeteria with all the drama.**

Me: **I'm sorry, babe. Would a nudie pic help?**

Cole: **It would solve everything.**

Me: **Give me time to shower first ;-)**

Cole: **Dirty can be hot.**

Me: **Not this kind of dirty. I miss you already.**

Cole: **I miss you too. What are you up to today?**

Me: **Writing. Right now I'm researching weapons that are legal to have in NYC. Did you know cane swords are illegal?**

Cole: **There goes your Christmas present...**

Me: **LOL hurry and fix everything so you can come home**

Cole: **Home...where we both live :)**

Me: **About that...we need a cat**

Cole: **Thor?**

Me: **He's too old. I miss him but couldn't do that to him. Plus he's an asshole.**

A few minutes pass before Cole's able to reply, and when he does, I can't stop smiling.

Cole: **When I get back, we can go to the animal shelter and pick out a cat.**

Me: **Really??**

Cole: **Yeah. I like animals. I never got a pet before since I was hardly home. But since you're there, it's a different** story. **I have to go into a meeting with these idiots...I'll call you when I'm done. Love you.**

Me: **Love you too. Good luck.**

I set my phone down and, instead of working, look up the animal shelters in the city. Five minutes later, I've decided that we need not one, but three cats and at least two dogs. And maybe that floppy-eared bunny someone dumped off in the shelter parking lot. This house is big. We have room for lots of animals here. And maybe even in years to come a baby or two.

Shaking my head at myself, but smiling as I do so, I close my computer and go upstairs to shower. I never thought I'd miss my vibrator while in New York with Cole, but with him away, I do. I'm in for a bit of manual labor then, because I'm fucking horny and missing Cole badly right now.

Keeping true to my word, I take my clothes off and snap a few pictures of my ass in the bathroom mirror before I'm satisfied enough with one to send to Cole. I add 'I miss you' to the image and text it to him, then get into the shower.

My shower?

Legally, I have nothing on this house, but it feels different now that I'm officially living here, and even more so knowing we want to get an animal together. I'm riding on a high, and enjoying the shit out of this moment.

Because it's only a matter of time before it ends. What goes up must come down.

chapter
eighteen

COLE

"*I*sn't it against company policy to keep us here so late?"

"Half the shit you do here is against company policy," I say, through gritted teeth. "Trust me, I want to get out of here as much as you do. Probably more, actually. Since I'm not going home to my girlfriend, but to a hotel room."

"Probably a fucking nice one," Dave mumbles and rolls his eyes. He's in charge of this imprint and I don't know if he's even old enough to babysit my nieces. I feel really fucking old standing here, trying to direct everyone on how to do their fucking jobs.

"It is a fucking nice hotel," I snap, surprising Dave and the other employees. "And once this is finally all sorted, I get to go home to a fucking nice house on the Upper East Side. I get to drive a fucking nice car to work on the days I feel like driving or have a company driver pick me up so I don't have to do shit myself. When I travel for work, I fly first class and stay in fucking nice hotels. And you know how I got all that nice shit? By *working*. Working hard and not slacking off on social media all day."

"Is that supposed to be a motivational speech?" another one of the employees asks. "Because I'm a minimalist and don't see the value in material items."

"Do you value a hard day's work? In doing your best and pulling your weight? Maybe you don't want your paycheck, but you could donate it to those who need it. Or invest it and save for your children's college years."

"You have a point, old man."

"I'm thirty-five," I grumble. "I'm not old enough to be your father, so shut it." I'm at my wit's end here, though the lack of professionalism here means I don't have to uphold the falsities that go along with work. "Bottom line, if this imprint doesn't get enough revenue, Black Ink will shut it down. You might not be interested in making more money or material things, but Black Ink sure as shit does. This is a business for them, not a political stance, not a way to get a voice heard. That might not be right, and sure as shit isn't fair, but that's how it is. If you want to keep spreading your message, you better get this place functioning like a business as well, or you'll all be out of jobs."

The last words seemed to hit everyone hard, and the tone of our meeting changes. I've been in LA all morning, trying to talk sense into the small yet brilliantly stubborn staff at this imprint. I went about things the usual way; polite, patient, trying to explain things in terms they can understand.

But my own patience ran out hours ago, and I realize now that I could have saved myself a great deal of trouble and a hell of a lot of time if I'd taken this approach the first time around.

"You haven't published anything in months, yet you've taken on new books almost weekly. Where do you think the marketing dollars come from?"

"Oh, come on. We know Black Ink headquarters has lots of money," Dave quips.

I resist the urge to bang my head on the wall. No fucking wonder Caitlin sent me. All the other publishers know how much of a headache this crew is to work with.

"They do, and they like to keep it that way. Which is why they won't hesitate to shut this down. You think I'm old and don't get what you're trying to say? Imagine a room full of the owners and operators of Black Ink, who are all bordering on retirement. They won't give a shit if you have three books lined up this summer to break through gender stereotypes and prove how blatant racism is. They might not see the importance of it. But I do. These books need to be read. The message needs to be shouted for everyone to hear. Which is why it's important to listen to me on this."

"You make a solid argument," Dave agrees. "That's all we want. To get the voices heard. Tell us your plan."

~

"I LEARNED today that the Brooklyn Zoo is *not* a zoo with animals," Ana tells me over the phone. "The cab driver probably thought I was the dumbest person in the world."

I laugh. "I can see how the mistake can be made."

"I know, right? The name is very misleading," she laughs. "It took like forty minutes to get to the right zoo, and your family was all running late so they only waited like ten minutes for me...and had a good laugh."

"Lexi is always running late," I say. "And Luke isn't much better. I honestly can't think of a single time when Lexi was early to work."

"I'm glad in this case. We had fun. The kids liked seeing the animals and it was nice talking with Lexi and your mom. Anyway, how's your day?"

"Fine. It's Sunday, so no work has been done at the imprint. I slept in today and then worked on editing. Doing this on top of my regular work is giving me a fucking headache."

"You should go out and sightsee! Or at the very least, take a break and enjoy the weather. It's cold here. It rained the last hour we were at the zoo, too."

"It's bright and sunny here, but I'm not a sightseeing person. Not here at least."

"What, the Hollywood sign isn't good enough for you?"

"No," I say with a chuckle. "Give me some ancient ruins and I'm happy. This isn't my thing."

"I miss you," she tells me. "You'll find out tomorrow when you can leave, right?"

"In theory. Hopefully everyone is able to stay on task and I'll be able to sit down with the editor in charge of acquisitions and we can get shit done."

"Poor baby. I'll make sure to take care of you when you get back. You'll be in need of a lot of TLC, after all."

"Fuck, yes."

I hear a door open and close and then voices, talking and laughing, coming through the phone. Someone calls Ana's name. "I have to go, dinner's ready. I'm still at Luke and Lexi's house. I'll call you when I get back to your house."

"It's yours now, too."

"Oh, right. It is," she says and I can tell she's smiling. "Bye, Cole. Love you."

"I love you too."

I hang up and toss the phone on the hotel bed, getting up to stretch. I sleep like shit when I'm not at home and have stayed up late every night working on edits, which kept me on schedule, thank the fucking Lord. I hate getting behind. Knowing there are a few more hours until Ana goes back to the house and is alone again is comforting. Despite how busy

I've been trying to sort out the mess at this LA-based imprint, there's been a constant ball of anxiety winding tighter and tighter inside of me as time passes. It would kill me if anything happened to her.

Remembering Ana's words about taking a break, I close my laptop and grab my wallet and room key. I make it down to the lobby before I realize I forgot my phone. Since I don't plan to be out long, I leave it upstairs and walk out into the sunlight. Unlike usual, I have no plan or end game, other than finding something to eat and heading back to my room.

Forcing myself to relax and enjoy the weather like Ana suggested, I wander down the street and find myself at some sort of art fair. The first booth I see has handmade coffee mugs, and two that are shaped like pineapples catch my eye. I buy them both, then walk around looking for anything else I could get Ana.

An hour later, I'm crossing the hotel lobby with a bag full of things for Ana and another full of food. It's been a while since I got to buy presents or surprise anyone. I missed this. Though what I have with Ana transcends anything I had before.

"Mr. Winchester?"

I look up to see one of the hotel's receptionists coming out from behind her desk.

"Yes?"

"Your friend was here looking for you. He seemed very concerned and tried to go into your room. It's against our policy and I need to remind you that outside guests can't have keycards."

"My friend?" I question. "I think you've mistaken me for someone else. I'm here on business and don't have any personal ties to the area. I'm not expecting anyone."

The woman—Jackie, as her nametag reads—pushes her eyebrows together. "You are Cole Winchester, right?"

180

"I am."

She smiles. "You have a face I knew I wouldn't forget. He specifically asked for you and said you two were supposed to meet and that it was really important."

I shake my head, wondering if it was Dave from the imprint coming to bug me. He has my cell number—fuck. My phone is upstairs. "If you see them again, I'll come down. No need to send anyone up." My dislike for Dave is growing by the minute. He couldn't be bothered to do his fucking job and now he's bothering me on my day off.

"All right, sir. And if you need anything…" Her eyes linger over me for a second too long. "Don't hesitate to ask. Customer service is very important to us."

I give a tight smile and hurry to the elevator and into my room. Setting Ana's bag down first, careful not to break any of the fragile items inside, I grab my phone with my free hand.

There are no missed calls.

No new texts.

And no emails from Dave or anyone at the imprint.

Weird.

I turn on the TV, flipping through channels as I eat. Ana calls when she leaves Luke and Lexi's and we talk her entire way back to the Upper East Side. I stay on the phone with her until she's safe in the house, armed the security system, and checked all the cameras. It's later there than it is here, and she's tired. We say goodnight, and I get back to work, editing until I can't keep my eyes open. I fall asleep with my computer in my lap.

Around four a.m., I'm startled awake by the sound of someone jiggling the exterior handle to the door leading into the room. I think. Maybe? I sit up, move my computer to the side, and blink through the dark, listening. It's too early for housekeeping, and they always knock.

I must have been dreaming. I turn my head to the side, stretching out my sore muscles, cramped from falling asleep sitting up. I turn the pillows down, getting comfortable for my remaining two hours of sleep.

And then I hear it again.

Someone is at the door. I spring up, annoyed more than anything at that moment, and go to the door. The chain lock is on, so even if someone did have a card, they couldn't get in. I reach to unlock it, sure that I'll have to direct someone's drunk ass to the right room, and then hesitate, moving my face to the peephole first to see what kind of mess I'll be dealing with.

I can't see out of it. I blink, move close again, and realize someone has their finger over it. What the fuck? Adrenaline surges through me and I don't think. I just act and throw back the lock and open the door.

He must have known. He must have been waiting. I step into the hall just in time to see him running away. The shock hits me and that moment's hesitation costs me my chance to catch him. I was so worried about Ana, I didn't see this coming. Steven isn't stalking her.

He's stalking me.

chapter
nineteen

ANA

"Welcome home, babe!"

Cole drops his suitcase and picks me up, kissing me with passion and twirling me around. My feet don't hit the ground, and instead, he pushes me up against the wall. My legs fasten around his waist, and I curl my arms over his neck.

"I take it you missed me," I breathe when we finally part for air.

"Just a bit," he pants and puts his mouth back on mine, kissing me hard and then moving his lips to my neck. A shiver works its way through me, and the heat builds between my legs. It's late Tuesday night, and I haven't been able to talk to Cole much since Sunday on the drive home from Luke and Lexi's.

Something seemed off when we spoke Monday, but I chalked it up to the stress he was feeling from burning the candle at both ends. I know he holds a high position at the publishing house, but I don't quite get why he'd go sort out a mess like that. Getting behind on his own work is stressing Cole out, and I hate seeing him upset.

"Please tell me you don't have to go into the office in the morning," I moan, turning my head to the side so he can access my neck. It's an instant turn-on to have his mouth against my flesh there.

"I do. But don't worry about that now." He runs his hands down my back and over my ass, curling his fingers into the material of my sleeper shorts. They're gray and patterned with pineapples and match the tank top I have on, and I debated changing into something sexy before Cole got in, but after his plane was delayed due to a storm in California, I passed out and only woke when he texted me to say he landed.

We stumble back, arms tangled around each other, and end up in the formal living room right off the foyer. Cole pulls my tank top over my head and admires my breasts for a moment before diving back onto me, kissing me harder than before.

As if he suddenly lost all control, Cole strips me naked and I desperately remove his pants. We make love on the couch, hard, fast, sweaty love, and stay tangled together once we're done.

"It's only been four days, but God I missed that," Cole breathes. "If I go out of town again, you're coming with me."

"I'll travel out of town with you just so we can fuck like I'm some sort of high-class mistress."

"As long as you're okay with it…"

I laugh. "Buy me pretty things and I will be."

"Speaking of that, I did get you something." He tightens his arms around me. "But I'm not getting up."

"You need sleep," I remind him. "It's one-thirty a.m. That's ridiculous you have to go to the office in the morning. At least go in late."

"I'll be fine," he says, though I can tell that's bullshit. He's tired as fuck, and he told me he doesn't sleep well away from home. And in this case—me.

"You can admit you're human." I carefully circle the tattoo on his shoulder with my finger. "Though I might not believe you after the very animalistic things you just did to me."

He responds by kissing my neck and snuggling into the couch, holding me against him. "Let's just stay here."

I grab a blanket that's neatly folded over the arm of the couch and spread it out, tucking Cole in. I sneak away to the bathroom and by the time I get back, he's asleep. I get dressed and get another blanket, then carefully lie down next to Cole. Being crammed on the couch is less than comfortable, but there's nowhere else I'd rather be.

$$\sim$$

I WAKE to the distant beeping of Cole's alarm. Blinking, I push the blankets to the side and get off the couch, stumbling through the dark house to find his phone and shut off the alarm.

"It is way too early to be up," I grumble when I go back into the living room. Cole is sitting up, head in his hands. "You only slept for like three hours. Please stay home."

"I can sleep for another hour," he mumbles. "That alarm is set early. I used to go to the gym before work." He gives me a small smile. "I haven't gone in a while, but the alternative is more than worth it."

"You better start going," I say seriously. "I fell in love with your muscles. If you lose them, you lose me."

Cole reaches for me. "I can't have that." His arms slip around my waist and we fall back on the couch together. Cole is still naked and his warm flesh against mine feels amazing and is sexy and comforting at the same time. I turn around, my chest against his, and hook my leg over him. Cole's eyes fall shut and

185

his breathing deepens. He's asleep again in minutes, and I'm out not long after that, sleeping soundly until Cole's second alarm goes off a little over an hour later. Cole reaches over me, feels around for his phone, and hits the snooze button.

Twice.

The third time, he gets up. Uncomfortable on the couch, I get up with him and make coffee while he showers.

"Want me to meet you for lunch?" I ask before he leaves.

"Yeah," he says, and the lack of hesitation actually surprises me. Cole's been so worried about Steven sneaking up on me, I half expected him to object. "That'd be nice. I'll try to take a break right around noon. Call me when you leave the house and I'll meet you in the lobby."

He puts on his coat and pulls me in for one more kiss before he leaves. Once the house is locked and armed, I go upstairs and into bed, sleeping for four precious hours before I get up, shower, and get ready to head out. I call Cole, talk to him for a bit as I walk down the busy sidewalk to catch a cab. He's busy and can't talk long, but says he'll meet me in the main lobby of the building to save me a trip up to his floor.

I take a seat near the doors and pull a small coloring book from my purse and a colored pencil, shading in the 'F' in 'fuck you'. My curse word coloring book is my fave.

"Scarlett?"

Someone stops in front of me and looks right at me as they say the name. My name.

"Uh, yeah?"

"I thought that was you." A pretty blonde woman smiles down at me. "We met at Gregory Lawrence's release party. I'm Lindsay."

"Right." Lindsay was Cole's date at that party. Not by his choice, but seeing her stirs up a bit of annoyance anyway. "Nice to see you again."

"You too. Are you going up? I am. I'm meeting my aunt for lunch." She raises her eyebrows. "Should be fun."

I smile back. "Sounds like it. And no, I'm not. I'm meeting Cole for lunch."

"Oh, right. He's editing your book. It must be so exciting to be an author. I've always looked at things from the other side. You know, growing up around this and all." She waves her hand at the building. "My aunt is pushing for me to be an editor, and I fought against it until I got to job-shadow Cole the day of that disastrous party."

"You shadowed Cole?" He didn't have to tell me, but after spending a day with this woman and then being her date, I'd think he'd mention it.

"Yes!" she gushes. "It totally changed my mind. Though I have a feeling Cole can change anyone's mind, am I right? I mean, you've seen him, so you know how persuasive he can be without even trying." Her cheeks redden and she pushes her hair behind her ear. "Anyway, I should probably get up there. I'm supposed to meet my aunt at noon, and it's five till, which according to her means I'm already late. Are you going to the Halloween party this weekend?"

"Yeah, I am."

"Awesome! Me too. This is my last year in grad school so I'm trying to come to as many of these functions as possible. Maybe I'll make some connections and if not, it's just great experience. I'll see you Saturday!"

"Yeah, bye."

She turns and heads to the elevator, leaving me with a weird feeling. She doesn't know Cole and I are dating, so I can't fault her for crushing on him…and admitting it in front of me. The last time I saw her, Cole wasn't my boyfriend anyway. Whatever. I shake my head and go back to coloring until Cole comes down.

"Hey, babe," I say, stashing my coloring book and pencil inside my purse.

"Ana, hi," he replies, smiling as he looks into my eyes. He takes my hands and leans in for a kiss. He pulls back quickly and looks all around the lobby. "I have a meeting at one-thirty. Sorry to make you rush."

"It's fine. I don't expect you to have the whole afternoon free. You are at work, after all." He falls into step next to me and we leave the building. The rain picked up force, and I pull my hood on and hunch my shoulders. "Our costumes came today. Though this cold is making me second guess my choice. I'm going to freeze. You'll be fine, at least."

Cole just stares in front of him and I wonder if stress from work is getting to him again.

"Cole?"

"Sorry," he says quickly. "Cold. Costumes. Right. You don't have to wear a costume, you know." He tips his head toward me with a smile.

"I know I don't *have* to, but I want to. It's been a while since I've dressed up for Halloween and it sounds fun."

"Yeah, it does."

"You sound tired," I say and feel bad for Cole. He hardly slept at all last night and he still has half of the day left.

"I am," he admits with a sigh. "But I'll be all right. I've pulled all-nighters many times trying to get last minute edits in. Coffee helps." He gives me a smile again, and this one seems more genuine. Still, something feels off, but I can't tell if it's with Cole or the world in general.

We walk down the block and into a restaurant. The feeling that something bad is going to happen grows, and I have a hard time forcing myself to eat my soup and salad. Since it's lunchtime, this place is busy anyway. Add in the rain everyone wants to escape from, and it's packed like a can of sardines. Loud sardines. I have to lean across the table to talk to Cole, which results in minimal conversation.

The rain stopped as we ate, and we walk a little slower back to the office. Cole takes my hand and gives me a gentle tug toward him, leaning in for a kiss.

"You know I love you, right?" he asks me, but it sounds like he's reassuring himself. The bad feeling that had started to fade comes back, and the hairs on the back of my neck stand up. I've often ignored my instincts, thinking that going off a feeling is stupid and the cause of a lot of my problems. And to tell the truth, it has been. But ignoring them has proved just as detrimental.

"You better," I tell him with a smile "Because I love you too."

Cole bends down for another kiss, and the second his lips press against mine the ill feelings disappear. Cole makes everything better. And then I see *him*, and it's like a cold finger slid down my spine. He's across the street, but there's no mistaking his blue-grey eyes.

Steven is watching me. Again.

COLE

I shut the door behind Ana and step back, watching the cab pull away from the curb and take off, driving the short distance to the house that we're now sharing. The rain starts again, coming down slowly and gently and gradually picking up force. It's cold, and the dampness in the air is the kind that sets into your bones, making it almost impossible to warm up without the help of a hot shower or another body pressed up against your own.

I should stand out here, getting drenched, and then deal with the shivers and chills the rest of the day. I deserve it. And Ana deserves better.

I turn my head up to the gray sky above, hating myself more and more as each drop of rain falls down on my face. My mind flashes back to this morning, back to when I first set foot into the office. Tired from all the fucking traveling, my guard was down. The Kentucky area code didn't raise a red flag, even though it should have. I get calls from all over the world, but I know where Ana is from...and where Steven comes from.

Yet, I answered. There was no exchange of words, but he

heard my voice and inhaled deep, as if he was taking in the fresh aroma of cookies right out of the oven. His exhale was one of pleasure, and until that point, I never knew how disturbing it actually is to hear nothing but breathing coming from the other line. Like a lame cliché from a B-grade horror movie, the panting left me feeling violated. Violated and pissed. Maybe I should turn the table and stalk him. Find him. Beat the shit out of him.

But that's not what's eating at me. That's not what's making me feel like the world's worst boyfriend and biggest piece of shit. I told Ana to meet me in the main lobby of the building so no one from Black Ink would see her and raise suspicions that we're together. Which was low of me in the first place, and my stomach actually fucking hurts from it.

I want that promotion. I want Ana. Why can't I have both?

On my way down, as luck would have it, I run into the one person who knows about the promotion...and who could blow my cover about Ana. That morning, Caitlin pulled me aside and said she wants to be done before the holidays, which means I only have a few more weeks until things become official.

Lindsay got out of the elevator as I was going to get in, and stopped me. She touched my arm as we spoke, happy we ran into each other and looking forward to the Halloween party. She asked me if I was bringing a date. Only a second passed between us before I answered, but a million things went through my head.

Ana and I are together. She's my girlfriend and I love her more than I've ever loved anyone. She makes me happy. Makes me a better person. Hell, she even makes me feel better about myself, which is why I feel like such shit now.

I said no.

I didn't have a date.

All because I want to be a publisher.

The rain falls harder, hitting me like the realization that I'm not a good person, no matter how you spin it. It wasn't direct, but it happened just the same. I picked work over her. I lied about the one thing in this world that's more important to me than anything...or so I say.

Maybe she's not.

And she deserves more than that. Ana is the kind of woman who deserves to be the center of someone's world. I thought I could give that to her, that I could be enough, but now...now I don't think so.

Again.

I should have fucking listened to myself the first time around. I knew I wasn't good enough for her, and was a fool to think someone as wonderful as Ana could settle for someone like me.

Even before I tried to break up Luke and Lexi, I've done things I wasn't proud of. Things to get ahead. Things to make myself look better. And what I haven't done can be overshadowed by what I've felt.

Jealous.

Thinking others are undeserving.

That I should be the one getting ahead.

"Cole?"

I blink, eyelashes wet with raindrops, and turn in the direction of the voice. I can't see her face, but I know that voice.

"What are you doing here?" I ask, looking through the sea of people and umbrellas for my ex-fiancée.

"I got your message."

My eyes settle on Heather's face. Her hair is pulled back into a ponytail, and she's wearing a bright pink raincoat. I used to feel so much when our eyes would meet, but now I feel nothing.

"I didn't call you."

She shuffles forward. "It was a text."

"I didn't text you either."

She pulls her coat tighter at the collar. "Can we get out of the rain?"

"Sure." Drops are making their way through my jacket by now and the cold is setting in, though I still think I'm deserving of the misery. Heather steps under an overhang, close to the building. She reaches inside her jacket and pulls out her phone.

"I didn't think it was from you," she starts, eyebrows pushing together. "The messages starts with 'Hi Heather' and there's no comma between the two. I know I'm not the best with grammar, so if I'm catching errors…" She shakes her head.

"If you knew it wasn't from me then why are you here?"

"I don't know." She looks up at me, eyes meeting mine. I used to trust and love this woman. Now I don't believe a word she says. "I wanted to make sure you were okay, I guess. Why would someone send a message pretending to be you?"

"Can I see it?" I ask. "I think I might know who sent it."

"Of course." She hands me the phone and her fingers grace my skin. I feel nothing.

The text is from a blocked number, reading as 'Unknown' on her phone. The conversation between them is short.

Unknown: **Hi Heather. Its Cole. Can we meet and talk? I miss you.**

Heather: **Okay. Where?**

Unknown: **Come to my office tomorrow after lunch.**

Heather: **What time?**

The unknown texter never replied after that.

"There's more than one grammar mistake," I start then shake my head. That doesn't matter. I take a screenshot of the conversation, send it to myself, and then delete the text from Heather's phone.

"You know who it is?" Heather asks, taking her phone back.

"I think so, and if this person tries to contact you again, don't answer." I look at Heather, noticing for the first time how much she's aged since ending things. I don't love her anymore, and there was a time saying her name filled me with hatred for everything she's done. Having to cancel the wedding hurt. My heart was broken and I had to call everything we had booked to tell them things weren't going to happen. I lost money, but that didn't matter. Mom had to tell all her friends her son wasn't getting married anymore. It was embarrassing for her. And for me. That right there is reason enough to hate Heather.

But add in all the shit she did after that...holding onto her obsession over Luke, desperately hoping he'd develop feelings for her...lying and making me think my own brother betrayed me. I know I cannot blame Heather for my actions. What she did to me caused the emotions I felt, but I and I alone acted on them. At the end of the day, the choices we make are ours, and cannot be blamed on anyone else.

Heather made me feel like shit, but it was me who sought vengeance.

Heather made me believe that Luke encouraged her to leave me, but it was me who tried to make him just as miserable.

She might not be any better of a person than I am, hell, she's pathetic enough for not being able to let go of her high school crush, but she's not to blame.

I am.

"I forgive you," I blurt.

Heather blinks and then shakes her head. "What?"

"The last time I saw you, you told me you were sorry. I forgive you."

She steps closer. "Thank you, Cole. I feel awful. Almost every day, to be honest. What I did was wrong and selfish. You were good to me and I took advantage of that. It's been hard moving on," she confesses and it hits me how similar we are.

"You should move on." The words leave and I feel a weight lifted off my chest. "The past is in the past. We're both different people now."

"Right. Thank you, Cole. Really." She steps in and hugs me. I stiffen, and then carefully bend my arm around her in a half-hug. She moves back, looks at me, and smiles. "You look good."

"Thanks," I reply and wonder if I should return the compliment. I don't get a chance because my phone vibrates in my pocket as a text comes through. Welcoming a distraction, I reach inside my jacket to check it. The number hasn't been added to my contacts, but I know who it is.

Steven.

He sent me an image, and when I open it, my heart pumps and rage fills me. He sent a blurry photo, but there's no mistaking the couple who's embracing. From a distance, the hug doesn't look as awkward as it felt. All you see are Heather's arms around me and a look of satisfaction on her face.

"Cole? What's wrong?"

"My girlfriend," I start and the words die in my throat. How can I explain what's going on when I can hardly fathom it myself? Steven set this up, but why? To get my ex and I together so he could take pictures and send them to Ana? Make her think I'm sneaking around with Heather? He's psychotic and dangerous, and believes if he can't have Ana, no one can. Fuck. He's trying to make her leave me, probably so he can get her alone and hurt her.

Rage takes over and I look across the street. Standing next to a park bench—the same fucking bench I've seen Steven on more than once—is a man in a gray hoodie, holding a phone. I don't think. Ignoring Heather, I take off, racing across the rain-soaked street. Brakes squeal and angry drivers honk and yell at me.

Steven sees me coming after him and turns to run, but bumps into someone and falls to the ground. The phone flies from his hand and he leaves it, scrambling to get up. I'm almost there. I scoop up the phone, scraping my knuckles on the cement in my haste, and jump over the park bench, grabbing Steven by the hood of his sweatshirt.

A woman screams, seeing me violently shove Steven to the ground. Not caring how much pain I inflict, I push him over, fist raised.

"Wait," he cries, covering his face with his hands. With the hood off, I see black, curly hair. That's not Steven.

"What the fuck are you doing?" I demand, and lower my arm.

The man slowly gets to his feet, and I let him, aware that people are watching us now. He holds his hands up in front of him, letting me know he won't try anything...like I'd ever trust him.

"Why did you take pictures of me?"

"Some guy paid me fifty bucks to do it."

"Some guy?"

"Yeah." The black-haired man before me is young, no older than twenty-one if I had to guess. "He just came up to me and said he'd give me fifty bucks to take your picture and send it."

"The phone?" I demand. "Where did you get it?"

"He gave it to me. Said to leave it on the bench when I

was done and he'd get it later."

"Where'd he go?"

The guy shakes his head. "I don't know. He already paid me, so I didn't pay attention."

"Fuck," I say and look around. Is he watching? Or is he—shit. Ana's alone. I look at the curly-haired kid once more. "Be more careful next time. There are some real psychos out there."

His eyes widen and he looks at me. "Yeah, I know." He turns and hurries away. My heart is about to break right out of my fucking chest. I call Ana, nerves on fire as I wait for her to answer.

She doesn't.

The call goes to voicemail. "Fuck!" I whirl around and hurry to the street. I need to find Ana. My head is spinning and I can't think. I raise my arm to get a cab when Ana calls me back.

"Hey, babe," she starts. "Sorry. I was in the bathroom."

"You're home?"

"Yeah, I just got in. Is everything okay?"

I close my eyes and exhale. "Yeah. I wanted to make sure you got home safe. And tell you I miss you already." And fuck, I do. I want to be home with her, wrapped up in blankets on the couch or in bed...it doesn't fucking matter where as long as she's with me.

"Come home early. You're exhausted, Cole. You need to rest. Though, if you do come home early, there won't be much resting."

"I'm okay with that. And I'll see what I can do. I might be able to leave early."

"I hope so."

I turn around, feeling more and more paranoid. And then I see Heather across the street, waiting for me to come back and explain everything. *Fuck.* "Me too."

chapter

twenty-one

ANA

"*I* didn't realize it rained so much here." I set a plate of tacos on the table for Cole and go back to fix one more for myself. "I don't know why I had it in my head that New York City was bright and sunny, but I did. Maybe from all the movies set here."

"Wait until winter," Cole says with a laugh. "You might miss Kentucky then."

"I'm excited for the first big snow," I remind him. "I don't have to leave the house anymore unless it's absolutely necessary, so it won't bother me. But don't worry, I will feel bad for you."

His smile grows and he gets up, coming over to the stove and puts his arms around my waist. "Speaking of home, I have something for you." He lets go of me and reaches into his pocket, pulling out a pineapple keychain. I set my plate down and take it. "For your house key."

"Cole," I say softly. "Thank you."

"I love you, Ana. I want you to feel like this is your home too."

"It's starting to. And once I start decorating with more pineapple stuff and pictures of cats, it really will."

"I think you're joking, but I need to be sure."

"Oh, I'm one-hundred percent serious," I say and nod. "I've already decided that a big picture of Thor should go over the fireplace in the living room, and I spent most of the afternoon researching photographers who do newborn photography *and* pet photography in the same style."

Cole laughs. "I bet that's a real thing."

"Of course is it! And when we get our cat, we'll need a good picture of the three of us for our baby announcement."

He puts his arms around me again. "I love you," he whispers and kisses my neck.

I close my eyes, wrap my fingers around the keychain, and hug Cole. We stay like that for a minute, and then separate and go to the table.

"This is good," Cole tells me after he takes a bite.

"Thanks. Tacos are hard to mess up. Though so is spaghetti and we know how that turned out. If we do Taco Tuesday every week, you're guaranteed at least one good meal."

"You don't have to cook for me at all, you know."

"I do know, and I'm cooking for both of us. Unless you want to hire a chef along with the housekeepers."

"I've considered it before," he tells me. "When I was serious about working out, I looked into it but it never panned out."

"That would be awesome, but they'd have to make me all sorts of junk food and dessert along with your healthy workout food. And probably sing "Be Our Guest" at least once while I'm wearing a blue dress and dancing with the dishes."

"You're so weird, Ana," he says with a laugh. "And I love that about you."

"Thanks. My mom always said it was either a trait you'd have to love or hate about me."

We both go back for seconds. "How was the rest of work?" I ask him, looking over my shoulder as I fill a shell with cheese and meat. "Anything exciting happen after lunch?"

"No," he says quickly. "Nothing."

"That's good. Sometimes a boring day is a good day, right?"

"Yeah. It is."

I sit back down across from Cole at the table in the kitchen. He's quiet again, and I notice the dark circles under his eyes. "Want to shower and then watch a movie or read together on the couch after dinner? You should really go to bed early tonight."

"Yeah, a shower sounds great. But I have a chapter to edit and send to an author. I meant to get it done at the office today but ran out of time. Sorry, Ana."

"Don't be sorry, Cole. Do your work then go to bed. Seriously. I'll work on my chapter while you work on yours. I was a little distracted today and didn't get much done."

"Distracted?"

"I keep looking at cats on the animal shelter's website."

Cole smiles. "We can go this weekend."

I raise my gaze across the table and reach out, taking Cole's hand. "I can't wait."

THE REST of the week passes by quickly. Cole works late almost every day and comes home looking even more worn out than before. We had plans to go out and see that movie we missed last weekend, but when he drags himself through the door Friday evening, I change plans for us. A night in is exactly what he needs, and falls asleep on the couch while watching a movie a little after eight p.m. At midnight, I gently woke him up and guided him to bed. He fell asleep quickly again and didn't get up until nine-thirty the next morning.

"You look better," I say, pouring myself a mug of coffee. I eyeball the kitchen windows, blinds still drawn, and sit by Cole at the table.

"I feel better. I guess I didn't realize how tired I was until I fell asleep. Then it was like I couldn't wake up."

"You needed to rest. I still can't believe you had to go to work after all that travel and then have to stay late. You deserve a raise."

Cole raises his eyebrows and nods. "I agree. Enough about work though." He puts his mug down and puts his hand on my thigh. "Tonight will be fun."

"It will. I haven't been to a Halloween party in a long time. I think you'll like my costume...and yours."

"Yay. I can't wait to wear spandex," he says dryly.

"I actually have a surprise for you," I tell him, wrinkling my nose. "About your costume."

"Should I be worried?"

"I'll let you decide. Stay here." I hurry upstairs to get a box and come back down to hand it to Cole.

"What's this?"

"Your costume."

"In here?" He picks up the small box and gives it a shake.

"Just open it." I watch, trying not to smile, as Cole opens the box and pulls out a pair of glasses and a name badge.

"Clark Kent from The Daily Planet," he reads and then turns to me with a smile. "So, no spandex?"

"I mean, if you really want to wear it, I'm sure we can find you something."

"This is perfect, Ana. Thank you."

"You're welcome. I do have a T-shirt for you to wear under a button-up if you want. It's blue with the Superman symbol on it. You can leave the top few buttons undone so people get the costume."

"You're a genius."

"Nah, I just have a Pinterest account, really."

"I want to thank you, regardless."

"I'll accept any form of thanks, too."

Cole sets the costume down and puts his hands on my ass. "I was thinking of licking your pussy."

His directness is such a turn-on. Fuck, I'm so lucky.

~

"You're joking, right?"

"I wish," Cole sighs. "It won't take long, and the office is a block away from the hall where the party is taking place. I already asked Luke if he and Lexi can swing by here on the way and pick you up."

"I don't want to inconvenience them."

"You're not. They're going to park here and take a cab to the hall anyway."

"Oh, I don't feel bad then."

"You shouldn't feel bad at all."

I nod and pick up the curling iron. I'm attempting to curl my hair before the party. It'll be flat in a matter of hours, but I'll get a few good pictures in before then at least. Just a few minutes ago, Caitlin Black called Cole about an issue with an editor and something about the wrong file being uploaded to Amazon, and he has to go into the office to oversee that the correct changes are made.

"Want me to come with you?" I ask, wrapping a section of hair around the hot iron. "For moral support, of course."

"I'd like that, but it's okay. Go to the party. If I can get ahold of the right people on the phone, it won't take long. But…"

"But it's Saturday night."

"Exactly."

"I'm sorry," I tell him and move onto another section of hair. "It sucks you have to deal with this."

Cole shrugs. "It comes with the job. I found out years ago the higher up you go in the company, the more responsibility you have. Unless you're Caitlin," he adds with a laugh.

"Must be nice to inherit the world's biggest publishing house. She literally got it all handed to her with no work."

"I know, right?" He sighs again. "I should go. I don't want to."

"You can't refuse, can you?"

"That wouldn't go over so well."

I curl the last strand of straight hair and turn to Cole. "You look hot as Clark Kent, by the way. I'm going to be waiting all night for you to rip that shirt off and reveal that you're really Superman. And then use your superpowers on me."

Cole kisses me. "I've never seen Wonder Woman look so fucking hot. Wait. Are Superman and Wonder Woman related?"

"If I said they are, would you still want to fuck me?"

"I'll always want to fuck you. But are they?"

I laugh. "There are fan theories that they are, but technically they are from different worlds, well, if you go off certain versions. So if you're into that sort of thing, we can pretend."

"I'm not." His hands land on my thighs. "I love you."

"Love you too."

He kisses me one more time and then leaves. Once I hear the beeping of the alarm and know the house is armed, I go back to fussing with my hair and makeup and then watch TV to kill the rest of the time before Luke and Lexi gets here. Based on what I've witnessed myself and by what Cole has said, I'm not counting on them being here anytime soon.

Cole calls, and I grab the phone eagerly.

"Hey, babe."

"Hey. Bad news. The wrong file has been uploaded everywhere, not just Amazon."

"Oh, babe, I'm so sorry. But, uh, what does this mean?"

"It means I'll be doing the same thing over and over."

"How long is it gonna take?"

"Depends on how long I'm on hold."

I frown, feeling bad for Cole. "Hopefully they at least play good music."

He chuckles. "Hopefully. Oh, and I left the Daily Planet name badge on the nightstand. Can you bring it for me?"

"Of course, Clark. I'll see you later. Love you."

"Love you, too," he says and hangs up. I go upstairs and look on his nightstand, but don't see the badge. I look on the other nightstand and find the badge. It's on the side of the bed I've been sleeping on, but since Cole's had the bed to himself for years, I guess assigning ownership to a side of the bed or a nightstand doesn't happen overnight. I grab the badge and then go downstairs, putting it in my purse right away so *I* don't forget it.

Twenty minutes later, Lexi texts me to say they're here. I unarm the house and wait at the front door, not unlocking it until I see Luke's face. Call me paranoid...fuck. I'll always be like this.

"You look amazing!" Lexi says as soon as she sees me. "And totally like you can kick my ass. I love it."

"Thanks. You look good too," I tell Lexi, who's dressed as Morticia Addams. "I'm seriously jealous of your boobs right now."

"They do distract from the baby bump." Lexi puts her hand over her stomach.

"You're right because I didn't even notice."

"That makes me feel good. I'm at that weird is-she-pregnant-or-fat phase."

Luke, who's dressed as Gomez Addams, slips his arm around Lexi. "I don't know why you're worried. Pregnant or fat, you're fucking hot and you're fucking mine. If anyone has a problem with any part of you, they have me to deal with."

Lexi turns her head up to him, heavily-lined eyes widening. "I love you."

"I love you more," Luke tells her and places his hand on her stomach. "You're growing our son. That's fucking amazing."

As if I'm not there at all, he kisses her, and now I understand even more why they annoy Cole so much. Hell, I like them both and they annoy me. I always thought couples who displayed an over-show of emotions were compensating for something, but I don't think it's true in Luke and Lexi's case.

"Shall we go?" I ask.

"Yeah. I need to pee first." Lexi hurries away and I go to the front door, pulling on my boots.

"Have you heard from Cole?" Luke asks.

"Yeah, a bit ago. The problem is worse than he thinks, so he'll be late, which sucks, but at least he'll be there."

"You'll probably have more fun without him."

Lexi comes down the hall and gives Luke a look. "Be nice. Cole can be fun."

"Name one time Cole was fun," Luke says seriously.

Lexi raises her eyebrows. "I'm not playing this game."

"That's because you can't think of anything," Luke laughs. "Though lately he's been much more tolerable. Thanks, Ana."

"You can pay me later. I do accept alcohol as a form of

payment," I say and head outside. It's hard not to smile when I pull out my house key, /attached to the pineapple keychain, and lock the front door. I still have to go back to Kentucky and get my stuff, but the overall feeling is that this place is home.

"Have you guys picked out a name yet?" I ask Lexi once we get into the taxi.

"It's either Ethan or Hayden," she starts.

"Not Hayden," Luke interrupts. "I'm not calling my son Hayden, and Lexi only likes it because of a character from a book."

"That's a real reason to like a name," I agree. "And dislike one."

"I had a neighbor in Chicago named Hayden and *she* was a huge bitch. Now that's what I think of when I hear the name."

"But Hayden Winchester sounds nice together," Lexi goes on.

"What about Aiden?" I suggest. "Aiden Winchester sound similar."

Lexi looks at Luke, eyebrows raised. "I like that."

Luke smiles. "I do too. I don't know why I didn't think of it before."

"Now we need a middle name."

Luke laughs. "We have time."

"Oh," Lexi says suddenly and looks at me. "Quinn asked me to talk to you and see if you'd be interested in doing an author takeover in her group."

"Oh my God, yes. That would be awesome but I'm totally going to be nervous."

"Don't be. She'll walk you through everything, and this can be great for you. Quinn has a big presence in the romance community and she knows how to use it. She's really excited to introduce you to her readers, actually."

My mind starts to get ahead of me, and instead of imagining things crashing and burning like I usually do, I imagine myself becoming friends with Quinn and having late-night talks where she shares her publishing wisdom and offers support. Writing an amazing book is only half of having a career in writing nowadays, and I'm worried my weirdness could be off-putting to fans.

I offer to pay the fare when we get to the venue, but Luke declines and hands the cabbie cash before he gets out and helps Lexi to her feet. The venue looks amazing just from the outside, and when we get in, I'm speechless. The decor is over the top yet classy, and is themed to make the entire place look like a haunted hotel from the 1920s.

I stick with Lexi as she goes around saying hi to people and introducing me to anyone I haven't yet met. I recognize Lexi's friend Jillian and start to feel like a third wheel when Jillian's husband and Luke get to talking like old friends. Lexi is way too nice to give off the slightest clue that I'm a burden, but I wonder if she'd be having more fun if she weren't constantly making sure I was okay.

Half an hour later, Cole texts and says he's finally on his way. Since the party is in Manhattan, it won't take him long to get here. Lexi introduces me to a newly-hired editor, a young woman named Ellie, and then I go off by myself, happily visiting the buffet table. I load up a plate with food and go to the bar for a drink.

"Are you here alone?" someone asks, stepping close behind me.

I turn to see a man, face painted like a zombie, standing just two feet away. He's clutching a plastic ax in one hand and smiling at me.

"Are you trying to be creepy?" I ask.

He laughs. "That wasn't my intention, but I get nervous

around attractive women. And you are making me very nervous."

"Oh." I realize he's turning it into a compliment, one that's supposed to make me laugh or blush or tell him I'm sorry that by standing here, doing absolutely nothing, I'm making him nervous.

"Maybe you didn't hear me. I get nervous around attractive women, and you're making me nervous."

"I heard you," I say with a polite smile, reminding myself that I have no idea who this guy is. He could be a publisher for all I know. But I'm going to hold onto my resolve and not fawn all over him just because he gave me a compliment. I did a social experiment in college and didn't giggle, blush, or swoon over compliments given to me by men, and a surprising number actually got mad about it, thinking I owed it to them to react the way they wanted me to react.

The zombie laughs. "And you're not going to thank me?"

"Why would I thank you for being nervous?" I push my brows together, trying to look like I really don't get it.

"Never mind. Superman's not here with you, is he?"

"Yeah, he is. Have fun tonight," I say to the zombie and happily take my drink from the bartender. I leave a tip and take my Moscow Mule and my plate over to a table, sitting by Lexi, who's working on a piece of chocolate cake, and ask her if she knows who the zombie is.

"He's wearing too much makeup," she tells me. "I can't really recognize him."

I nod and take a drink, and then it hits me: this is a costume party. Not everyone is what they appear. There are people in heavy makeup and masks. It's all too easy to hide yourself tonight.

Fear makes its way down my spine and the room spins. I put my hands flat on the table, and close my eyes. I can't freak out now. I take a deep breath in and slowly let it out. I press my feet hard down onto the floor, reminding myself that I'm right here, right now. I'm surrounded by people. I'm safe.

And then I feel his presence, and everything is okay. I open my eyes to see Cole walking across the room. A purple strobe light dances across his face and our eyes meet. He smiles and my heart flutters. The panic goes away. The fear subsides.

Cole gets stopped by someone on his way over, shooting me an apologetic look. I don't mind because he's here now. I reach into my purse for his Clark Kent name badge.

"Hi, Scarlett!" a woman in red high heels says my name. I straighten up and see Lindsay pulling out a chair at the table. She's dressed as a sexy nurse and looks hot and adorable at the same time. "Oh my gosh, I love your costume!"

"Thanks. I like yours too."

"Please." She waves her hand in the air. "This was last year's. I wore it to a sorority party and spilled rum and Coke on it. The stains are still there but you can't see them in the dark."

"It's perfect then."

"I just got here, have you been here long?"

"Maybe forty-five minutes? Not that long."

"It's amazing in here. I expected things to be over the top, but this…" She looks around. "This is breathtaking. I sound lame, don't I?"

I laugh. "Not at all. I thought the same thing. I'm from a small town in Kentucky so pretty much everything in New York City has been breathtaking for me." I take another drink and try not to shudder. Whoever made this was very generous with the vodka. I look at Cole and can tell he's trying to politely get away, taking a step back every now and then. Whoever he's talking to moves along with him, laughing boisterously and not picking up on the social cues that Cole is ready to be done with the conversation.

Lindsay follows my eye. "Cole didn't wear a costume?"

"He's Clark Kent," I explain. "He forgot his Daily Planet name badge." I hold it up so she can see.

"Who's that?"

I blink. Once. Twice. Three times. "Superman."

"Superman has a human name?"

If I had taken a drink, I would have spit it out. "Yeah, he does."

She looks at me, and then at Cole. "What about Wonder Woman?"

"Diana Prince."

"Interesting," she says and watches Cole come over. She fusses with her hair and pushes her shoulders back. "Hey, Cole," she says as soon as he's at the table. I stand and walk over to him.

"Did you get everything taken care of?" I ask and slip the name badge over his head, then go in for a hug. Cole brushes me off, and out of the corner of my eye, I see Lexi nudge Luke. She thought it was weird too.

"I did, thankfully. Everything is fixed, and the new versions of the book are uploading now."

"I knew you'd fix things." I take Cole's hand, but he pulls it out of mine. Lindsay saw and is giving me a weird look. "Want a drink? I can go get you something."

"I can get it myself, but thanks. Enjoy the party."

"I'll enjoy it more with you."

Cole just gives me a tight smile and sits down in the seat between mine and Lindsay's. I sit back down as well, grabbing my drink and taking a few big gulps.

"Is my aunt driving you nuts?" Lindsay asks Cole.

"No more than usual," he answers.

"I can only imagine. She's such a hardass anyway, but

with her wanting to make you a publisher, it has to be ten times worse."

"You're being considered for a publisher?" Lexi asks, leaning closer.

"I am," he says.

"Cole, that's awesome! Why didn't you say anything?"

I look at Cole, feeling more and more like that third wheel again. I'm his girlfriend. We live together. I'd think this is the kind of thing you'd share, right?

"It's not a done deal yet," he explains. "I don't want to get excited until it's actually happening."

"Oh, it will happen," Lindsay says. It bothers me that she knew and I didn't. She's Caitlin's niece…maybe she told her directly. "I've heard her talk about it. She really does think you're the best to take over her spot. The board is meeting in two weeks to make the final decision."

Cole smiles and then shakes his head. "That doesn't mean anything."

"It does. You are so modest. Which is so nice to see in a man." Lindsay bites her lip and laughs. "You will be perfect for the job."

I put my hand on Cole's thigh, feeling more and more uncomfortable as time goes on. Lindsay is openly flirting with him, and I'm right here. Maybe she didn't know we were a couple before, but now that Cole's here next to me, shouldn't he say something?

"We should celebrate. Want to get a drink and then dance?" I ask and give his leg a squeeze. He tenses, and it's like he wants to jerk his leg away. Okay…does he not want Lindsay to know we're together? He's certainly acting like it. But why?

Cole turns, smiling. He looks me in the eye and his whole body relaxes, but only for a moment.

"I'll take a drink but you know I don't dance."

211

"I have a quarter with your name on it."

Lindsay leans in, eyeballing my hand on Cole's leg. "What about a quarter?"

"Long story," Cole says quickly. "I'm going to get drinks. Want anything?"

"No, thanks," I tell him. "I still have this left."

Lindsay asks him to bring back a glass of wine. Before Cole gets up, I go in to kiss him, but he stiffs me and turns away. What the fuck is going on?

"You seem very friendly with him," Lindsay says to me once Cole is gone. "Is there something going on between you?" She wiggles her eyebrows and offers a smile. The innocent girl-talk isn't sitting right with me.

"Yeah, there is. He's my boyfriend."

Lindsay laughs. She actually fucking laughs. When I don't laugh with her, the smile disappears from her face. "Oh, you're serious."

"Yeah, I'm serious. I've been staying with him at his place for the last month too."

She turns her head, watching Cole, and then looks at me again, "Really?"

"Yes."

"I asked Cole if he was bringing a date tonight," she says slowly, as if she's trying to piece things together. "And he told me he wasn't."

My stomach drops. "When did you ask him?"

"The day I saw you in the lobby. Wait. You were there to see Cole?"

"Yeah, we met for lunch. He told you he didn't have a date tonight?"

"Yes. I'm sure. I...I thought he was single. Sorry if I overstepped," she apologizes but sounds like she's not sure if she should believe me, or if I'm delusional and making this all up.

I keep my eyes on Cole. "You didn't. Excuse me," I say and get up, going to the bar where Cole is.

"Ana," he says and looks around, making sure no one is watching. Then he leans in as if he's going to kiss me. I hold up my hand, stopping him. "What's wrong?"

"Did you tell Lindsay you're single?"

"No."

"Weird. Because she looked at me like I was an idiot when I said you were my boyfriend. She's under the impression that you don't have a date tonight, which is strange since we were supposed to be here together."

"Ana, I didn't—"

"Maybe you got confused and told her about the promotion but not your girlfriend."

"I can explain, Ana."

My stomach drops. "Just hearing you say that...just knowing that you have to explain..." I shake my head, fighting back tears. "I don't understand why you'd lie about me. Are you ashamed?"

"Of course not, Ana. I love you."

"Then why would you tell her you didn't have a date tonight? Why won't you kiss me or hold my hand?"

"Ana..." he starts. "Please let me explain."

"Explain why you lied about having a girlfriend? Or why you thought telling me about the promotion wasn't important enough to mention." I angrily wipe a rogue tear away.

"Yes, explain that," he says, brown eyes filling with worry.

"You know what, don't bother. You told me you loved me, and I believed you. God, I'm an idiot."

My words are like bullets, hitting Cole with the truth. Pain radiates across his face and he steps forward. I back away.

"Ana..."

I look into Cole's eyes, heart yearning for him. He could

have a good reason, right? No. I can't make excuses for him. Is lying to Lindsay about me enough to walk away? Was he hoping to hook up with her? That just doesn't seem like Cole. Why would he ask me to move in if he wanted to sleep with other people?

"Cole," I breathe.

He steps away from the bar and cups my face. I close my eyes, taking in the heat of his hand, the way his rough skin feels against my flesh. "I love you, Ana."

"I want to believe you."

"Believe it."

Someone stops behind us. "Are you in line?" a woman dressed like a cowgirl asks.

I blink and look up, having forgotten we were in the middle of a party. Cole has a way of making everything else disappear. My heart thumps in my chest and emotions flood through me.

"No, we're not," Cole tells her and we step to the side. Lines of worry form on his handsome face. My phone rings and I reach into my purse with the intention to silence it. I see the number and the familiar tingle of fear makes its way through me, along with anger.

Can't he just leave me alone?

"Ana? Is it him?"

I decline the call. "Yes. But I'm not answering." I shake my head and sigh. "I guess I'll be calling that police officer. It's been a while since Steven has pulled anything. I almost felt normal."

Cole looks away and nods. The screen changes on my phone, reminding me about the call I declined and letting me know I have three text messages.

All from Steven.

My fingers shake as I unlock my phone. The first text simply reads "Happy Halloween" and the two others are pictures. One is of Cole standing close to a woman in a pink raincoat, and the other is a blurry image of Cole at some sort of market.

"What's wrong?" Cole asks and shuffles closer.

I swallow my pounding heart and hold the phone up for him to see. "He took pictures of you."

Cole's gaze moves to the phone, eyebrows pinching together. "I know."

"What do you mean, you know?"

"Maybe we should sit down."

"No!" I say a little too loudly. "What's going on, Cole? You knew he was watching you?"

"Yes. I did."

His words are like a slap in the face. "What the hell? How long?"

Cole inhales and shifts his gaze to the party. "Let's sit down, Ana."

"Tell me what's going on, Cole," I say each word slowly, but my heart is racing.

"I realized he was following me when I went to LA. He showed up."

"What the fuck?" I exclaim, not caring the pitch of my voice caused several people to turn and look. "And you didn't think it was important enough to mention?"

"I didn't want to upset you."

"Upset me? It's a little late for that, don't you think?" I bring my hand to my face and shake my head. "And do I even want to know who that woman is in that picture?"

"She means nothing."

"Steven is a fucking psycho but he has reasons. He wouldn't send me a picture of you with some random person."

Cole's shoulders sag forward. "Her name is Heather. That's my ex."

"What the fuck, Cole?"

"He set it up. Pretended to be me to get her to show up at the office."

"And telling me this never crossed your mind?"

"Ana, I—" He cuts off and looks away. "You were so happy and I couldn't bring myself to ruin that."

"I'm not some child that needs to be protected from the truth. Shit happened, and yeah, it still scares me. But I'm not weak. I don't need to be lied to in order to spare my feelings. If that's the kind of person you think I am, then this—what we have together—is all a sham. I'm not a damsel in distress waiting to be rescued. I want a partner. An equal. I thought that's what we had. I guess I was wrong."

Cole stares at me, desperation and sadness on his face. But the doesn't speak. Doesn't tell me he's sorry and that he was stupid and not thinking. He just stands there.

"Aren't you going to say something?" I ask, slowly moving my head from side to side.

Cole opens his mouth but no words come out.

"Cole. Please! Say something." Fat tears fall from my eyes. I shake my head. "I guess I know where I stand." I turn and walk away, past Luke and Lexi who are trying to act like they didn't see what just happened. I don't know what to do other than go home and wait for Cole. I'll have calmed down by then, and he'll have had time to think of another lie.

No. I can't think like that.

I'm mad. Upset. *Scared*.

I know I get impulsive, so leaving and cooling off is exactly what I need. I get my coat and step outside. The cool, fall air on my face is sobering. I walk past a group of people smoking and try to remember what Cole told me on how to see if a taxi is available or not. It had something to do with the numbers and the lights. Shit. I don't remember. I'll just stick my arm out at any taxi that drives by, not caring if I look like a typical tourist. Hell, I'm already dressed like Wonder Woman.

"Hello, Ana."

I know that voice. My heart races and my stomach flip flops. My fight or flight reaction kicks in and I reach for the lasso on my belt. I don't know what I'll do with it, but I won't give up without a fight this time. I turn and come face to face with Steven. I haven't seen him since the trial, and it shocks me how he looks exactly the same.

"What do you want?" I spit out.

"I just want to talk to you." He smiles and runs his eyes over me. "I always said you made a good Wonder Woman."

"Fuck you."

He laughs. "You have fucked me. Many times. Do you remember how good it felt?"

"Go to hell."

"Always with the insults." He moves closer and looks me right in the eye and smiles. "How are things going with your boyfriend, Ana? What's his name again? Oh, right. *Cole.*"

A chill goes through me and I realize that everything that happened tonight fell perfectly into Steven's plan. He knows me and knows I get impulsive when I'm angry. That I have a tendency to blow up and need alone time to let off steam. He sent those pictures of Cole with his ex hoping to get me right where I am.

He inches forward again.

"One more step and I scream," I threaten.

"No, you won't. In fact, you're going to do exactly what I say."

"Why the fuck would I do that?

I move back, trying to get into the group of smokers' line of sight.

"Love makes you do crazy things." He tips his head, watching me. "And you do love Cole, don't you?"

The blood drains from my face. "What did you do?"

"Nothing. Well, nothing yet." He holds out his hand. "What happens or doesn't happen is up to you. Come with me, Ana, and everything will be all right."

My heart hammers in my ears and I look at his outstretched hand. I can see the snake tattoo peeking out from the sleeve of his jacket.

"Ana," he repeats sternly.

I'm mad at Cole right now, but I love him. I love him so fucking much. I have no idea what Steven is planning, but I know the shit he's capable of. A tear rolls down my cheek and I slowly extend my arm.

What other choice do I have?

chapter twenty-two

COLE

I blink, the image of Ana's hurt face burned into my mind. How can she expect me to say something when I can't even breathe? I fucked up. I know it, but I don't know how to make it right. I did what I thought was in her best interest and was wrong. She left, and I feel like history is repeating itself from that night Heather called off the engagement.

Only this is worse.

I did the thing I was most afraid of. I hurt Ana. I caused her to walk away.

"Is everything okay?" Luke asks quietly, coming over to where I'm standing. I haven't moved since Ana turned and walked away. I watched her, rooted to the spot, feeling like the life got sucked out of me.

"I don't know." I blink and look at my brother. "I'm an idiot."

"We already know that." Luke puts his hand on my back and guides me to the bar. "What happened with Ana?"

"I withheld the truth about something I should have told her and—"

EMILY GOODWIN

"You lied?"

"Yeah."

Luke orders two drinks and looks at me. "I heard some of it. That blonde chick asked if you were single and you told her you were?"

"Not exactly," I say and Luke raises his eyebrows. "She's my boss's niece." I let out a breath, feeling like the scum of the earth. "I'm being considered for a promotion to be a publisher and if my boss found out I'm dating an author I'm directly working with, it could very well be a deal breaker."

Luke nods. "So you lied about your relationship because you wanted a promotion, not because you wanted to shack up with that chick."

"Yes. But, fuck, it still sounds bad when you say it like that."

"It does because it's a dick move. Especially since it seems like Ana didn't know."

I look down at the bar. "She didn't." The bartender brings us our drinks and I take mine, downing a big gulp right away. "I thought I could do both. Get the girl of my dreams and land the promotion. My boss leaves in less than a month. All I had to do was keep my personal life separate from work for a few more weeks. I really thought I could do it." I down more of my drink. "I fucked up, but maybe it's for the better. Give Ana a chance to find someone new."

I can feel Luke's eyes on me. "You really care about her, don't you?" he asks softly.

"I do."

"Then go to her."

"I don't think she wants to be around me right now. Or ever."

"You made a mistake. Who hasn't? You're human, after all. We mess up. We do it again. And sometimes again after that. The point isn't *not* messing up. It's what you do after you

220

mess up. Start with apologizing. And follow up with showing that you're sorry."

"You make it sound so easy."

"It's not, but that's what you do for the ones you love."

I look up at Luke for a second and then finish my drink.

"As much as you like to act like you're fucking perfect, you're not. No one is, and fucking up is part of life. It happens, and you have to deal. Not dealing—trust me on this —makes things a hell of a lot harder in the end. Things don't get better on their own. And if Ana loves you, she'll understand. You forgive people when you love them."

"With exceptions," I clarify. "What if Ana doesn't—"

"You don't know unless you try," Luke interrupts. "Even though you've been an asshole most of my life, you're still my big brother and I've looked up to you. I used to be jealous of how you'd succeed in everything you did."

Was my drink spiked or did Luke really just say he was jealous of me?

"And then I realized that you were very selective in the things you did. You only took on something you knew you could handle."

I sit back in the barstool, wanting to tell Luke he's wrong. But he's not.

"Fear of failure holds more people back than actual failure, but I don't need to tell you that. Find Ana, have makeup sex and show her how sorry you are. Because you are sorry. I can tell."

I finish my drink and set the empty glass down on the bar top. Luke's only getting half the story. He only knows half the shit I did, and now's not the time to get into Steven. Because Luke is right about one thing: I love Ana and need to prove it to her.

"Thanks," I say to Luke and get up. I stride right past Lindsay, who calls my name and don't stop until I'm outside.

I call Ana. Her phone rings four times then goes to voicemail. I know she's mad, but Ana doesn't seem like the type of person who would hang up on me.

I move down the walkway in front of the building, looking for Ana. A small crowd is gathered outside smoking, and I go over to them.

"Excuse me, I'm looking for a friend," I start, asking a man who's dressed like Hugh Hefner. "Wonder Woman."

"I think I saw her," another person answers. "I think she went to get a cab."

"Thanks," I say and hurry to the street. I call Ana again. The phone rings once and someone answers.

"Ana?"

A muffled voice says something but is too far away for me to make out what's being said. Then someone breathes into the phone.

It's like the floor opened up beneath me and I plunged into icy water, getting pulled down so deep the pressure is closing in on me. Fuck. It's Steven.

"Hello, Cole. I'm afraid Ana can't talk right now."

chapter twenty-three

ANA

"*I*'m not going anywhere with you," I sneer and push Steven's hand out of the way.

"You really don't want to test me." Steven takes a step closer and I move away.

"Get away from me, Steven. I mean it."

He laughs. "What are you going to do about it? Drug me again? Go ahead. Maybe I can get your ass arrested this time."

"So this is about vengeance?" I slide my foot back, thinking if I can keep him talking, I'll have a better chance of getting away. I'm in the worst spot possible, between a fence and parked cars. I need to get to the road or get back to the venue. "You're mad I turned you in?"

"I'm mad about the lost time, Ana. Over a year went by. We should be planning our wedding by now."

"You're fucking crazy, you know that, right?"

"And you're a fucking bitch. I know you know that."

"Maybe I am." I start to move my hand down the straps of my purse. If I can't get away, then I can call 911. "So why want me?"

"Because I love you, Ana."

"You don't know what love is."

Steven takes a quick step forward and I jolt back, hitting the fence. I use the collision to grab my phone from my purse.

"And you do?" he growls. "You know all about love from the short time you've been with your loser boyfriend."

I know he's trying to make me upset by insulting Cole, and my lack of reaction will piss him off. I've been a pawn for so long I can play the game.

And win this time.

"Cole's a better man than you'll ever be." I put the phone behind my back, pressing the screen against me to shield the light. I blindly tap the screen, trying to unlock the phone without looking at it.

"That might be true. But he'll never love you the way I love you. I care about you more than anyone. And how do you repay me? By sending me to prison. But I'm willing to look past that."

"Fuck you." My phone vibrates, letting me know I put in the wrong passcode. Fuck. Steven moves closer.

"You didn't comment on my costume."

"You're wearing a—" I cut off when I see the blood splattered on Steven's white shirt. It's more brown than red now, but I remember it perfectly. That was the night he hit me and broke multiple bones in my face. He hit me in the nose first, and I bled instantly. I stumbled forward and blood splattered on him. He got mad that I ruined his favorite shirt and hit me again, with the blow that fractured my cheekbone. He wiped his hand on his shirt after that, and when the police looked for that shirt to be used as evidence, it was gone.

"So you remember?" He smiles, but his eyes are empty. Then my phone rings, and I bring my hand in front of me to answer. Steven shoves me hard in the chest and takes the phone, nails scratching my flesh in the process.

He hangs up.

"It's Cole," he says. "Probably wondering where you are. Which is a good question. Because why are you out here, Ana?"

"That's none of your fucking business."

"It is. Your business is my business."

The phone rings again. Steven grabs me, wrapping his hand around my neck in a chokehold, and answers the phone.

"Cole!" I scream only to have my voice die in my throat as Steven tightens his grip. I can't get any air and my body goes into a panic to breathe.

"Hello, Cole," Steven says coolly. "I'm afraid Ana can't talk right now." He hangs up and throws my phone over the fence. I'm gasping for air and not thinking. I jerk my head back and the metal Wonder Woman headpiece falls over my eyes.

I'm only dressed as a superhero, but that doesn't mean I have to be a victim. I gather the remaining strength I have and dig my fingernails into Steven's arm that's around my throat and lift my foot up, kicking behind me and nailing him right in the balls. Steven pitches forward, grip loosening enough for me to get an arm free. I elbow him hard in the face and take off running.

And then I see him with his back turned and cell phone pressed to his ear.

"Cole!" I call, tears filling my eyes. He turns around and runs to me, pulling me into a protective embrace.

"Are you okay?"

I'm shaking from head to foot, my neck hurts, and my hand burns from where Steven scratched me. But I'm alive.

"I think so."

"I'm so sorry, Ana," Cole says, pushing my hair back. The headpiece fell off in the struggle, and my loose curls are in my face, sticking to my sweaty flesh. Cole pulls me to him again, and right now the apology can wait. "You left and then he answered your phone and I thought he...fuck. Are you sure you're okay?"

"You're here," I whisper. "I'm okay now."

Cole kisses my forehead and I close my eyes, trying to get my pulse to slow down before I have a heart attack.

"Did he hurt you?" Cole looks over my shoulder, surveying the darkness behind me.

"He tried." I close my eyes, still able to feel the force of Steven's arms around my chest, pulling so tight it hurt. My hands tremble even harder now. "I kicked him in the balls and broke away. He'll come back. He always comes back."

Cole holds me tighter, gently running a hand over my hair. Steven will run away with his tail tucked between his legs, take a day to come up with another plan of attack, and then will hit harder. And harder. Until I break.

But I won't this time.

"We should call the police," I say.

"I already did," Cole starts and holds up his phone. "I should let the dispatcher—" He's cut off when something hurdles through the air and hits me on the shoulder.

"Ahhh," I exclaim, hand flying to the pain.

"Ana?"

I bring back my hand and see blood on my fingers. On the ground near our feet is a jagged shard of metal.

"Fucking hell." Cole whirls around, hands curling into fists. A dark shadow dances behind a parked car, and Cole takes off, ready to beat the shit out of Steven. Everything happens so fast: Cole is right there in front of Steven, fist raised. And then a bright light blinds us both. I close my eyes and look down, and the next thing I know, someone grabs me, dragging me off the sidewalk and into the bushes. No one from the venue can see me now.

"Ana!" Cole yells and sprints forward. He jumps through the bushes and onto Steven, knocking him to the ground. I go down with them and break free from Steven's grasp. Steven tries to make a dash for it, but Cole grabs him by the back of his collar, spins him around, and punches him in the face.

"If you fucking come near Ana again, I'll kill you," Cole says through gritted teeth and hits Steven again. Steven falls to the ground and Cole kicks him, and then drops to his knees, hitting Steven again. Blood splatters the grass. "You worthless piece of shit!" Cole raises his fist to hit him again, but I grab his arm.

"Stop, Cole." I tug him back and point to the flashing blue lights that are racing down the street. Cole steps back, shaking out his hand. His phone is on the ground, and the 911 dispatcher's voice can barely be heard. With trembling fingers, I pick up the phone and tell her what happened.

~

"Well, Ms. Ventimiglia, I think it's safe to say we have enough to put him away for a long time."

"Thank God. And thank you," I tell the police officer. I'm not sure what was more satisfying: seeing Cole beat the shit out of Steven or seeing Steven get handcuffed and shoved into the back of a police car. I've been at the police station along with Cole, giving statements and taking care of paperwork.

"We found what we consider a Hit List in his wallet. Conspiracy to murder, stalking, attempted kidnapping, and two counts of assault are not things that can be easily dismissed in court. Pair that with the fact his shirt had your blood all over it and you have a solid case."

"That's a relief," Cole says and puts his hand on my thigh. "Can we go?"

"Yes," the officer says. "You're good."

Cole stands and offers a hand to help me to my feet. I take it, and walk behind him to his car.

"Are you okay?" he asks as we pull out of the station's parking lot.

"I'll be fine."

Neither of us talk much on the drive back to his house. Cole opens the door and shuts off the alarm. I take off my boots and stand in the foyer, looking at the house that's supposed to be mine.

"Want to take a shower and lay down?" Cole asks, sounding hopeful. Things went from bad to worse in a matter of minutes, and it's easy to feel like the reason I left in the first place is no big deal compared to the shit Steven pulled.

"Yeah, but I want to shower alone."

"Okay. Do you want me to make popcorn or anything?"

"Cole…" I start, and my heart hurts all over again. "Saving me from Steven didn't make everything between us okay. Because it's not. You lied to me. You made me look like an idiot. I trusted you." My voice breaks and I turn away, not wanting Cole to see me cry.

"Ana," he starts, sounding just as emotional. "I'm so sorry. I was wrong to lie. I messed up. I'm sorry."

"I'm sorry too."

He slowly shakes his head. "Why are you sorry?"

"I'm sorry this isn't going to work."

"No. Don't say that, Ana."

Tears roll down my cheeks. "Being able to say I trusted

you—completely trusted you—was a huge thing for me. After what I went through before, I needed it, Cole."

"You can still trust me."

"But you lied! For a week, you lied about Steven. We went to bed together, ate together, *lived* together and you pretended like everything was fine when it wasn't." I let out a shaky breath and wipe my eyes. "I think I should go."

"Where?"

"Home. To Kentucky." I rub my forehead, feeling a killer headache coming on. "I'll find a flight in the morning."

The blood drains from Cole's face and he backs up into the wall. "Ana, please. Don't go."

I look at Cole, heart breaking. "I'm sorry. I have to."

chapter twenty-four

COLE

*T*hey say all good things come to an end, and I guess this is mine. Maybe I'm getting what I deserve and was a fool to think I could change my story. I'm the villain. The bad guy. And I'm not even the one you love to hate. The darkness in me is of my own creation, brought forth from every bad choice I've made, and I've made a lot. Even when I try to do the right thing, the world laughs and throws in another plot twist. And not even the best storyteller can get me out of this one.

I lied to Ana. Destroyed the one thing that most solidified our relationship. The trust has been broken, and I can never get it back.

She's gone.

I want to be gone too.

I woke up this morning alone, and found the pineapple keychain on the kitchen table, along with a note that I haven't brought myself to read yet. I hold the keychain in my hands, the metal warm from my skin, and concentrate on breathing. It's hard to do that right now. I feel broken, like part of my soul and all of my heart has been ripped out.

I flip the keychain over in my hands, missing Ana so much it hurts. She printed her flight info in my office, and I was able to see when she's leaving, and it's not for another three hours...and the flight isn't full.

Sunlight reflects off the gold keychain. I close my eyes. I want to go to Ana. I want to tell her I love her. I don't want to live without her. She's made me a better person without even trying.

But I'm still not good enough.

Which is why I'm sitting here. I love her enough to let her go.

I hang my head, not knowing how I'm going to go on after this. Ana gave purpose to my life, more than getting up and going to work.

"Fuck!" I yell and pound my fist down on the table. I'm so fucking pissed at myself for screwing this up. I throw the key across the room as hard as I can. It hits the tiled backsplash and falls into the sink. I ball my fists and let out a breath, eyes going to Ana's note.

Certain it tells me to leave her the fuck alone for the rest of my life, I didn't pick it up before. Not allowing myself to think, I reach for the folded piece of computer paper. A quarter falls out and rolls away, coming to a stop under the oven. I look down at the paper and read what Ana wrote.

Cole-
You control your own destiny.

I READ her words over and over, trying to make sense of it all. And then it hits me, and I know exactly what I have to do. I don't need to flip for it this time because no matter what, I'm going to her.

~

I LOOK down at the ticket to find what gate I need to go to. The plane leaves in half an hour, and boarding will start soon. My heart is racing and I know this moment right here will define the rest of my life.

Because Ana is my life.

I pass by a group of slow moving people, not caring that I bumped into one of them. I need to get to Ana. Finally, I see her sitting at the gate, twisting her dark hair around her finger and looking out the large window. I'm not sure why she turns and looks the moment she does, but our eyes meet and she stands.

"Ana," I call and rush to her.

"Cole." Her eyebrows come together. "What are you doing here?"

"I can't lose you. I'm an idiot who doesn't deserve you, but I'm madly in love with you, Ana."

She blinks, not knowing what to say. "You bought a plane ticket?" she finally asks, looking at my boarding pass.

"It was the only way I could get through security to see you."

She turns her head up, tears in her eyes. "Cole...I don't know what to say."

"You don't have to say anything. Just know that I'm so, so sorry for lying. I should have told you about the promotion but didn't want to mention it in case I didn't get it. Call me self-absorbed but I didn't want to go through the letdown of not getting it in case things didn't pan out. And I should have told you that Caitlin Black wouldn't approve of an editor dating an author. I thought I could keep my work life and personal life separate, but I know now that's not possible because you are my life, Ana, and I want you in every part of it."

Ana clasps her hands on her elbows and nods.

"I did lie to you, back when we first met."

"You did?"

I nod and reach into my back pocket. "That night in the bar...the first time you flipped the coin you told me heads we go home, tails we go out."

"I remember."

"It landed on heads."

"But you...

I open my palm, showing her the quarter that I saved from that night. "I lied. You had an impact on me from the start and I tried so fucking hard to resist it. But for some reason, I couldn't, and the moment that coin got tossed into the air, I knew no matter what, I didn't want the night to end."

Ana takes the quarter from me, looking at the running horses stamped in to represent the state of Nevada. "It's the same one."

"I never believed in love at first sight, and I wasn't sure soul mates existed, but you...you've changed everything. You changed me, and I don't want to go back to the person I was before I met you. You make me see the good in things, and you make me want to be a better person. I can't imagine my life without you, Ana, and frankly, I don't want to. I love you, Ana. Before I met you, I didn't think love was real. But you changed that. You make me believe not only in love but in magic. I love you."

A tear rolls down Ana's cheek. "I love you, too."

She throws her arms around my neck and I hold her close. We kiss, and just like the first time, everything around me fades away.

"Now what?" she asks once we part.

"I...I don't know. What do you want to do?"

Her eyes meet mine. "Go home."

chapter
twenty-five

ANA

"*H*ow's your hand?" I ask Cole.

"It's okay."

"Really?" I lift my head off Cole's chest to incredulously eyeball him. We got back from the airport a few hours ago and had immediately gone upstairs and into bed.

"It kind of hurts, but every time I feel the pain it reminds me of how fucking good it felt to finally hit that asshole."

"I enjoyed seeing it," I tell Cole and rest my head back on his chest, listening to his heart beating. "It's finally over."

"There's no way he's getting out early for good behavior now," Cole reassures me and runs his fingertips over my shoulders. "Have you told your mom?"

"No. She doesn't even know he was in New York. I think telling my mom that Steven attacked both of us should be said face-to-face. Right?"

"Probably. She'll be able to see you and know you're all right. But I wouldn't wait too long."

"Right."

Cole rolls over, spooning his body around mine. "Are we okay, Ana?"

His lips land on the back of my neck. I close my eyes and consider everything that's happened. "We will be."

He holds me tight and kisses my neck again. "I love you, Ana."

"I love you, too."

~

"ANA," Cole says with a smile. He stands from his desk and comes around, meeting me by his office door. He puts his arms around me and gives me a kiss on the lips, not caring who sees. I'm his girlfriend and I brought him lunch at work. That's worthy of a kiss. I told Cole I understood his reasoning for downplaying our relationship, and that in itself wasn't what upset me, but being kept in the dark.

I was all for keeping things secret until Caitlin Black made her decision, but Cole wouldn't have it and said if it's a deal breaker, then he doesn't want to be a publisher anyway. I'm more important to him, and he wants to make sure I know that.

"Hey, babe," I say and come in. "Is Lexi here today? I got an extra cupcake for her."

"She is, but she's having lunch with an author. I can put it on her desk if she's not back before you head out. Are you going to the coffee house today?"

"Yeah, after this. I think I can get the last chapter written on this book."

"You're the best author I've worked with for many reasons. Having your book done early might be the best one."

"Better than the fact I'm also the only author you're sleeping with?"

"It's a close contender. You know how much I like punctuality."

I laugh and pull up a chair to Cole's desk. "And you know how much I like to come early." I bite my lip and smile.

"God, you're hot."

Someone knocks on Cole's door and he waves Jillian in.

"Hi, Scarlett," she says and comes over to the desk, handing Cole a paper to sign. "You rocked that Wonder Woman costume Saturday night. I would kill for your legs."

"Thanks. I was a little worried about wearing a skirt that short, to be honest."

"You have nothing to worry about."

"That's what I told her," Cole says with a shake of his head. "You looked good."

Jillian takes her papers back from Cole. "Any chance you want to call and yell at an author for me later?"

"Fairchild?" Cole asks with an eyebrow raised. "Again?"

Jillian sighs. "I would love to get him for breach of contract and cut ties. That last book was not good. I think I rewrote half of it." She rolls her eyes. "You know, I'm willing to trade. Scarlett for Fairchild."

Cole looks at me and slowly shakes his head. "Not a fair deal. Scarlett is easy to work with and has her books done months ahead of time."

"I'll edit anything else Gregory Lawrence writes."

"Deal."

We all laugh, and Jillian says goodbye and goes back to her office. Cole and I talk as we eat. He has a meeting at one-thirty, and the time goes by quickly.

"I'll bring home dinner," Cole offers, walking with me to the door of his office. "So you don't have to cook."

"That's fine with me. I need a day or two to go Pinterest crazy and find some good recipes."

Cole wraps his arms around me and plants a kiss on my lips. I think he's hoping someone will ask about us, or at least make it obvious they witness the kiss. I have to give him credit for trying. He feels bad, and I hate that he's beating himself up over this, even more so than before.

We all make bad choices. Hell, I've made more than my fair share, and I'm sure I'll do something stupid again probably sooner rather than later. Cole covered up the truth thinking it would spare my feelings, that he could draw out the high I was riding and keep me happy. He didn't lie to trick or manipulate me.

Still, it's not something I can forget overnight. Which is why we decided it's best to not officially move in together until my lease is actually up at the end of the year. I'm staying in the city for another week, and then am going back to Kentucky to manage my own shit. Cole is flying out Thanksgiving week and is spending the holiday with my family and me.

And then, assuming things are still going well—we're taking things day by day—I'll be here with Cole and his family for Christmas. My lease on my apartment is up at the end of this year—which isn't far away, and Cole and I will reevaluate where we're at then, though I already know things will be okay.

Because I love Cole. And he loves me.

"Love you," Cole says and gives me one more kiss.

"Love you, too. See you later."

I leave after another kiss, and spot Lexi in her office. She catches my eye and waves.

"I have a cupcake for you in Cole's office," I tell her. "With blue frosting, since you're having a boy. I realize now how lame that was."

"It's thoughtful. Thank you. I've had the worst sweet tooth this whole pregnancy."

I go inside her office, which is hardly anything more than a cubicle with a door.

"Is everything okay?" she asks softly. She and Luke are the

only ones who know the truth about what happened Saturday night. Only a few people associated with Black Ink witnessed what happened, and were lead to believe Cole was dealing with someone who drank too much at the party. Luke came outside to find Cole and make sure things were okay and saw us talking to the police.

"I think so."

"And you and Cole are..."

"Still together. We're taking a little step back, which I think will work out in the long run."

"I think so too. And I hope so. I've known Cole a while, and if I had to pick out his biggest flaw, it would be that he cares too much, as cliché as that sounds. When it comes to protecting the people he cares about, nothing is off limits."

"I'm realizing that now."

"He's a good person, even though he can't see it. Did he tell you about, uh, the drama between him and Luke?"

"Yeah, he did. And he still feels bad about it."

Lexi shakes her head. "I know. I wish he'd let it go. Luke and I both have. Anyway, even when he thought Luke caused his fiancée to call off the wedding, Cole still welcomed Luke here in New York when he needed to get away. Cole pretty much hated his brother, but he still opened the house for him." Lexi lets out a breath. "That cupcake is on my mind and I'm not sure if I'm getting my point across so I'll just say it. Cole will do anything for someone he loves. He's a good person with a big heart, and sometimes I think he just needs a little reminder that you aren't going to leave him."

I turn, watching Cole walk through the office to greet the author he's meeting. My heart flutters, and I look back at Lexi. "I don't think that's going to be an issue."

Lexi smiles. "Good. Because we all really like you. Grace and Paige are pretty possessive of their Uncle Cole, and even they are hoping to see you around again."

"Well, I can't disappoint them now, can I? Mrs. Winchester—Cole's mom, I mean. You're Mrs. Winchester too—texted me this morning about a family dinner Friday. So, I'll see you all then. And Cole mentioned something about coming over Thursday to see the girls in their Halloween costumes too."

"Only if you guys want to. I know it's a bit of a drive. Though Harper looks so fucking cute as Snow White. It is worth seeing." She shrugs. "I guess I might be biased."

"I'm sure she's adorable."

"Be prepared for Mrs. Winchester to try to get you to go to Disney this summer too." Lexi puts her hand on her stomach, lovingly rubbing her small bump. "Little Aiden here will only be a few months old and she wants us to go."

"You guys are going with Aiden?"

"Aiden Matthew Winchester. We agreed on it last night. You pretty much named our baby. Thanks."

"I can't wait to meet him."

"Me neither." Lexi's phone rings and she says a quick goodbye and then answers the phone. I readjust the strap of my laptop bag on my shoulder and get into an elevator, going down to the main lobby and then out onto the busy Manhattan street.

Cole and I are taking things day by day, but for the first time in a long time, I'm excited about the future.

chapter twenty-six

COLE

"*G*ood evening, Mr. Publisher," Ana greets me with a smile.

I smile and shake my head. "It's been a week since I got promoted. You can stop calling me that."

"I'll never stop calling you that. It's hot."

I take my boots off and leave them on the rug by the front door. "Looks like we're going to have a white Christmas."

"Is that rare here?" Ana asks, looking out through the front window at the big snowflakes that are gently floating to the ground.

"It seems like the last few years it's been cold with no snow. I didn't pay much attention though," I admit.

"I'm excited for the snow. I feel like I'm in a Hallmark movie right now. It's snowing in Manhattan and Christmas is three days away."

I unbutton my coat, shake off the snow, and hang it up. Christmas can't come soon enough. I haven't looked forward to a holiday this much in years. In fact, the last time I was this excited for Christmas I still believed in Santa.

"How was work?" she asks, tearing her eyes away from the window.

"Great. You know that book I was telling you about? The one Paramount was interested in?"

"Yeah. Did they buy the rights?"

"Fuck yes. For books one, two, and three."

Ana's face lights up. "That's awesome, Cole!" She throws her arms around me. We kiss just as the oven timer goes off. Ana hurries away, checking on the meatloaf she's been perfecting over the last week and a half. She has her grandmother's recipe and wants to make sure it's perfect before we have people over here for Christmas Eve dinner, which is a tradition in Ana's family.

I follow her into the kitchen, noticing that she added more decorations. I never knew my house could feel so much like home until Ana moved in just a few days ago.

"You're really not sick of this yet?" she asks, taking the dish from the oven.

"It's been good, so not yet. Though today might be pushing it."

"This is the last time I'll make it," she promises. "Well, until Christmas Eve."

I put my hands on her slender waist and kiss the back of her neck. Ana closes her eyes and tips her head up to me, taking a step back so her ass presses right against my cock.

"It'll be perfect, I promise."

"I hope so. I've never cooked for a party like this before. I want things to be perfect."

"We could have burned spaghetti again and it would be perfect. Because you're here. That's all that matters."

Ana turns around in my arms and is about to kiss me when a loud bang comes from the basement. She startles and makes a move for the screen that's mounted on the kitchen wall. I've upgraded the security around the place since Ana moved in, even though Steven's preliminary trial promised lots of jail time for that loser.

"I told you there's really a ghost," she says.

"There is no ghost. But, uh, stay here. I'll go check it out."

"Not alone! Take a knife or some salt or something."

"Have you developed those super powers yet?"

"Not the ones that can take down a ghost," she says. "You're not really going down there, are you?"

"Something is down there. I need to see what it is."

"Cole, no!"

"I'll get the knife, you get the salt."

"Fine," she agrees and grabs the biggest knife from the block along with a canister of salt. We head down into the basement, looking around for something that could have made that loud sound. There are lights down here, but it's dark. I pull out my phone and look in the shadows.

"Ana," I whisper when I see something moving. "It's not a ghost." I put my phone down and silently step over a box of junk.

"What is it?"

"Look," I say, reaching down to grab the source of the noise.

Ana's eyes widen and her mouth falls open. "Kittens!"

"I see four. Plus the mama who's hiding under that table."

"They are so fucking cute. Oh my God." She comes over and gently picks one up. "Their eyes are open, but they can't be very old." Her eyes meet mine. "Can we keep them?"

"All of them?"

"And the mom?"

"That's five fucking cats."

The smile is still on Ana's face. "It can be my Christmas present?"

I laugh. "I already got you a present, but yeah. We can keep them. They've already been living here anyway."

～

"Can you get that?" I ask Ana when the doorbell rings. It's the day before Christmas Eve, and my vacation has officially begun. I'm fully capable of answering the door right now, but this is the first part of Ana's surprise.

"Sure." Ana sets down a sheet of cookies and goes through the foyer, looking annoyed. I'm in my office, pretending to be working. Ana looks through the window before she even thinks about turning off the alarm. Steven is being held without bail until his trial, but old habits die hard.

"What?" she shrieks and puts her hand over her face. She turns to me, a huge smile on her face. "Did you—what? Are they?"

I laugh and stand, going out of my office to meet her in the foyer. "Open the door, Ana."

"Right." She opens the door and the alarm sounds. I punch in the code and step aside so Ana's mother, sister, and sister's fiancée can step inside.

"Mom!" Ana cries and hugs her mother. "What are you guys doing here?"

"Merry Christmas, Ana," I say.

"You did this?" Ana blinks away tears and lets go of her mother to hug her sister.

"It was all his idea," Ana's mom tells her. "And he paid for our plane tickets. I never knew how much I was missing out until I flew first class."

Ana hugs her sister and then comes over to me. Her eyes are wet with happy tears. I put my arms around her waist and kiss her forehead.

"Thank you, Cole." Ana's eyebrows pinch together and

243

she blinks away tears. "I was sad about not spending Christmas with my mom, and now she's here." Ana covers her face with her hand and then turns, facing me. "I love you, Cole Winchester. So fucking much."

"I love you, too."

We're not standing under mistletoe, but we kiss anyway.

epilogue

ANA

TWO YEARS LATER...

"*I* can't tell who is who." Cole's eyebrows come together, and he looks down at the babies, guilt on his face.

"I have a hard time with it too," I say softly and put my hand on his. "Especially when they're all wrapped up like this."

"What are we going to do when the hospital bracelets come off?" Cole reaches into the bassinet and picks up one of our babies. "How will I know this is Amelia and that one is Madelyn without proper ID?"

"They won't always look alike," I assure him and lean back, wincing slightly as I move. The girls aren't identical twins, but the surprise of having two babies instead of one was just as big of a shock. I stopped taking birth control pills the month Cole and I got married, going with the attitude of 'just seeing what happens.' We got quite the surprise when we found out I was pregnant only three months later. And then had an even bigger surprise at my first ultrasound and found out we were having twins.

"Are you okay?" Cole asks, cradling Amelia to his chest. "Should I get the nurse?"

"I'm okay," I say. "Well, as okay as I can be after delivering twins via C-section twenty-four hours ago."

"You were a rock star, by the way," Cole says. "I almost passed out."

I laugh, then regret it and put a hand on my abdomen. "I know. At least it offered a distraction from having my stomach sliced open."

Cole makes a face and gently hands me Amelia. "She looks like you."

"You think so? I think they both look kinda squishy. Adorable, but squishy."

Cole helps me position pillows and get Amelia set up to nurse, and then he picks up Madelyn, smiling down at her. The love in his eyes as he gazes on his daughter stirs up emotions, and I blink back tears.

I yawn and carefully lean back, making sure Amelia is comfortable. After twenty hours of active labor and one emergency C-section later, I'm exhausted. The sun is starting to rise and I'm having a hard time recalling the last time I slept.

"You should try to sleep," Cole says, and it's as if he can read my mind. "After they each take a turn nursing. I'll be here, and your mom is in the waiting room. We can handle the girls for a few hours."

"Yeah," I agree. "I'm tired, but I don't know if I can sleep right now. I just want to hold my babies."

Cole checks his watch. "You're due for more pain medication soon. It would be a good idea to try and pair that with a nap. You deserve it. Plus, I want to hold my babies." He looks at me with a smile. "Our babies."

"Ours," I say, looking down at Amelia's face. She's half latched on and the pain I'm feeling is more than I expected. "I think I'm in a bit of shock." I look up at Cole with tears in my eyes. "We've been waiting for so long for the girls to get here. And now they are. We made them."

Madelyn lets out a small cry and Cole shushes her, slowly swinging her back and forth until she falls back asleep.

"We did a good job."

"Yes," I agree and hold out my hand. Cole comes over and takes it, lacing his fingers through mine. "We did."

HOT MESS

The Love is Messy Duet series started with Luke and Lexi's story in Hot Mess. A complimentary sample has been added to Battle Scars for your enjoyment.

1

ALEXIS

*S*omeday, I'll get my shit together. Today, however, is not that day. I bring my coffee to my lips and whirl around, tripping over the dog. The mug hits my teeth, and hot coffee sloshes down the front of my ivory blouse.

"Really, Pluto? You have to lay in the middle of the kitchen during rush hour?" I glare at the little mutt who looks at me, and then at his empty bowl. "I didn't forget to feed you," I say and grab a towel from the kitchen counter. It's damp from drying last night's dishes, but it'll work. I rub the front of my shirt, swearing under my breath. I'm going to have to change, and I'm already running late.

I take a sip of my coffee and fly to the pantry. "Son of a bitch," I say when I stick my hand into the big bag of dog food. I only feel crumbs.

"Mom, you said a bad word," Grace points out, little feet slapping on the cold tile as she comes up behind me.

I let out a breath. "That's a mommy word. Only mommies can say those words." I grab the dog food bag and look at my six-year-old. "Did you feed Pluto last night?"

"I did," she says proudly.

"How much did you feed him?"

She shrugs and looks away, a move she mastered years ago. "I don't know."

"You fed him all of it," I say with a shake of my head, closing my eyes in a long blink. I had it mentally planned out to give him the last of his food this morning and pick up a bag on the way home from work. "He's on a diet, remember? We have to only give him one scoop in the evening."

"But he was hungry!" Grace says, and her shoulders sag. "I'm sorry."

"It's okay, baby," I say and smile. She's as sweet as she is sassy. "Thank you for helping last night. You take good care of your puppy."

That brings a smile to her face. "Can you do my hair?" she asks, holding out a brush.

"Yes, let me find something for Pluto first. Did you brush your teeth?"

She nods and pulls out a bar stool, climbing up to wait for me. I get three-day-old chicken and rice from the fridge and stick it in the microwave. While the food is heating up, I fly over to Grace, taking another drink of coffee as I walk. I set the mug down and pick up her brush, running it through her brunette locks.

"Your hair is getting so long," I tell her, carefully brushing through her tangled curls. "And so pretty."

The compliment makes her sit up a little straighter, and I can tell without looking that she's smiling. "I want a bun like you," she says and I internally cringe. My own dark blonde hair — a shade or two lighter than hers — is up in the usual messy bun. I'm not talking the cute and stylish kind. I'm talking the if-I-put-on-a-hoodie-I'll-look-like-a-drug-dealer kind of messy bun. But hey, at least my hair is clean.

"What about a braid?" I ask and lean back, looking into the living room for my three-year-old. Paige is curled up on the couch watching cartoons. A wave of sadness and guilt hits me when I see her. Like her mother and older sister, she's naturally not a morning person. Yet she's up, dressed and fed before seven a.m. so I can drop her off at daycare before work.

"Okay," Grace says to the braid. I turn my attention back to her, heart aching. I worked part-time when Grace was little and did the majority of my work from home. She didn't have to go to daycare or get up early. I spent my mornings and afternoons with her, playing and snuggling, living out the life I always imagined.

And then I got divorced, and everything changed.

I carefully braid Grace's hair and then grab the leftovers from the microwave, taking them to Pluto's dish.

"I'll get you dog food tonight," I promise him. "But don't act like you don't prefer this."

He gets up and trots over to his bowl, scarfing down breakfast. I pat him on the head, glad I got to keep him. Russell, my ex, and I adopted him for Grace's birthday three years ago.

"Okay, girls," I say. "Coats and shoes, please!"

Grace hops off the stool and goes to the hall tree by the back door. Paige needs a little more coaxing and asks me to sit and snuggle her for a minute. I can't resist. I sit on the couch, turning off the TV, and pull her into my arms.

"I love you to the moon and back, sweet pea," I whisper in her ear. She looks up at me, golden brown hair falling into her eyes.

"I love you too, Mama," she says back and hugs me. "Can I stay home with you? Please, Mama?"

My heart breaks. "What about your friends? Don't you want to see them?"

"Oh, yeah. Friends!" She perks up and climbs off the couch, jibber-jabbering away about her friend Olivia from school. That's my saving grace about this whole thing. The girl is a social butterfly, though I don't know where she gets it from. I'm not exactly what you'd call a "people person" most days.

I let Pluto out into our small fenced-in backyard while we go through the process of dressing for the cool spring weather, putting on shoes and loading backpacks and lunches into the car. The girls start fighting over who gets to hold the stuffed monkey that was discarded on the floor of the car and forgotten about for weeks. Well, until now.

"Take turns," I say, putting the monkey in Paige's hands. "When Paige gets to school, you can hold it," I tell Grace, too tired to tell her kindergarteners shouldn't be bickering like this over a plush monkey.

I glance at the clock, cringing when I see that we should have left ten minutes ago. Dammit. I snap Paige in her carseat and check Grace's seatbelt. Then I fly back into the house, let the dog in, grab my shit, and slide into the driver's seat.

"You smell like coffee," Grace says after we've backed out of the driveway and made it two miles down the street.

Dammit. I look down, tears threatening to form, and see the caramel-colored stain on my blouse. I can't go into work like this, and I don't want this stain to set in and ruin the shirt. I don't have a choice, seeing there isn't time to turn around. How the hell did I forget to change? An even better question might be how the hell did I forget my shirt was sopping wet? Am I that much of a hot mess having some sort of food or beverage spilled on me is the norm? This is going to be a long day. Hell, it's already been a long week. And it's only fucking Monday.

"Mommy?" Grace asks, leaning forward in her booster seat. "Are you okay?"

"Yeah, honey," I say and blink back tears. "I'm okay." I flick my gaze to the rearview mirror and see both of my precious daughters.

And I really do feel okay.

～

"Long night?" Jillian asks me as I rush into the office.

"You could say that again." I set my purse down at my desk and hesitate before taking my coat off. I had left a black cardigan in the car at least a month ago. It was a little wrinkled and smelled like the stale Cheerios it was piled on, but it was better than my stained blouse. I buttoned it up the top and hoped no one would notice I didn't have a cami on underneath. "Paige has been having nightmares again." I sink into the rolling chair and fire up my computer, looking up at Jillian, who's perched on the edge of my desk.

Her hair is brushed to perfection, falling over her shoulders in a wave of blonde curls, and her makeup is flawless. She's been at Black Ink Press almost as long as I have, and we've become good friends as we bonded over books.

"I was up late reading my last submission. The book is great, by the way, a little slow in pacing, but nothing I can't fix. As soon as I laid down, Paige woke up screaming about the man in her doorway. I know they say it's a phase, but this is starting to creep me out."

I unzip my coat and brace for Jillian to say something. Books are her first passion, and fashion is a close second. She's always put together and doesn't hesitate to point out those who aren't. But in the year since my life fell apart, she's gone soft on me. I kind of hate her for it...as much as I love her for it.

"You need to get that place blessed. I swear Russ is sending voodoo vibes your way to make you want to leave."

I shake my head. "I wouldn't put it past him." Who got the

house after we split caused more grief than anything. Well, other than who got the kids. He fought tooth and nail for them at first, and swore he'd be in their lives as much as possible. He did great for the first six months, and then he started dating again.

If only he acted like a deadbeat dad *before* the divorce, we might have ended things sooner and spared the heartache. Though, if I left the first time I thought we were broken beyond repair, I might not have Paige. Or Grace. Or have gotten married in the first place.

Having hope that things will work themselves out is my biggest flaw. Live and learn and all, right?

"I don't know how you take care of your kids and work full-time," Jillian says, as we walk to the break room. I can't start the day without a bagel and some coffee. "It's just me, my cat, and sometimes my boyfriend at my house. And I don't have to commute from the suburbs. Seriously, I don't know how you do it."

I shrug and fill a paper cup with coffee. "I don't either. But I just do. I have no choice but to keep going, and it's only by the sheer grace of God I've gotten this far." I spread cream cheese on a bagel and shake my head. "And to be honest, I don't feel like I'm doing a very good job. I'm struggling so much, Jill."

She puts her hand on my arm. "Besides that rat nest on your head and your interesting choice of clothing, it doesn't look that way. I don't know if that's helpful or not, but know the rest of the world can't tell."

"Thanks."

"You're doing great, Lexi. Don't be so hard on yourself, and don't forget to take care of yourself either. You deserve some happiness."

"Are you talking about masturbating again?"

"Not this time, but don't forget to do that either. I know

how long it's been since you've had sex. What I meant was you should go out and have fun. Maybe think about dating again."

I pour creamer into my coffee, shaking my head as I stir. A million arguments rush into my head, listing out reasons why I'm not ready to start dating. I open my mouth to spit them out but stop. Because I do want to date again. I wanted to date again before the divorce was official. I spent the majority of my last pregnancy avoiding my husband, the father of my unborn child, because being around him was more painful than being alone.

No one warns you how painful falling out of love is.

"You're right," I say.

"Now I knew you'd—wait, did you just agree with me?" Jillian flips her hair over her shoulder, long lashes coming together as she blinks.

"I did. You're right. I think it is time. I'm ready." We snap lids on our coffee cups and slowly make our way back to our offices. "I'm lonely," I admit. "I've been lonely for a long time."

"I know," she says softly. "Let's go out on Saturday, just for fun. You can practice your flirting skills and let off some steam. Russ has the kids this weekend, right?"

I carefully sip my hot coffee. "He does."

She smiles, blue eyes going wide with excitement. "I got a new top that's too long for me—the curse of being five-foot-two strikes again—but it will look *killer* on you. Come over Saturday, let me do your hair and makeup, and you'll be turning down hotties left and right."

I laugh, snorting into my coffee. "Sure I will."

"You're a MILF, Lex. Don't sell yourself short."

"So, when I meet these hotties, do I tell them I have kids or not? Because they need to know I'm a mom to be one they'd like to fuck, right?"

"Yes. But make sure to tell them you had your vagina stitched shut extra tight each time you pushed a baby out."

Gerry, one of the assistant editors, raises his eyebrows as he walks past. I sigh. As much as I want to find a partner again, the thought of dating scares me. Russell and I met in college, were married at twenty-two, and got pregnant just months after the wedding. Flash forward to now, and it's been a while since I've been on the market.

"Don't stress," Jillian says, reading my mind. "This is just for fun. Find a hot guy to go home with and use him as practice."

"I've never had a one-night stand before."

"I'm well aware."

"If I did, would you think I'm slutty?"

She stares at me, unblinking. "No, and you know how I feel about that. You're a grown-ass woman. If you *want* to sleep with a different man every night, more power to you. You own your body and your sexuality. Do what you want."

"I love it when you talk feminism to me."

She smiles. "I'll text Lori and Erin and see if they want to come too. The four of us haven't been out like this in a long time. It's so overdue."

I can't dispute that. Lori and Erin were also involved in the book world, like us. Lori works in marketing for Black Ink Press, and Erin recently made the move from being an editor like me to a literary agent. She has kids as well, and though they're in high school, it's nice to have another mom to hang out with.

We go into our small offices and get to work. I pick at my bagel while I open my email, shuddering when I see my growing inbox. I skim through, flagging the important ones, move them into a folder, and then check Twitter and Facebook as I finish my coffee. I get sucked into a public temper tantrum between two agents from rival agencies, wasting fifteen precious minutes of my morning.

Then it's back to the emails, replying to authors and agents about the projects I'm working on. I open a document from Quinn Harlow, an author I've worked with since my start at Black Ink Press, happily surprised she sent over changes to her novel already. I lean back in my chair and start reading through them, getting pulled into her romance novel about a billionaire heiress and an ex-convict all over again.

Before I know it, it's time for lunch, and the number of emails in my inbox has doubled. Again. I stretch my arms over my head, refusing to let it stress me out. I'm going to stay on top of things this week, so much I'll be able to either leave early on Friday or take the whole day off and spend it with my favorite three-year-old.

I load Quinn's book onto my Kindle so I can read while I eat, and after checking Twitter and Facebook again, head out, meeting Jillian in the lobby.

"Erin's in the area," she says, not looking away from her phone. "She's at The Salad Bar. Want to go?"

"Sure," I say but feel guilty. The food is good, but I hate paying over twenty bucks for a bowl of lettuce with light toppings. It's healthy for your body but not for your wallet. I didn't bring a lunch for myself today, anyway. I had time to make the girls' lunches or mine, but not both. They trump me every time.

The bright sun has warmed up the day enough that we get a table outside, soaking up the cloudless day. Erin hugs us when we see her, and I can't help but smile at the sight of my friend. We order our food and swear we won't talk about work, but just minutes later, Erin is telling us about a new author she signed.

"She has a few self-published books that did really well," she tells us. "And has a decent fan base already, but…" She shakes her head and pulls up the author's Facebook fan page. "She'll be a hard sell to marketing. She posts a lot of drunk videos on her fan page." She holds up the phone so we can see a video of the author talking to the camera, waving a drink around. "And she doesn't play nice with the other indies in her genre. I found a lot of other authors posting that she uses them to get ahead, then throws them aside like garbage."

"Ugh," I say. "No one likes a bully."

"She'd have to have a fucking amazing book to make me take her on," Jillian admits. "Have you tried talking to her?"

"Yes, and it's gone nowhere. Like I said, great writer, but an asshole of a person." Erin sighs and sets her phone down. "Enough about work. How's life. Did Aaron propose yet?"

"Not yet," Jillian says, shrugging. She acts like it doesn't bother her, but after five years together, the lack of commitment gets under her skin. "How are your kids?" Her deflection only proves how much it upsets her.

"Driving me fucking insane," Erin admits. Her eyes meet mine. "People say it gets easier as the kids get older. It's a lie. Don't buy it. They just get moody and mean, and Mom is the last person they want to be seen with. I'll trade you."

"There's no way I'm giving up my babies. They're hardly even babies anymore."

"It goes fast," Erin says. "Savor it. Before you know it, you have two teenagers who only care about what you're making for dinner and how much money they can con out of you."

We laugh and the subject changes to books and publishing again. We say our goodbyes, and go back to work. Back in my office, I answer a few more emails and lean back in my chair to hopefully read through the rest of Quinn's changes. One of those changes is an added sex scene, and oh my God, it's hot. I don't realize I'm biting my lip and leaning closer and closer to my Kindle screen until someone knocks at my office door.

I blink, feeling a bit disoriented—Quinn will be happy to know that—and look up, expecting to see Gavin or even Jillian. The smile on my lips freezes in place and my cheeks flush even more than before. My stomach flutters and I momentarily panic that I have lettuce stuck in my teeth. I didn't check, after all, so it's entirely possible.

"Cole," I finally say, still smiling like an idiot to my boss. "Hi." Getting caught reading a naughty sex scene is one thing. Getting caught reading a naughty sex scene by someone you've fantasized about acting out those naughty sex scenes with is another.

Especially when that person happens to be your boss.

"Hi, Alexis," he says, smiling right back at me, his brown eyes shining in the afternoon sunlight. He's one of the few people who always calls me by my full name. It annoys me when others do, but it's sexy when it's coming off his lips. "How are you?"

"Good. I'm just going through what I think are the last changes for Quinn Harlow's latest book."

"Perfect," he says and comes into the office, leaving the door open. "That's actually what I wanted to talk to you about. I just got out of a meeting with the marketing team and they wanted to bump the release date up." He leans over the desk, staring down at my Kindle. Black Ink is one of the biggest publishers in the business and is no stranger to erotic or taboo novels, but I suddenly feel shy that my Kindle is open to a page—the entire page—devoted to oral sex. Maybe it's because I've wondered what Cole's head would look like between my legs?

Stop it.

He's right fucking in front of me. I'm already hot and bothered from the sex scene. I don't need the image of Cole's handsome face slowly trailing down my body as he kisses my neck, my breasts, the soft skin on my—*stop!*

"How soon?" I ask and clear my throat. "When do they want to release, I mean. And how has that changed the marketing plan? Quinn will want to know."

"They want to move the release date up by a month, and the marketing has already started."

"I think we can do that, then."

He smiles at me, and my panties melt right off. "I knew you'd be able to handle this. And between you and me, I'm glad it's you working on her book. You're one of the best we have here."

I shake my head. "You're too kind."

"Really," he says and moves in a little closer. "Do I need to bring up *The Fake Wife*?" he asks with a laugh. I blush and shake my head. I took a gamble on a debut author's thriller not long ago, and the book blew up. The movie came out over the summer and was a hit. "You've yet to advocate for a bad book. How do you do it?"

I shrug, looking up at him. "I just know what I like and go for it." I don't mean for it to sound as flirty as it does. I'm about to divert my eyes and blurt out something random to take the tension away, but Cole speaks before I have the chance.

"I like that about you," he says coyly, giving me a sexy-as-hell smile. "You'll talk to Quinn Harlow or her agent today?"

"Yeah. I'll email them both right away."

He goes on to tell me the details of everything, and I do my best to listen. I even jot down notes so I can explain everything in perfect detail when I talk to Quinn's agent.

My mind starts to drift to Cole's perfect cheekbones and the alluring way he smells. Cole Winchester is the Editor-in-Chief at Black Ink Press, and is the subject of many office fantasies. The moment you meet him, it's obvious as to why.

Besides his looks—tall, athletic, handsome-yet-rugged face that's covered in a perfect five o'clock shadow all day—Cole is a diamond in the rough. He's respectful of his employees. He's responsible and always has his shit together. He's an overall nice guy but can still command the room without even trying. Cole meets all the criteria on my to-date list.

Yet, he's made it abundantly clear that he'll never date anyone from work. Don't shit were you eat and all, I guess. Though I like to think I could be his exception, like one of the leading ladies in the romance novels. And there's that hope again rising in my chest. I've been told that not all is lost when you have hope. But enough of that optimistic bull-shit. Having hope only prolongs the heartache.

2

LUKE

Is murder always a crime? I push my shoulders back into the leather behind me and grit my teeth. I push the buttons on the controller in my hands, taking satisfaction in pummeling virtual zombies to death with a splintered piece of wood. That's the only murder that's happening today.

"Luke, I know you can hear me," my brother says again. He stands to the side, arms crossed over his chest. "Luke," he repeats. "You were home all fucking day. Why are there dishes in the sink?"

It's taking effort to maintain the guise that these headphones cancel out all noise. I didn't do the dishes because I'm not his fucking maid. I cleaned up after myself, but I draw the line at doing his dirty work.

"Luke." Cole moves in front of me, blocking my line of vision. I'm half tempted to keep staring forward, pretending he's not there. I did go three weeks pretending he was invisible when we were kids. Ten years later, and nothing has changed. But I'm close to leveling up on my game. I hit pause, and look up, blood boiling.

Inhale. Hold it. Let it out slowly. I can't lose it, not completely. Cole might be older than me, but I can take him in a fight. Easily. And he knows it.

"I'm not washing your dishes," I say calmly, proud of my level tone.

"I work all day. You don't. Pick up the slack around here if you want to live here."

The controller clatters to the ground. I leap up. So much for keeping my cool. "Did you forget I work at night? You wanna play this game? Really?"

I stare him down, wondering where the hell we went wrong. Cole is two years older than me, and he's always hated me. Chalking his behavior up to typical sibling rivalry doesn't begin to cover it. I don't get it either. Cole and I are as different as brothers can be.

Physically, we share a slight resemblance. His hair is lighter and his eyes are darker. I'm taller by several inches, with pounds of more muscle. Cole excelled academically and I was good at sports. We went our separate ways at college and he was tolerable for several years.

Yet here we are, together again. Fuck my life.

Cole takes a step back. "You came here. To my house. You have to follow my rules."

"You've got to be fucking kidding me!" My nostrils flare as anger pulses through me. "This isn't *your* house." It had to be some sort of a sick joke for our grandmother to leave this ostentatious Manhattan house to us.

Us.

Mom says it was Grandma's final attempt to do what she couldn't: make Cole and I get the fuck along. Unlike my brother, knowing the discord between us caused our mother —and grandmother—angst, upset me. I never wanted to hurt either of them, but I'm not one to sit idly by while my narcissistic brother thinks his shit don't stink. Though I do regret

265

shoving him four Thanksgivings ago. But only because he knocked over a bottle of red wine on Mom's antique armchair.

"You're such an asshole," I hiss, picking my controller up off the ground. I readjust the headphones and sit down. *Keep your cool.* It's not worth it. Not anymore. "After everything that happened, you'd think you'd cut me a little slack." I look right into my brother's eyes. "You're just like Dad."

"Take that back!" he snaps. "I'm nothing like him!"

I ignore Cole, taking satisfaction in the insult. Our father was not a good man. I resume the game, and eventually Cole leaves the room, muttering on and on about how he can't stand living with me.

A wave of sadness goes through me, not uncommon as of late, and I wish for just a second Cole and I got along. I've been in New York City for only weeks, and after all the shit that happened just months ago, I could use a friend.

Whatever. This is temporary. I'll go back to Chicago eventually. My life is—was—there. Someday I'll be ready to go back. Problem is, I have no idea when. The fire was still ablaze when I left, burning every aspect of my life, taking everything I held dear to me, and turning it into ash.

ACKNOWLEDGMENTS

I need to take a moment to thank everyone who has loved the Love is Messy series from the start. I started Hot Mess with the intention of writing a standalone romance, and the book became bigger than I ever expected, and the response has left me breathless. 🤍 Now to thank my friends...Christine, TL, Kristin, and Erin: thank you for always lending an ear, calming me in my (many) times of panic, and for your overall support and friendship. To my beta team: you all are rockstars. I cannot express how grateful I am to have you. And to my family: thank you for putting up with me after I pulled an all nighter (more than once) to meet deadlines, and for being understanding that the voices in my head are real.

ABOUT THE AUTHOR

Emily Goodwin is the New York Times and USA Today Bestselling author of over a dozen of romantic titles. Emily writes the kind of books she likes to read, and is a sucker for a swoon-worthy bad boy and happily ever afters.

She lives in the midwest with her husband and two daughters. When she's not writing, you can find her riding her horses, hiking, reading, or drinking wine with friends.

Emily is represented by Julie Gwinn of the Seymour Agency.

www.emilygoodwinbooks.com
emily@emilygoodwinbooks.com